A Wide
and
Capable
Revenge

A WIDE AND CAPABLE REVENGE

by THOMAS McCALL

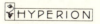 HYPERION

NEW
YORK

Library of Congress
Cataloging-in-Publication Data

McCall, Thomas.
 A wide and capable revenge / by Thomas McCall.—1st ed.
  p.   cm.
 ISBN 1-56282-864-9
 I. Title.
PS3563.C3342P38   1993
813'.54—dc20   92-28413
                                   CIP

FIRST EDITION

10 9 8 7 6 5 4 3 2 1

FOR DIANE AUGUSTA

Harrison Salisbury's moving work, *The 900 Days: The Siege of Leningrad* (Harper & Row), was a valued source for this book.

I would like to thank Judith Weber, my agent; Patricia Mulcahy, my editor; and Christine Archibald, assistant editor. Beyond their hard work and encouragement, each of these women displayed that rarest of all virtues: careful, line-by-line attention to an unpublished novelist.

Finally, and most deservedly, I would like to thank Diane, my wife. Writing means squirreling away, and she granted me that freedom while she tended to our five children. I may have had faith and hope, but she came up with the charity.

We have known everything . . .
That in Russian speech there is
No word for that mad war winter . . .
When the Hermitage shivered under bombs . . .
Houses turned to frost and pipes burst with ice . . .
The ration—100 grams . . . On the Nevsky corpses.
And we learned, too, about cannibalism.
We have known everything. . . .

—Daniel Leonidovich Andreyev,
a survivor of the Siege of Leningrad,
writing of the Leningrad apocalypse

A WIDE
AND
CAPABLE
REVENGE

1

CHICAGO

MAY, 1988

Fifteen minutes after the shooting, I climbed the wide, concrete stairs to Holy Name Cathedral. Behind me, State Street hummed and honked with the push of Saturday afternoon traffic. My blouse felt puffy in the stiff breeze, in the sudden and surprising warmth pouring in across the city that afternoon.

My name is Nora Callum. I am a tall woman, and I think that when I am on my crutches my height gives me a modicum of grace, a deflection of attention away from my disability. Yes, that's it, deflection of attention. I use similar reasoning when I wear my blond hair pulled so snugly back across my scalp that it becomes striking. I hope conspicuous hair might siphon notice from my prairie-flat cheekbones, humped nose, pale green eyes, and too wide mouth. I claim nothing delicate in my face, only, I suppose, a look of maturity and purpose that some may never acquire, even with age. Although I am only thirty-three, my face easily vaults me into my forties.

A pink-cheeked police officer met me outside the Cathedral doors. As I neared the top step, he tipped his hat to me, then labored to pull open a door. His effort was not only out of deference to a superior, but because I required his help to get myself and my crutches through safely. The Cathedral doors are something to be reckoned with: large, cast-iron slabs on automatic closers—doors that, like the Gates of Heaven, can crush mortals not nimble enough to slip through quickly. Once inside, I thanked the cop, a courtesy I wasn't required to extend to rookies, then asked, "Where is she?"

"Up there, Lieutenant. In the confessional." He pointed toward the front of the church.

I moved through a narrow foyer into the church itself, one I had driven past hundreds of times but rarely entered. Struck by the quiet—the place had an eerie, uncommon peace for the scene of a shooting—I stood still and scanned the expanse in front of me. Rows of empty pews stretched ahead in geometric perfection; the ceiling, a cavernous dome of dark wood, towered over the sanctuary. Sunlight ran through grand stained-glass windows to splatter over the pews and across the ornate woodwork that trimmed the walls. The church air smelled faintly of its polished lumber and somehow, I thought, of intimidation, the intimidation a young woman feels while on her knees at the feet of a priest. I'll wager even Magdalene felt it.

I turned back to the officer and said, "When Lieutenant Campbell comes, send him up to me, will you, please?"

He nodded.

"And have the church roped off. All entrances."

"Yes, ma'am."

I started up the center aisle, my crutches biting off long, sweeping strides. My gait on crutches is a three-point affair, the two crutches leading the way, going out in tandem, then my right leg, following behind, catching up. As soon as my foot plants safely between the crutches, I swing the sticks forward again for another stride, my right leg following once again.

My agility with crutches smooths my passage, making it less choppy than one would expect with my disability: my left leg is off at mid-thigh, and has been so for three years, since a shootout during a drug raid. On this Saturday, my prosthetic leg was broken, in the shop for the kind of repairs occasionally demanded by all mechanical things put to hard use. Sometimes I kid my partner, Art Campbell, that, even on crutches, the Chicago Police Department's only one-legged woman detective could outrun more than a few of her male counterparts. Art laughs at this, but admits there's more than a sliver of truth to it.

Near the altar, under the huge wooden crucifix hanging solemnly from the ceiling, I turned left. The confessional stood just ahead of me. It looked common enough: wood construction, boxy shape, a central door for the priest's compartment, and two flanking doors for penitents. Four widely scattered, jagged bullet holes in a penitent's door were the confessional's only unusual features. This wrecked door, the left-side one, stood half open, and through it the victim spilled out. Her cheek lay in a wet patch of blood on the carpet, her legs still wedged in the confessional.

Two standing policemen guarded the scene. A priest sat quietly in a nearby pew. I glanced at him briefly, then turned to concentrate on the woman on the floor. Looking to be twenty or thirty, she was dressed in a blood-soaked white T-shirt.

"Who is she?" I asked.

"We don't know," one of the officers said. "We knew we shouldn't touch the body till a detective came. We opened the door and she fell out. Dead. She must've been leaning against the door."

"You two were the first here?"

"Yes," they said, in foolish unison.

"Who reported this?"

"We were driving by, on State Street," an officer said, "when a lady came out of the church and flagged us down. That's her back there." He pointed at a solitary figure hunched in a shadowed rear pew.

Art had arrived and was now up to the confessional. Squinting toward the dimness at the church entrance, I said, "Looks like we need her."

"I'll get her," Art said.

I went down on my knee, close enough to the victim to smell her sweet perfume and study her face. Her skin was blemish-free, smooth, and of dark complexion. It was a face of perfect balance, each feature beautifully wrought, none calling undue attention to itself.

I gently touched the woman's cheek—it was still warm. I frowned, then looked down at her chest. Nothing seemed to move under her baggy shirt. Not satisfied, I bent lower and placed my open hands on her ribs, one under each breast, on the blood-wet part of her shirt. Her chest was moving.

"Goddammit!" I shouted. "She's still alive! Call an ambulance!"

"What?" an officer said.

"Call an ambulance! Now, for chrissake!"

The man jerked a small radio from his belt and called his dispatcher. While he did so, I said to his young partner, "Look, a piece of advice. Next time, worry first if they're dead or alive. Feel them if you have to. Touch them with your fingers. You see? It's okay, you won't disturb anything."

I rolled the woman onto her back and loosened her jeans. I fingered a thready pulse at her wrist, then fished out a purse from under her rump.

When two paramedics arrived minutes later, I stood out of their way while they bent over the woman. "She's got breath sounds," one said coolly. "Everything's abdominal. Nothing's thoracic. Good, good."

"Pressure's seventy over thirty," the other said. "Let's get an IV going and get her the hell outa here before she codes."

In seconds, they had perforated a vein at the woman's elbow with a large-bore needle and hung a plastic bag of fluid to run through clear tubing into her arm. After they hoisted her onto a stretcher, they headed out the church's side entrance. The whole job took less than five minutes. When the stretcher passed through a shaft of sun, a small diamond on the woman's dangling left hand caught the light and flashed it in my eyes.

I picked through the woman's purse and found a wallet with identification. This barely vital, bleeding lady was Eva Ramirez, age twenty-nine, of 722 North State Street, just a block south of the Cathedral. In the wallet were three rumpled dollars, some change, and a small, worn picture of the Sacred Heart. Where the credit cards belonged there was no plastic, but another picture, this one of Eva, a man, and three small children, all boys, all dark-skinned. In the picture Eva wore a summery white blouse with lacy sleeves. The others, even the baby, wore neatly pressed, open-collared shirts. Behind the group stood a wall of dull blue painted with smudges of white. I recognized the photograph as the kind hawked for a dollar or two at department-store specials. I had a half-dozen pictures at home of my daughter Meg and myself with the same sickening background.

With Eva gone, I went to the priest in the nearby pew. He looked for a moment as though he were going to stand, but he didn't. "Your name, please, Father?" I asked.

"James Ritgen."

Balding and sweating, Ritgen was all pouches—under his eyes, at his loose cheeks, under his neck and throat. He wore a floor-length black cassock and a stiff Roman collar, a fold of pendulous neck burying the collar's edge. He looked to be in his sixties.

"What happened?" I said.

"Who are you?" Ritgen asked.

"Lieutenant Nora Callum. I'm from Area Center Six, Violent Crimes. Belmont Avenue at Western."

"I know the place," he said.

"They called me from the Eighteenth." The Eighteenth District station house was only two short blocks from the Cathedral. "Can you tell me what happened?"

Ritgen looked up to the hanging crucifix, his somber eyes

momentarily embracing the corpus of Christ. Ignoring my question, he asked, "What time is it?"

I checked my watch. "Almost four o'clock."

"We have Mass in here at five. Could you be cleared out of here by five?"

"Impossible. It'll take us several hours to go through the church."

"I see." He paused, then said, "We can hold Mass in the basement, yes. That wouldn't disturb you."

"That's fine," I said impatiently. "Now I need to know what happened here."

Ritgen wiped his fingers across his eyes, briefly smoothing away their flaccid bags. "Would you like to sit?" he said, noticing my crutches if not my single-leggedness.

"I'm fine, no. Please go on."

"I was hearing her confession," he said, "when I heard a bang—a shot, I guess. From somewhere beyond my door. I thought it was loud and close . . . but I didn't find out what loud and close were till the other shots came."

"You heard a single shot first?" I asked.

"I think it was a shot. At the time, I wasn't sure what it was."

"If it was a shot, then it didn't hurt the woman?"

"No, she asked me what the noise was," Ritgen said. "I didn't answer her. I suppose I was too confused, or frightened."

He slipped a forefinger under his rigid collar, looking for a fraction of an inch more room for his fat neck. His face glistened with perspiration, though the Cathedral felt cool to me.

"You couldn't see anything, could you?" I asked.

"No. My door was closed as always."

"Was anybody in the other penitent's box?"

"I have no idea."

I looked back to the confessional, to the lights over each of the three boxes that indicated which were occupied. A lighted red bulb still glowed over the door to Ritgen's compartment, while two green bulbs, both off, marked the penitents' boxes. In spite of the darkened light over the right-hand door, I asked the officer to open it and check inside anyway. The box was empty.

My leg was tiring now—the call for this shooting had come at the end of my day, just before shift change. I had been ready to collapse then, but protocol required me to follow this through. I sidled into the pew in front of Ritgen's. I sat and scooted in, then spun on the slippery wood to face him again, my normal right leg comfortably up on the bench. "Go on, Father."

"After the first bang, the more distant one, the woman continued with her confession. In another fifteen or twenty seconds, the other shots came pouring into the confessional."

"Okay, good."

His hands flew up from his lap. "Three shots, five, ten," he said excitedly. "I don't know how many. It was a shooting gallery in there. It sounded like the shots were exploding inside my head." His hands came back down and squeezed each other tightly.

"But you weren't hurt."

"Would I be sitting—? I'm sorry, Lieutenant."

"It's okay," I reassured him. "You're doing a fine job of remembering. Really." I reached over and touched the rough fabric of his cassock sleeve.

Ritgen said, "That's all there is. The shots went off close to me. I dropped from my chair to the floor. I was afraid to come out till I heard the officers speaking. When I finally did come out, I ran here and sat."

"Did you—"

"Don't ask me why I ran here," he interrupted, his head quivering just the slightest bit. "I should have been giving the poor woman the Last Sacrament, not shriveling in this pew."

"With any luck she won't need the Last Sacrament," I said.

"Yes, please God. Who is she?"

"Her wallet says 'Eva Ramirez.' Do you know her?"

"No." He touched his lips with the back of a hand.

I pushed on. "Did she say anything to you?"

"You mean after she'd been shot?"

"Yes."

"She groaned. No words."

"And you didn't hear anything either outside the confessional or in the other box?"

"Nothing."

I pulled a small notebook and pen from my pocket. I scribbled a few notes, looking up once to give Ritgen a smile.

"May I leave now, Lieutenant?" he said. "I have to arrange for the Mass in the basement. And somehow—good God, I don't know how—somehow I have to preach at that Mass."

"Just one more thing. Did Eva have anything to say in her confession, anything that might tell us why she was shot?"

"I can't say what she confessed. That's privileged, even by law."

"Yes, I know, but—"

"Are you a Catholic, Lieutenant, a believer?"

My attention wandered. Was I? Could I be a believer, with one leg off and a husband gone? Should I believe in anything beyond myself and my crutches?

"Lieutenant?"

"Oh. Am I a believer? Of sorts, I suppose. Yes, of sorts, Father."

"Then you respect the dictum that requires my silence."

"I'm not after specifics. I just want to know if she spoke about an affair, or drugs, or anything that might push someone to shoot her."

Ritgen's lips framed a small smile. "I can tell you she made a good confession," he said. "She was shot while filled with God's grace. Nothing she said would help you."

He wiped his eyes dry. His face jerked reflexively toward the crucifix.

2

Art and I approached each other in the center aisle. Art isn't a tall man, not even as tall as I am, but he's stout as a bull terrier. His skin is black, his hair close-cropped and going gray. His heavy features have nothing subtle about them, but his smile will dazzle the unwary.

Fifty-three years old and a three-decade veteran on the Force, Art possesses common sense that runs through him like a deep vein of coal. On the street, as a partner, he shows prudent courage, knows when to be a hard-ass and when not to, something some cops never learn. Helen, his wife of twenty-five years, contends that the only unreasonable behavior the man has ever shown was the puritanical house rules he enforced when their three daughters became old enough to date. Art and I understood what Helen didn't: anything can happen on the street.

On our team of two, Art is my link with convention, the partner who has smoothed our way through countless police routines prescribed by Headquarters. Art calls it "keeping down with Downtown." And it's Art who helps me with Raymond Melchior, our chief at Area Six, the man who deeply resented my return to the detective corps following my amputation.

Now Art and I faced each other across the aisle. Art's interview of the woman in the rear pew had been less than standard.

"Goddamn, Nora, who you giving me to question?" he said,

his voice a rich, deep baritone. " 'Cause I'm old and black, you think you can give me a shit job like this? This old lady's crazy as a hoot owl!"

"What's the matter, Arthur?" I chided.

"What's the matter? You talk with her and find out. I'll take over with the padre." He loosened his tie and opened his collar. "I'm hot already, and we haven't even started here yet. Shit, and I'm supposed to take the kids to a Sox game tonight." Beyond his family, the White Sox were the other objects of devotion in Art's life.

"What did the woman say?" I asked.

"Who knows? It's not English."

"What is it?"

"It's not a language problem, Nora. It's a nonsense problem."

"Who is she?"

"Wouldn't say."

"She tell you anything?"

"She said—I think she said, it was half goddamn gibberish—she said that while she's kneeling on the floor in the back of the church—"

"What's she doing on the floor?" I broke in.

"Scrubbing it. Does it regularly, I guess. Shit, who knows?"

Art looked up, studied the vaulted ceiling as if searching for secrets nesting in the dark beams.

"Sorry for interrupting," I said.

"Okay, so she says somebody comes into the church—a man, probably. Then she says, oh, no, maybe it's a woman, or maybe it's one of each, she doesn't know for sure. But she does know that all of a sudden there's a loud noise. A shot, lady? I ask, and she can't say. Doesn't know, but she does know that after the noise she's got a piss-hole in her water bucket, the bucket she's using for scrubbing the floor."

I struggled to stay with the prattle, wishing it were eight in the morning instead of four in the afternoon.

Art wet his lips and leaned his upper body toward me for emphasis. "Notice the flow of logic here, Nora? A man or a woman, or maybe both, maybe some shooting, definitely a hole in a water bucket. You're with me, aren't you, girl?" He shook his head comically, rubbed his nose with his knuckles.

He was rolling. I wouldn't break in.

"Anyway, then the old lady hears more shots. Sounds like several more, but, naturally, she's not sure. So she looks up again and maybe she sees someone running in the front of the church." A quick, deep breath. "That's it, Nora, that's all I can make out of her. Just a shade less than we need to arrest and prosecute." After another pause, he finished quietly: "Shit, Mother, I can't dance."

Shit, Mother, I can't dance. I'd learned this fragment of black vernacular during my first few weeks with Art; he'd used the expression when his considerable personal energy was spent and bewilderment rampaged within him. Sometimes, for reasons foreign to me, he would add a final tag: "Shit, Mother, I can't dance; wake me up for the screwin'." I knew nothing about what the words meant, yet I understood their message perfectly.

"Let me try the lady," I said, and slid down the pew to where she sat waiting.

Ragged and elderly, she was dressed like a Gypsy and smelled profoundly of days-old urine. Her face was narrow and pinched, and her dark, deep-set eyes jumped continually, unable to look directly at me. She rocked forward and backward incessantly, like an autistic child.

I started softly. "My name is Nora. What's yours?"

No answer, only a slowing of her repetitive rocking.

"I'd like to talk with you if I could," I said. "Lieutenant Campbell tells me you saw somebody come into the church. Is that right?"

The woman twisted her head sharply toward me, a quick

spasm. "Aaiiii, aaiiii!" she howled. "Dirtee people, dirtee people!"

"What?"

"Dirtee people, in Gód's house, hah! Shooting! Hah!"

An understanding of Art's troubles turned me toward him. He sat at the end of the next pew forward, his chin in his hands. He offered a grin in consolation. Exasperated already, I looked back to the woman, who now sat with her spine flexed and her face tucked between her knees.

"Can you tell me where the man or the woman came from?" I asked her, looking at the greasy hair on the back of her skull. "Do you know who was shooting, or where they went?"

No response, but she surprised me by raising her left hand, filthy and closed, into midair. When I placed my own hand underneath hers, she dropped a dented, scratched bullet into my palm.

"Thank you," I said, rolling the slug between my fingers. I reached forward and handed it to Art, who dropped it into a small cardboard box he carried in his pocket.

"Where did you get the bullet?" I asked.

The woman didn't answer, not even with more nonsense. She began another round of rocking. Staring at her, I decided that if this poor creature's face and body reflected what was in her soul, then her life was nothing but turmoil, a perpetual fracas.

I slid back to the aisle, took the bullet from Art, and put it in my purse. Ritgen was passing by, headed for the basement, so I stopped him.

"Father," I said, nodding toward the old woman, "do you know her?"

"Of course. She's Rita Pesgevich. She's been scrubbing the Cathedral's rugs and floors for twenty years. Sometimes she'll scrub the same square foot of carpet for a week. A week, mind you."

"She's an employee?"

"No, God, no. A parishioner."

"She doesn't make much sense of our questions."

Ritgen lifted his eyebrows. "She's schizophrenic. Confirmed. Incurable, even with barrels of medication, I'm told. She can't make sense, but she's harmless. She only knows the church and her room in a boardinghouse a few blocks from here. She's one of those members of society who should have a bed in a mental hospital. We owe these people that much, you know, but tell that to the Legislature."

"I'll be able to find her again if I let her go?" I asked.

"Find her?" Ritgen said. "We can't get rid of her. She's here every day. I know where she lives if you need her. She might talk to me."

When I told the woman she could go, she stood and started for the vestibule, walking with the hunch of an aged, broken female. At the rear of the church, she stopped, knelt next to a water bucket, and began scrubbing the carpet with a blackened washrag. Her face was so close to the floor that I thought that she might kiss it.

"What's with the bucket?" I asked Art.

"Like I told you," he said, "she said there's a hole in it. A shot made a hole in her bucket."

"So," I said, "we've got several bullet holes and a nearly dead woman up in the confessional, and one bullet and a wounded water bucket back here with crazy Rita."

Art said, "God bless you for your perceptiveness."

For the next three hours, our homicide team—Eva Ramirez wasn't dead yet, but the expectation was there—searched the Cathedral, photographing, probing, measuring, and fingerprinting. We finished at eight o'clock in the evening, and the church was reopened. None of the faithful came at that time of day, but at least the church would be ready for the string of Sunday Masses the next morning, a fact that heartened Father Ritgen immensely.

We discovered that, indeed, there was a bullet hole in Rita's water bucket, and that the bucket was near a point of ricochet where a bullet, presumably the one Rita had handed me, had struck and bounced off metal grillwork on the rear wall of the church. I decided this must have been the single first shot, the quieter shot Ritgen and Eva had heard before the firing of the several shots pumped through the confessional door. We searched the center aisle and retrieved a single empty casing, likely ejected from an automatic weapon, on the floor against a pew.

The confessional showed a jumble of fingerprints and the holes four bullets had ripped through the oaken door, all at close range. They had entered in a scattered pattern, three of the four at waist level or below, the fourth a wild one near the top of the door. Three slugs—one high, and two of the lower ones—were dug out from deep inside the blood-spattered plaster wall that made the back of the confessional. The fourth, not found, was thought possibly to be still inside Eva. No empty casings were anywhere to be seen, so unless the shooter had stopped to houseclean, he or she had used a revolver.

As the team packed to leave, I noticed that the red light over Father Ritgen's door was still lit. I opened the door and turned off the light at a wall switch next to his chair. I started away, then looked back and stared at the bloody destruction. I tried to remember my own last trip into a confessional box, but I couldn't. The Church had lost the power of guilt it had wielded over me as a youngster.

Art would return to Area Six, log in the evidence, and run a check on Eva Ramirez. I would stop at the hospital to see if there still was an Eva Ramirez. My watch said eight-thirty. I knew that Anna Skrabina, my baby-sitter for Meg, wouldn't mind staying as late as ten o'clock.

The spring evening was a boastful visitation of summer, warm and breezy, with even a trace of steamy haze around State Street's pale orange streetlights. The hospital was close, only three blocks east, toward Lake Michigan, on Superior Street. I thought about walking, but not for long and not seriously—my leg ached with fatigue. I slid into my squad car, a Plymouth Fury, and tossed my crutches onto the passenger seat. Before turning off State onto Superior, I glanced southward to see about where Eva Ramirez's address would be, but it was too dark to decipher much from a distance.

Traffic plugged Superior Street, especially where it crossed the gridlock of cars and pedestrians on North Michigan Avenue. Of all the avenue shops, only the ice-cream and popcorn stores were still open, yet thousands of people meandered along the sidewalks anyway, lured by the weather. Most of the walkers were young and from the city. They strolled with a slow and easy swagger, unimpressed by the glitzy street but enchanted by the tropical smell of the air. The tourists were the ones who stood still in the flow of traffic and craned their necks upward to find the brightly lit tops of eighty- and hundred-story skyscrapers.

At the hospital, Northwestern Memorial, I parked near the emergency-room entrance, in a slot reserved for clergy, then flipped down the sun visors, with the words "Chicago Police Department" showing. Inside, I walked to the police room, a tiny cubbyhole next to a row of treatment rooms.

The police visited this emergency room all the time—for murders and rapes, assaults and child abuse, dog bites and drunks—but if the appearance of our room reflected the esteem in which we were held, then we had nothing to brag about. It was crammed with three metal chairs and a metal desk, all scratched and battered and looking even worse than what we complained about when I had been a patrol officer at the Eighteenth. A few half-empty coffee cups and parts of the last three days' Chicago *Tribune* littered the desks. A wooden rack holding a stack of police reporting forms leaned against a wall, and a broken slot spilled "Report of Rape or Attempted Rape" forms onto the floor. The city's perpetual grime blackened the beige linoleum underfoot.

I sat and waited patiently in the room. I had learned not to disturb the pace here: information came more easily if I didn't bristle anyone. A nurse would see me soon enough, and nurses were always more helpful than physicians. This was the teaching hospital of a medical school, so its emergency room was staffed by interns and residents, young lions who strutted and preened between patients. They were too solemn and inflated to want to talk to police, especially female police.

In a few minutes, Mary Calder entered. Mary was the p.m. shift's head nurse, a scrawny, tough, black-haired fifty-year-old who had been in nursing two years past the quarter-century mark, all in this emergency room. When her current roster of physician-bosses were still in diapers, she had already been mopping blood, resuscitating heart attacks, dressing burns, and comforting the sobbing relatives of the newly and suddenly dead.

And it was Mary, three years before on a warm, thick night like this one, who bent over a bloody cart to gather my wounded self into her arms, to enfold me against the horror when they told me that the wreckage of my left leg would have to be lopped off above my knee. Since that night, I had never seen Mary without recalling the smell of the woman's hair in my face that evening, a smell that summoned my memory of her compassion, that act of pure human kindness I had never expected. I couldn't forget Mary's smell if I had wanted to: it rose from the most primitive part of my brain, the area where memories are fire-branded into the cells.

Mary affectionately squeezed my shoulder as she passed, then dropped onto a chair and lifted her skinny legs to the desktop.

Her legs were hairy, even through white hose. "I'll bet I know why you're here, sweetie," she said, her dark eyes staring out over half-frame glasses.

"I'll bet you do."

"Who'd shoot a beauty like that?"

"I don't know, Mary. I haven't a clue."

"Must be drugs," she said. She pulled a long cigarette from her pocket and lit it. Smoke haloed her thin face. "What's her name, anyway? She came in a blank."

"Her wallet said 'Eva Ramirez.' "

"Pretty name, Eva." She paused to inhale. "Bring any family with you?"

I shook my head slowly as I felt my face warm with embarrassment. "Guess what?" I said. "I forget to check." I picked up the phone next to me and dialed information. There was no listing for a Ramirez on North State. "No phone. I'll drive over there from here, after I find out how she is."

"Send somebody," Mary said.

"No, I'll go. That's the least I can do."

Mary sucked in another lungful of smoke. "We didn't even make up a chart on her, didn't have the time. Just pumped some O-negative blood in and got her up to surgery." She pulled her glasses off her nose; they dangled on her chest from a red cord. "Where'd it happen?"

"In the Cathedral. In a confessional."

"Oh, Christ! Don't kid me about that, Nora."

"I'm not. Ask Father Litgen, or Ritgen, or whatever his name is."

"It's Ritgen. I know the old gasbag. He used to be a tough bird in the box, you know, before the church eased up on everything."

"You must have told him a few things across that screen."

"A few, maybe a few. Before I was married. But that wouldn't be any of your business, now, would it, sweetie?"

"Of course not," I intoned.

Mary brought her legs back off the desktop and smiled, her cigarette-stained teeth poking through her open lips. "How about some coffee?"

"No, thanks," I said. "I'm going home to bed after this. So Eva's still alive?"

"I think so. I'll check with Fiester, Dr. Big Shot, when I finish this smoke. He just went up there to check. I'll ask him."

"Who's Fiester?"

"The new intern for the month down here. A real jerk."

"That bad?"

"That bad. You know, most of these guys who rotate through here will be okay, eventually. But I'm not sure about Fiester. Walks on hallowed ground, you know. Lies, too." She shook her head. "Dr. Big Shot, I mean Dr. Big Shit. Pardon my French, Nora."

I laughed.

She took in a final draft of smoke, then tossed the live butt into a coffee cup, where it sizzled. She stood, slipped her glasses on, and said, "Be right back, sweetie."

A few minutes later, she returned to report: "She's still alive, still cooking. I guess it's not murder yet."

"How is she?"

"A few holes in her bowel. Spleen has to come out, but that's okay."

"Did they find a bullet in her?"

"I didn't think to ask. I'll check again later with Fiester. You go now, Nora, see if there's any family to bring back here. And when you get home, kiss your little girl for me. She doesn't really know me, but kiss her anyway."

"I will."

We touched hands.

"Say, why are you back on crutches?" she asked. "Where's your leg?"

"Busted. They're making me a new one."

"Oh, swell."

A cart with a moaning old man on it whizzed by, and Mary hurried after it.

Before leaving the hospital, I phoned Art. "What do you have on her?"

"Nothing," he said, "not even a driver's license. She doesn't exist."

"Did you check through any family?"

"Not yet. Do you know how goddamn many Ramirezes there are in this computer?"

"I guess. Sorry, Arthur. Let's start tomorrow."

"Sounds good. You going home now?"

"I think I'd better look for some family at that State Street address."

"They're not at the hospital?"

"No," I said. "The hospital didn't know who to call."

"I never thought of that. I should have thought of that, not you. Procedure, simple procedure."

"Just keeping down with Downtown, Arthur."

"Good night, girl," he said.

3

The Ramirez address on North State Street was easy to find, even in the dark and haze. Number 722 was the only standing building on the block, the others having been recently leveled to make way for a skyscraping apartment complex. Rocks and bottles lay strewn over the empty lots on each side of the building, but the land was productive nonetheless. The developer had ingeniously fenced it off for temporary parking spaces, eight dollars a day, best of luck with your tires. No sense in losing a buck in the months before construction began, during the time it would take him to secure 722, evict its residents, and demolish it into powder and splinters.

The building was a square redbrick, three stories tall, probably a century old. Lovely, intricate concrete cornices graced the building's top floor, and at street level a brightly lit, garish yellow sign with black lettering stuck out over the sidewalk, over a shop that one day may have sold sweet rolls, or chocolate candy, or flowers. Now the sign boldly announced VIDEO ART GALLERY. Rentals were available, minors need not enter, the degree of pleasure to be rented could be assessed by the number of "X"s. For those who couldn't wait to return home, short subjects could be viewed on the premises for half a dollar. Poor Eva, I thought.

I parked a short block from the building. The sidewalk was deserted except for three people who stood in a clutch between the fence of the parking lot and the building's south wall. I shut off the Fury and stared at the moonlit figures. They were hatless young men, two white and one black. The odds that they were doing a minor drug deal were overwhelming, probably a few packets of cocaine that they would discard to the wind if I rushed them. I didn't care about the drugs—this was probably just one of a hundred such transactions occurring that very minute throughout the city—I just wanted to be inside 722. The trick was to do it safely.

I took my gun from my purse and placed it inside my right-hand coat pocket. Outside the car, I shut the car door with a hard slam. The noise forewarned the men: to surprise them would have been stupid.

I started toward the building, eyes downcast all the way. A female civilian on the street at night does not look at men, but a lady cop does; she needs to look directly at people, needs to make eye contact. I knew that playing the woman, not the cop, would probably get me past the druggies safely. To hopheads, coke means more than sex, but if I was wrong, I could drop my right-hand crutch and be on the trigger of my .38 in a second.

As I approached and passed the men, I kept my eyes so glued to the sidewalk that all I could see of them was what flickered at the periphery of my vision. They stirred and turned toward me furtively, but then quickly reformed their tight circle; they had no interest in the cripple. I was happy to disappear past the corner of the building unchallenged.

The building's tiny lobby was darker than the street, lit only by sad reflections of the video parlor's sign. A row of scratched and dented mailboxes highlighted one wall. The name Ramirez was taped over one of the boxes. I pushed the call button, and a man's voice, thickly Hispanic, answered.

"I'm police," I said, "Lieutenant Callum. I have news of your wife."

The lobby door buzzed open. I trudged the darkened staircase, a pro with my crutches, but nearly exhausted by the third floor. Mr. Ramirez waited at his door. He was a big, sweaty man with a square face and hair as black as oil. He invited me into his apartment, where a television glimmered in a corner, bouncing color through the otherwise darkened room. I felt a night breeze spin around me from the open windows.

"Where is Eva?" Ramirez said.

"She's been hurt," I said. "She's at the hospital."

"What?" he said, suddenly frightened.

"She was shot," I said.

His chin jerked upward, as though he had taken an uppercut. "She just went to church," he said awkwardly. "Shot at the church?"

"Yes."

Ramirez backed up to a battered couch. I looked away to the windows to grant the man a moment of privacy. Suddenly, like sparks from the darkness, two small boys appeared, and rushed across the room to their father. Each boy wore nothing but white underpants; both were as dark and beautiful as their mother. One of the boys carried an even smaller, diapered brother, a child so young he didn't yet have the sense not to smile at strangers like me.

Ramirez pulled all the boys close to him, corralling them with great, protective arms. For a moment, I thought he would get up from the couch, but, instead, he dropped back, as though the weight of my news was too much for him to handle. He made the sign of the cross over his face and shoulders, kissing his thumb in a swift movement.

"She's all right?" he asked. His voice sounded too slight for so large a frame.

"She's having surgery now," I said as calmly as I could, "at Northwestern Memorial Hospital. I just spoke with a nurse, and she said Eva's doing fine so far." Even if Eva was already dead, I didn't have the courage to be blackhearted in front of this man.

"You a police lady, you said?" Ramirez said.

"Yes."

"With those?" He pointed to my crutches.

"Yes."

He nodded as though he understood. "I don't know what to do now. Sometimes Eva, she goes to a girlfriend's by the church. But she was too late. I can't go to look because of my kids. And I don't have a telephone to call anybody." He squeezed the baby before going on with the explanation he needed to get out. "The kids couldn't stay here. Too dangerous alone."

"I understand," I said.

"I was ready almost to take the kids and walk to the police, you know, by that station." He pointed at the north wall of the room, toward the Eighteenth station house.

"I've worked there. I know it."

"Okay. Now we walk to the hospital. The one by the lake, over there?" This time he pointed east, at the windows.

"Yes," I said, "but I'll drive you and the kids."

"You would?"

"Sure, of course. Dress them. If they're not afraid, I can help."

The two older boys pulled shirts and pants from a tangle of clothes at the end of the couch. Ramirez walked to a back room and returned with a small cotton gown. He laid the baby on the couch and tugged the gown over his head and shoulders. He was a handsome, round-faced child, with hair as black as his father's.

"This is all the baby needs to wear," Ramirez told me. He started to change the diaper.

"What's his name?" I asked.

"Emilio."

"Oh," I said, smiling widely, "I like that."

In the car, the bigger boys went to the back seat, while Ramirez held the baby in the front, my crutches between us. It was near ten o'clock, and traffic was easing. Michigan Avenue pedestrians were moving more slowly now; a few were already drunk.

"Who might want to shoot your wife, Mr. Ramirez?" I asked while waiting at a stoplight.

"Nobody," he said. "Eva was no trouble for nobody."

"Did she have anything to do with drugs?"

"Dope?"

"Yes," I said.

"Never."

"Was she ever arrested?"

"Never," he said resolutely. He adjusted the baby in his arms. The child's huge black eyes stared out at the galaxy of city lights.

"Does Eva work?" I said.

"Sometimes she's a waitress at a restaurant downtown. When I can watch the kids."

"Do you work?"

"I clean buses, the city buses. The big yard on the South Side."

"Did your wife have problems at work that she told you about?"

"No." He shook his head for reinforcement.

My training told me to suspect each of Ramirez's answers as he delivered them, but I seemed unable to. His responses were quick and matter-of-fact. Nothing seemed contrived.

At the hospital, I escorted the family to the surgery waiting room, a low-ceilinged, dimly lit dungeon furnished with worn magazines and a television. While we waited for word about Eva, the boys played on the chairs and the floor, and Emilo slept in his father's arms. I asked Ramirez a few more questions and discovered nothing.

Soon the surgeon, a short, bespeckled man still in his bloody gown, came to assure Ramirez that Eva was still alive, even improving a little, and was expected to survive. He dutifully explained what he had done to Eva, but the anatomical intricacies of Eva's injured belly sailed over both Ramirez's and my head. The doctor said the family could see Eva in an hour or so. He shook Ramirez's hand and left, but not before rubbing his hand over the scalp of the sleeping baby. "Beautiful child," he said. "Like his mother."

Ramirez smiled, the first break across his face since I had met him.

"Doctor," I said as he began to leave, "did you find a bullet in Mrs. Ramirez? I'm Lieutenant Callum from Violent Crimes at Area Six."

"Oh," he said, surprised. Then, "Yes, we did find a slug, only one, near the right kidney. Must have bounced off a rib to stay inside her. I've sent it to the lab. Hospital regulations—anything we take out has to be sent to the pathologist, a way of checking on us." As an aside, he added, "Don't ask me who checks on the pathologist."

"I need the bullet as evidence," I said.

"It'll have to be in the morning. Pathology sleeps at this time of night."

"Fine. I'll pick it up then."

When the surgeon left, I gave Ramirez a number he could call when he wanted a ride home. I would alert the Eighteenth to send a squad whenever he needed it. I told him I would try to see Eva in the morning.

I sped my Fury home through thin traffic on Lake Shore Drive, the curving, antique expressway that hugged Lake Michigan's beaches and parks. A wet, fishy smell from the lake blew in through the open car windows. I knew the odor: that year's collection of dead alewives. Every spring, to the great displeasure of the city's sunbathers, the lake spits up the small, silvery fish in a ritual cleansing of its waters. The Park District skims the carcasses from the beaches of the downtown and Gold Coast neighborhoods, but farther north and farther south, where the per capita income dwindles, the fish are left to rot in the sand.

Halfway up the Drive, I raised my thoughts from dead fish to Megan, my seven-year-old daughter. It was nearly eleven o'clock, and Meg would surely be in bed and asleep by now. A day spent without seeing anything of Meg seemed wasted, a day when I had given everything to the Force and nothing to my blood. That inequity always disturbed me.

And then there was my worry over Anna, my baby-sitter. I knew she liked to be home by ten, in bed to watch the nightly news, then off to sleep after that.

Dear Anna Skrabina. A seventy-five-year-old widow who, conveniently, lived one floor above me, she had been my baby-sitter for seven years, since Meg was an infant. Before Richard, my husband, left me, Anna's visits were only occasional, but after I was alone, I needed her almost daily. And once, three years before, when I lost my leg, she came day and night for two months, nursing me like a mother, indulgent and sympathetic, yet never allowing me to wallow in easy grief. Overwhelmed by Anna's generosity of spirit, I vowed I would repay her if I was ever given the chance.

Anna and Meg had always gotten along wonderfully, adopted grandmother from the old country and granddaughter from the generation of *Sesame Street* and Madonna. Anna's stories from her own childhood were never-ending, although Meg had certain favorites that she pleaded to have repeated over and over, and Anna always obliged. The stories were generic fables, never a story rooted in a specific village or country, never anything about Anna's own life or family.

Anna's husband, Andrei, was a soaring, reedlike man who sometimes accompanied Anna to our apartment. During the first difficult weeks after my amputation, when Anna virtually lived with us, Andrei came to see me frequently. I relished his afternoon visits, I on the couch, he in a chair close by. A saintly listener, he could sit for hours without squirming, even as I rambled on. Andrei's sympathy for my loss of a leg to street scum was as genuine as Anna's. He bolstered me, telling me

stories about World War II amputees he had known who re-
bounded from injuries similar to mine.

One afternoon, when Anna and Meg were off for groceries,
I asked Andrei about the war. Opening a surprising crack to me,
he told me how he and Anna had been forced to work in a German
munitions factory during the last years of the war; how, from a
cave cut into rock above the Rhine, they had watched the Allies
pound Germany from the air; how their factory had been fire-
bombed down to molten metal; how the camp where they lived
had been blown from existence with half its residents still in their
beds. In 1950, he and Anna had emigrated to the United States
from the French Zone in divided Germany.

As Andrei spoke about the war that day, I saw the small fires
that burned in his eyes: they didn't focus on me, but searched
for something unspeakable in the blaze of sun at my back. After
he'd finished, I knew his story had been given to me as a gift. I
sensed we would not be passing that way again, and, indeed, we
didn't. When, sadly, Andrei dropped dead of a stroke two years
later, he went to his grave without ever having said anything
more to me about Europe.

Andrei's death gave Anna a sudden abundance of free time.
With Meg in school all day, Anna worked hard to fill her empty
hours till classes ended and she could pick up Meg. She began
taking long, tiring walks along the lakefront, walks that she said
would help her nod off to sleep at night more easily. She cleaned
her apartment incessantly—way too clean, embarrassingly clean,
I kidded her. And she visited museums and libraries, attended
lectures, things she had somehow never done when Andrei was
alive. For the most part, she did well, although I knew she cycled
through days of blank despondency.

I followed the Drive to its end, Sheridan Road, where I turned
north and passed a row of gaudy high-rise condominiums, then

the Loyola University campus. At Fargo Avenue, my street, I turned east and, with luck, found an empty parking space in front of my building. I was just three buildings from the lake.

This was Rogers Park, a neighborhood thick with low, square apartment buildings, all yellow or orange or brown brick. Decades ago, Fargo had been a street for the gentry, but as the city matured, the well-to-do deserted the lakefront for the more fashionable suburbs. A mixture of race, nationality, and age arrived to fill the void: some Central and Eastern European immigrants; a few blacks and Hispanics; a large number of older and not wealthy Jews; and some student renters—mostly Catholics— from nearby Loyola. I enjoyed the diversity of my neighbors, as did Anna, although she felt strongly that the unmarried men and women students from Loyola should never, no never, be living together.

I turned the key quietly. When I inched open the door with a crutch, I heard a late-night talk show chirping on the television. Anna wasn't to be seen. I walked up to the couch and peeked over its back. Shoes off and knees tucked up, she slept peacefully on her side.

I circled the couch and sat on its edge. "Anna, Anna," I said, tapping her forearm, "wake up, old lady." "Old lady" was a gentle epithet that I used and that Anna enjoyed. Proud of her seniority, she accepted my chide with the good nature that was intended.

Anna twisted her face from the cushion. Her gray hair had gone haywire in her sleep, and the faint swelling that sleep brings to the cheeks softened her usually sharp features. Her eyes were clear blue and determined, still lustrous at her age.

"Nora?" she said. "Oh, my God, Nora, I'm falling asleep! I'm some no-good baby-sitter." She bolted to a sitting position. "Where is Megan? Where is she? Oh, wait—I put her in the bed."

"I'm sure she's fine, Anna. I'll check in a minute. Are you okay?"

"What time is it, dearie?"

"Nearly eleven. Sorry I'm so late. A shooting came in at the end of my shift. I didn't have a choice."

"Okay, forget that," Anna said, waving her hand. "We went up to my apartment, and we cook some frozen pizza for dinner." She smacked her lips: "Delicious."

I smiled.

"You need me for something tomorrow?" she said as she stood and straightened her skirt.

"It's Sunday, but I'll have to work on this case. Can you sit for just a while?"

"What time, dearie?"

"Nine?"

"Anna will be here," she said, with Old World pride in her sense of duty. She started toward the door, then turned back to say, "Nora, please, was it the shooting at a church, at the Holy Name Cathedral?"

"It's been on the news already?" I said.

"Oh, yes, just before I'm falling asleep. The girl? Dead?"

"No, 'still cooking,' as a nurse said."

"It was drugs?" Anna asked in the style of seasoned police, not an aged woman who wouldn't know a key of coke from a sack of powdered sugar. "The newswoman says it is probably drugs."

It seemed that no big-city evening newscast was complete without a drug murder. Amused by Anna's tone, I shrugged. "I have no idea," I said. "I wish I knew half as much as the broadcasters."

She made her second start for the door. "I worry for Megan, even at her age. Good night, dearie. I'll be here at nine."

"Good night, Anna."

My first stop was Meg's bedroom. The closet light, the one Meg insisted be on as she went to sleep, faintly lit the room. Meg was tangled in a sheet, her nose pushed deep into a pillow, a sweep of blond hair crossing her left eye and cheek. I sat on the floor close to the bed and studied her breathing. Her build, long and gangly for a seven-year-old, was all mine, but her face was her father's: round, every corner soft, nothing harsh or pronounced. I watched her carefully for a while, touching her only with my eyes, my thoughts tightly focused on how much I loved this child. Before standing up, I brushed a kiss across her cheek. For some reason, when I left the room, my eyes brimmed with tears, secret tears a parent knows but can't explain.

In the kitchen, I ate an apple, a mound of stale potato chips, and half a bag of chocolate-chip cookies. I washed everything down with a warm orange soda. In my bedroom, I slipped from my clothes into a nightgown, then hopped to bed, leaving my crutches close by, on the floor. Before pulling up the sheet, I reached for my bedside phone and dialed the desk at the Eighteenth. Mr. Ramirez had called a few minutes ago; a squad had been sent to the hospital to take the family home. The desk sergeant knew nothing about Eva's condition.

I looked briefly out the window to the lake's black pitch. A breeze, mildly fishy, freshened the room and hurtled me into sleep.

4

My father, Albert Dybzewski, was a brake-and-front-end specialist at an auto repair shop. His formal education ended with high school. As a young husband, he agreed one day to accompany his glad-handing, hard-drinking brother Stanley to a community college outreach program—on the Great Books, mind you. Only the Lord knew what moved Stanley to attend the course; even my mother could not venture an opinion. But she did claim that my father's motivation had been brotherly: to keep Stanley out of the Higgins Avenue taverns for at least a few nights each month.

Stanley abandoned his quest for Higher Knowledge by the second week: the Rationalists had nothing on icy, foamy mugs of Schlitz. But my father continued the course for two semesters, then sailed off on his own reading program fed by the Chicago Public Library. Evenings for him meant a quick dispatch of the *Sun-Times* while at the kitchen table, then a couple of hours of deeper work in his easy chair. He read intently; distractions angered him.

Even as a young girl, I understood that my father's reading habits were a confidence the family held as closely as Holy Grail. Only my mother, myself, and my younger sister, Caitlin, were in the know, for my father was somehow embarrassed about his self-improvement. I could guess at his logic: residents of our neighborhood shouldn't be caught contemplating Spinoza or re-veling with Joyce. Some of our brethren in Jefferson Park were too narrowly blue-collar to admit to brain waves. After all, we had settled far west of the gentile Swedish enclave of Anderson-ville at Clark Street and Foster Avenue. No little herrings, pickled or jellied, were found on our tables, no pancakes oozing with lingonberries. For us, it was gut-busters: *kielbasa* sausage and *pirogi* and cold beets with horseradish. Oh, yes, and Bears foot-ball. Dostoevsky? Forget it.

As my father's senior-born, I was designated to be the first Dybzewski to carry the academic torch, and Literature, not Sci-ence, would be the discipline. It would have been the better choice to wait for Caitlin, but I gave no argument. By that time, my father's bony frame carried mostly loose skin; the muscle for performing ten thousand front-end alignments had long been drawn down by a pulmonary malignancy. If Albert wished me to knock around the Loyola University English Department, then so be it—I hadn't anything better to do anyway. Then, about the time I naïvely equated college with inanity, Albert died, so I quit Loyola and looked to the Chicago Police Department for my inspiration and sustenance.

Since I'd neglected to pull the shade the night before, the morning sun filled my window. I wanted to fall back to sleep, but I could not with the intrusive brightness, and not with Eva Ramirez now pecking at my brain. I grabbed my crutches and went to the bathroom, then returned to bed. I would go in to work on the Ramirez case, but it was Sunday, my supposed day off, so I wouldn't report in at 7 a.m.

I mulled over the shooting. "Find a motive and you're halfway there," my ex-partner Jack Flaherty used to say. Sex or drugs didn't seem to fit, in spite of their prevalent association with the city's violence. Maybe the shooting was a score being settled, but if so, the scene seemed improbable. One would think that such payment would have involved a bit more planning than an attempt on a Saturday afternoon in an open church. And squeezing off the shots through a closed door seemed equally foolish.

In another quarter-hour, the sun had crept fully across my bed; I rolled from my stomach to my back, still thinking. I tried to make something of crazy Rita's story but couldn't, and I bristled at the thought of another interview with the mad-woman.

Meg came quietly into the bedroom, looking for me. "Hi, honey," I said, smiling. "Here, get into bed. It's nice and warm." I tossed back an edge of covers and Meg ducked in.

With my arms wrapped around her, I asked, "How'd you sleep? Like a rock?" It was a question I would ask her often, a small joke between us.

"No, Mom," she said with feigned exasperation.

"Like a log?"

"No, Mom. I slept like a Meg."

We both laughed. I took her hands; they felt cold.

"Will Dad call today?" she said. "It's Sunday."

"Don't count on it."

She forced a weak smile of understanding.

Richard hadn't phoned Meg in a month. The man failed to understand that as forgiving as estranged children are, even they sometimes abandon ship. He was forfeiting his future with this bright and shiny piece of himself.

"Hungry?" I asked.

Meg nodded her head. "Can we have pancakes?"

"Pancakes it is."

"Great!" She beamed.

"I heard you had pizza last night, in Anna's apartment."

"Yeah, pizza. It was great, Mom."

"Did Anna eat it?" I said, joking. "Pizza?"

"Sure, some. But mostly she was on the phone. Somebody called her for a long talk."

"So Anna's turning into a telephone person, eh?"

"What?" she said, confused.

"Never mind. Let's get some pancakes."

My first stop was Northwestern Memorial's intensive care unit. The nurse in charge confirmed that Eva was not only still alive, but doing reasonably well. But she was "not out of the woods," as the nurse put it, and certainly not ready to be interviewed. Eva was still deeply asleep, the effects of her long surgery and anesthetic barely worn off. Maybe I could return in the afternoon, the nurse suggested.

As I turned to leave, the nurse said someone else had called to check on Eva's condition. "Her husband?" I asked. "A Mexican man?"

"I do think the caller had an accent," she said.

Now I was after the bullet from Eva's belly. No one manned the pathology lab's reception desk in the basement, probably because it was Sunday morning and things were only running at half-speed, or not at all. I walked past the desk into the lab itself.

A haggard young woman with lifeless brown hair stood at a lab table, with a dozen or so specimen cups—opaque covered plastic containers as big as coffee cups—stretched neatly in front of her. She was cataloguing the cups, each with a number, onto a computer. These were the specimens, the tissues removed from the previous day's surgeries, each to be studied by the pathologist.

"Good morning."

The woman pushed out a small "Hello," obviously a great effort for her. The effects of a late Saturday night, I decided.

"My name is Lieutenant Callum. I'm from the police." I flashed my ID that no one ever studied, only glanced at.

"Oh," the woman said, her eyes mildly surprised, her face otherwise stony.

"I'm looking for a bullet found in surgery last night. It's evidence in a shooting. The doctor told me it was sent here."

"It's in that cup there," the woman said, and pointed at one of the soldiers in the row. "I've already catalogued it."

"Good, then I can take it with me." I knew what the woman's response would be.

"No, not today. The pathologist has to see it yet and make his report. He doesn't come in on Sundays."

"Yes, but I—"

A wall phone on the other side of the room rang and interrupted my dissension. The woman walked toward the phone. As soon as I saw her back side, I made my move. Quietly picking up the cup that contained the bullet, I lifted the lid and saw the slug. I was still not out of bounds—the woman could not object to my just looking at the bullet—but then I picked it up from the cup and closed it into my hand. I turned an ear toward the phone.

"But you never told me about her," the woman murmured into the mouthpiece, her back still to me, her head held disconsolately down. "I don't—I don't think it's very fair of you to . . ."

I dropped the slug into my skirt pocket and reached in my purse for a fifty-cent piece, then set it into the plastic cup. I shook the cup gently: the coin rattled as the bullet might have. I replaced the opaque lid and returned the cup to its position on the table.

I turned toward the woman and said, "Thank you. I'll come back tomorrow."

She was whining into the phone, leaning against the wall, looking as though she needed the support.

This was West Lake View, a community where stores and homes were frugal one- or two-story structures often built right to the sidewalks. As many of the shop owners had their overhead signs in Spanish as did in English, and you might attend a service spoken in German at an Evangelical Lutheran church, Missouri Synod. You could buy groceries and insurance here, be educated, visit a doctor, eat out twenty-four hours a day, browse for antiques, secure a loan for a used car, be waked and buried, and all without ever having to leave the precinct for one of the city's more resplendent areas.

The neighborhood's rich diversity took anchorage in the Area Center Six station house at the corner of Belmont and Western Avenues. As architecture, Area Six was about as good as it got for us Chicago police. A relatively modern, dark brick two-story, the building offered a sampling of angles and corners and window placements that elevated it above the shoe-box motif shared by so many other Department buildings. Nevertheless, the station house wasn't without blemishes: the acres of parking on three sides of it; an unkempt lawn and ailing trees; and the front plaza's huge, unsightly, paint-chipped abstract sculpture—The Pastel Monster, we had dubbed it—whose creator hadn't had the audacity to sign.

I parked the Fury on Belmont. The station's south entry doors, propped open to the warm morning, swallowed washes of bus fumes into the lobby. Inside, a drunk fidgeted at a big red Coca-Cola machine. He looked as though he needed the hydration, if he could just get a can to drop from the machine's bowels. A few other people, human leftovers from the Saturday night patrol, sprawled in chairs along a wall.

I stopped at the lobby desk, a square of countertops with an enclosed central work area. Frankie Luchinski, desk sergeant on duty, stood behind the counter. "Hi, Frankie," I said.

"Hey, Nora, baby," Frankie said brusquely, looking up from

a sheaf of papers, beaming. "How are you, baby doll? Oooo, I knew you'd come back to Frankie someday."

Frankie Luchinski was a young Chicago Pole whose muscular arms and shoulders bulged under his shirt. Although moody at times, he was generally an unashamed kidder and perpetual optimist, a perfect policeman to greet the public. Besides, his strength could overcome any lobby visitor who didn't succumb to gentler forms of persuasion.

"I'm fine, Frankie," I said. "Has Art been through yet?"

Frankie slid his elbows across the desk, closer to me. "Hey, Nora, it's you and me, babe, not old Art, not Art the Fart."

"Frankie—"

"You can lean on me, Nora. Throw down those crutches, and lean on Frankie." He sizzled a gleaming smile at me. "I'll be your sugar daddy. Forever. You know that."

In a flash, I jerked a crutch toward Frankie's face, stopping just an inch short of his nose. Startled, he jumped back, nearly falling. A clump of hair dropped down over his forehead. "You're full of shit, Frankie," I said. "Now, did Art go through?"

Frankie straightened to mock attention. "Yes, ma'am. I believe Lieutenant Campbell passed by this desk at 0800 hours. He was wearing a yellow sport shirt, a cheap Hawaiian one I think, ma'am. I observed him to be heading upstairs."

"Thank you, Sergeant." I smiled and left for the staircase.

Detective Division shared Area Six's second floor with Juvenile Division. Our room was expansive, lit by fluorescence, and full of desks and work-counters, typewriters and the odd computer terminal. Art and I had pushed our desks together so they faced each other—good for hashing over our work as partners, bad if we weren't getting along for a day or two, but that rarely happened. Besides the desks, we had commandeered a metal file cabinet and an extra couple of chairs; I had contributed a pot of fake flowers I'd rescued from a rummage sale.

Our view was east to an overpass that took traffic up and over the congestion at Belmont and Western. Beneath the overpass was a barbershop, then Margie's Grill, an all-day, all-night operation that featured the North Side's best inflation-beater: three eggs with potatoes and toast for a dollar forty.

I dropped into my chair. "What do we have, Arthur?" I straightened a framed photograph of Meg on my desk. Art's shirt may not have been cheap, but it certainly was Hawaiian: an explosion of huge yellow flowers on a red background.

Art said, "First, we have a collection of fingerprints that need sorting. There were probably twenty or thirty different ones found in and around the confessional." He paused. "Who says that Catholics don't go to confession anymore?"

"Are the prints any good?"

"They're lousy, all of them. The wood surfaces weren't glossy enough for good prints."

I sipped at a cup of coffee Art had had waiting on my desk. He knew I didn't mind—in fact, even liked—cold coffee. "Thanks for the brew."

"Sure."

"What'd the Sox do last night?" I asked.

"Lost. Ten, three. They got three runs in the first, then . . . I'd rather not talk about it."

"Cubs, Arthur, Cubs, Cubs," I said. "Think Cubs."

"Cubs, my ass."

"I won't tell. Nobody on the South Side will be the wiser."

"Wouldn't matter. They could tell just by lookin' at me. You know, the eyes of a traitor."

I smiled and sipped again. "How about the bullets?"

"There's four of them, three dug out of the confessional and the fourth from the hand of schizo Rita. Oh, and there's the empty casing found in the center aisle. Now, I'm no ballistics guy, but the bullets don't look very common to me."

He dumped the casing and bullets from a small cardboard box onto the desk. They rolled across the metal, then settled. I picked up one of the bullets in my fingers, but it meant nothing to me.

"I've got the one from the hospital," I said, "the one they found inside the Ramirez woman." I pulled it from my skirt pocket and held it side by side with the one in my other hand.

"How'd you get that so quick?" Art asked. "I always get that stuff about 'the pathologist has to inspect it,' or 'it won't be ready till tomorrow,' or, 'where's your warrant, Lieutenant?' They never give me—"

"They didn't give me anything."

"You took it?"

"Yep."

"Jesus," Art said, with a shake of his head. "Why do you do those things? You know it's not procedure. Somebody from the hospital is sure to call here. Shit."

He downed a swig of coffee; then, waving a forefinger at me, he said, "I'm telling you right now, Nora, you're talking to Smilin' Ray by yourself this time." Raymond Melchior was Deputy Chief of the Area Six detectives. "I'm not going in there with you this time. No, ol' Arthur's not listening to any more tirades about stolen evidence. I'll come drag you out after the hurricane."

I didn't rise to the bait.

Art hesitated, staring at my blank expression. Then, chuckling, he said, "At least it's metallic this time. It won't rot in the drawer."

He referred to my last theft of evidence from the same hospital. Several months before, the victim of a gangland killing had been found in a dumpster, hands and feet dismembered in a bizarre ritual understood only by gangs. The man had been carrying no identification. The body was taken to Northwestern Memorial for the forensic pathologist to do an autopsy—once again, on a weekend. Nobody—neither the pathologist nor the police—except me felt there was any rush; the victim was almost surely a gang member, whose demise would mean one less headache for the police. After all, what policework was more efficient than one criminal killing off another? But I hadn't been satisfied with waiting through a weekend for identification of the body, so I sneaked into the hospital morgue on the Saturday afternoon and left with one of the victim's butchered hands wrapped in paper towels.

Back at the station, I fingerprinted the hand without anyone seeing me, but when I returned it to the morgue that evening, I was spotted. My police ID cleared my way out, but didn't prevent a call the next day from the hospital administrator to Chief Melchior. Immediately after the call, Melchior invited both myself and Art into his office where he delivered a roaring, thirty-minute diatribe, once even heaving a weighty copy of the Chicago *Yellow Pages* against the wall.

Not thinking now about Melchior or my theft of the bullet, I said, "Okay, we've got the bullets and casing, a few third-rate fingerprints, and some testimony from the Father and Rita what's-her-name. What's it all add up to?"

"Jack-shit."

"You're right." I sighed.

For another hour and three more cups of coffee we reviewed what we thought had gone on in the Cathedral, but came up with nothing but ideas in flux. We knew we were sputtering; it was time to head back to the streets. Solutions to violent crime rarely walk into the station.

I decided Art would talk again with Father Ritgen and Rita the rug-scrubber. Would these witnesses have anything to say worth more than they had yesterday? Probably not, but one never knew what the soothing hours of sleep might help resurrect.

Art protested comically, saying, as usual, I gave him the worst jobs because of his age and his race. We both knew he meant neither charge.

I would go to the Crime Lab in the Headquarters Building downtown, then visit Eva Ramirez.

The Loop, the loose designation for that part of downtown Chicago bounded by raised commuter train tracks, the El tracks, was nearly deserted. This commercial heart of the city bustled for six days of the week, but never on Sundays. Offices and stores were closed, the consumer action switching to the Near North Side, where North Michigan Avenue and the Gold Coast didn't know about—or at least didn't admit to—the Sabbath.

I zipped through the Loop's streets and stopped at Police Headquarters on South State Street. I rode an elevator to the seventh-floor Crime Lab and stopped at Ballistics. The only person working that day, an ancient security guard named Otto, sat at the front desk. I knew Otto from my frequent visits to the lab. He was a warm and humorous man whose dried-out face was creased with deep, convoluted wrinkles. A stack of Sunday newspapers sat on his desk; a portable radio blared out the Cubs game, the radio's high volume an accommodation to his hearing.

"I have some bullets and a casing, Otto," I said as I pulled them from my purse. "Mark this slug separately. It's from the victim's body."

Otto tagged everything, dropping things into appropriate envelopes.

"Can I get these done tomorrow?" I asked.

"You can if I put them at the top of the ledger," he said, with an old man's twinkle.

"Thanks."

"Sure. Say, Lieutenant, how come you're using your crutches today? Where's your leg?"

"It's broken. It's in the shop."

"You should have an extra one, then, for times like this."

"Can't afford the luxury, Otto. It's two thousand dollars for a new one."

"They charge you two grand for a new leg?"

"Yep."

"Goddamn robbers!"

5

Eva Ramirez's face was bloated and stretched—she wasn't the same beauty I had seen bleeding on the Cathedral carpet the afternoon before. A thin, clear plastic tube exited her nose and led to a large glass suction bottle on the floor. Clumps of bloody mucus tracked their way along the lumen of the tube, following the pull of the suction. An IV sprung from each arm, and from under the sheets, one final tube, the one to her bladder, drained urine into a plastic bag hung from the bed frame. Eva had been plied with all the dehumanizing technology of modern medicine, and because of it she was still alive.

The nurse had granted me fifteen minutes. Eva, her swollen dark eyes opened narrowly but bright nonetheless, seemed to understand when I introduced myself.

"Who did this to me?" she said, her voice as dry as old leaves. Her accent was less obvious than her husband's.

"We don't know," I said. "I thought you might help us with that."

"No. I can't."

So as not to threaten, I started obliquely. "Did you see your family today?"

"They came for a while."

"The baby, too?"

"Yes."

45

"Your Emilio is a beautiful child."

She smiled weakly; her lips were like cracked parchment.

I hesitated a moment, then carefully said, "Have you been involved with anyone lately, Eva?"

"Involved?" she said, my question driving the sweetness from her eyes.

"With a man, I mean."

"With two little kids and a baby?" she answered scornfully, as though I were ignorant of the constraints of motherhood. "There's no extra energy after that, believe me. And I have my husband."

I continued with my litany of questions—drugs, gangs, illegal aliens—and found nothing. Then, "Did anyone talk to you while you were in the confessional?"

"Just the priest."

"Did you think anybody was outside the door, someone ready to hurt you?"

"No."

I lifted my face to the ceiling, searching the dusty, celery-colored tiles for my next question. "Did you hear a gunshot a minute or two before you were hit?"

She scrunched a nostril to move it away from the stomach tube. "I heard one shot first. I didn't know it was a shot then, but it must've been."

"Where was that shot?"

"Not close. Out in the church somewhere."

"But you didn't make anything of it?"

"No."

"The next shots were close?"

"They hit me in the stomach."

Tending to believe everything Eva had said, I broke from my routine of questions, talking instead about her children, especially the two older boys. Eva seemed heartened by the switch in tempo; her limbs lost some of the stiffness I had noticed when the subject of her shooting was center stage. After twenty minutes of wandering, easy conversation, I thanked her and left.

As I crutched down the hallway, I wondered if Eva realized how close she had come to death in that shattered confessional. I thought of a passage I had once read, words about how every one of us spends every second of our lives standing at the brink of eternity. I was glad Eva hadn't toppled over that edge, glad she hadn't left Juan and her young sons behind without her. For the briefest of moments, I thought of my own grand fortune, leg or no leg, husband or no husband. Me, alive and healthy on planet Earth, a daughter joyously at my side, and that chance for shameless new love always before me.

After Eva, I headed home. It was early afternoon. Art and I had agreed that when we each finished, we would take the rest of Sunday off. There wasn't anybody else to talk to that day, and all the Crime Lab work was on hold till Monday. I hoped for a break from the ballistics tests.

Lake Shore Drive crawled with cars and motorbikes. It was the first warm Sunday of spring, the temperature already eighty degrees, and still rising. The beaches and parks that sprawled between the Drive and Lake Michigan were even more crowded than the roads. People of all ages, dressed for the weather in brightly colored swimsuits or summer shorts and tops, lounged in the sand or bicycled at the edge of the beaches or jogged on the parks' gravel paths. A few brave ones waded and played in the lake, in water still icy with winter. Hot-dog stands and balloon salesmen drew long lines of customers; an occasional dog meandered among the legs, sniffing for its master. On the horizon, a scatter of sailboats made tiny white triangles against the sky and the deep azure lake. The smell of the day was from water and sand, not from cars or garbage or factories.

At home, I thanked Anna and paid her for the week. While Meg and I sat at the kitchen table and ate peanut-butter-and-lettuce sandwiches, I said, "How about the zoo, Meg?"

"Today?" she answered with enough surprise that I felt a twinge of guilt.

"Yes, today."

"Well, yeah . . . but, Mom, I have to finish this sandwich before we can go."

"I know that, Meg."

"Should I change?" She was in a white blouse and yellow jumper.

"I'd put on some shorts. It's warm enough."

"Should we wear our sunglasses, Mom?"

"Definitely."

"Can we get some decent music on the car radio? I mean, instead of that police stuff?"

"Sure, sure."

"Great!" She beamed. "Are we gonna rock, Mom?"

"Right down to our bones, kiddo."

"Okay! Hey, can Anna come?"

"Good idea," I said. "I should've thought of that."

I reached for the wall phone next to me, and dialed Anna but got a busy signal. Meg tried again, a few minutes later. "It's still busy, Mom," she said.

"We'd better go," I said. "We'll take Anna another day."

We headed south on the Drive, the Fury's radio blasting Rolling Stones and Grateful Dead songs at misdemeanor levels of volume. Meg, her sunglasses drifted halfway down her nose, bounced rhythmically in the front passenger seat.

The parking spots at the Lincoln Park Zoo were mobbed. I pulled in to a no-parking zone and flipped down the visor with my Police Department sign.

"Are you supposed to do this, Mom?" Meg asked. "I mean,

park here?" Meg's recent ability to read had brought with it a host of new problems for me.

"Not exactly. See, I can park here, but, ah . . . not, I guess, when I'm not on police business."

"Is this police business?" Meg asked innocently.

I smiled. "No," I said gently.

Meg tried to save me. With great seriousness, she said, "Well, Mom, if someone in the zoo is being mean to the animals, then you might have to take them to jail."

My embarrassment made me restart the car. "No one is being mean to the animals. I guess I forgot I'm not on duty."

I backed out and found a spot a block away. As we walked a rocky path back to the entrance, I prayed that my new leg would be ready as scheduled.

The zoo was as jammed as the beaches and parks. The heat made the ape and lion houses acrid, the smell of the animals' urine whacking people in the face as soon as they entered. The outdoor displays, especially the seal pool, were the big hits of the day. Children and parents clustered at the fence around the pool, but nobody pushed or shoved. A bag lady sorted through a garbage can at the edge of the crowd.

By four o'clock both Meg and I were hot and tired. We plunked down on a bench being watched by a fenced elephant. "Hungry?" I asked.

"Yeah," Meg said.

"Me too. Want to go to Ed's?" *Ed Debevic's* was a restaurant just north of the Loop. A reconstruction of a nineteen-fifties diner, it had become the new darling of the Near North Side.

"Ed's!" Meg yelped. "Really?"

"Really."

We were back in the Fury in ten minutes and close to Ed's in another ten. Just a half-dozen blocks away, I drove past the Cathedral. I slowed at the front entrance, started to speed up, but then stopped completely. The Cathedral's Gothic face, a collection of beautifully arched windows and spires, gleamed in the afternoon sun, the light burning the usually pale yellow stone to a dazzling whiteness. The effect reminded me more of a Monet painting than the real stone in front of me.

"Meg," I said, "I want to go into that church for a minute. Okay?"

"Are we still going to Ed's?"

"I promised, didn't I?"

The heavy front doors to the church were unlocked. Almost, but not quite overwhelmed by their weight, Meg held them open as I passed through with my crutches. The church was empty; even crazy Rita was gone. It was refreshingly cool inside; the huge, vaulted rotunda of a ceiling held the hot afternoon sun at bay. When the great doors clunked shut, the city's street noises magically ceased behind us.

I gazed around the Cathedral. Though at first I hadn't been sure why I wanted to come in, I now decided to try to act out what might have happened there twenty-four hours before. I located the torn metal grillwork, six or eight feet up the back wall where the first shot had hit. "Meg," I said, "stand over here. You're going to be Rita."

"Who?"

"Never mind."

Meg came and looked up at the metal. "What happened?" she asked.

"A bullet hit there."

"In a church?"

I walked toward the front of the church, then turned around. Meg stood dutifully under the bullet-creased metal, very near the center aisle. She was a foot or so shorter than Rita, but I could still pretend she was a target. I started to point my forefinger at her in a mock gesture of shooting when it suddenly struck me that this was all wrong. Rita's wounded bucket and, almost surely, the kneeling, scrubbing woman had been twenty feet to the left of the center aisle, nowhere near the point where the bullet first struck before its ricochet to the left.

"Meg," I said, "move over that way." I pointed her away from center; she walked slowly to my left. "More, Meg, go further away from the aisle."

Meg poked a bit, but was soon at the spot where Rita would have been the afternoon before. Now, repointing my finger at my daughter, I eyed the damaged grillwork on the back wall, then swung my finger to aim at the point of ricochet. The difference in the angle of aim between the two targets was forty or fifty degrees. Only a blind man would have missed Rita by such a distance. And besides, it now occurred to me, she had probably been on the floor, behind the pews, safely out of sight.

The weekend's warm weather unraveled violently. At two o'clock Monday morning, a swarm of dense clouds slid relentlessly across the city from the prairies to the west, and clouds piled themselves up against the moon, occluding all its light. Then came the pyrotechnics: blue-gray flashes of lightning mixed with the steady hammer of thunder. The rain fell through the glow of streetlights in glistening, pounding sheets of water and sound. Curbs were flooded in an hour.

I was up half the night. For a time, when Richard was with me, I had been better during electrical storms: in bed, I was able to take solace against his bulk. A storm's hash of light and noise would rarely waken Richard, and just his sleeping presence reassured me. When I was young and first married, I took his composure to signify personal bravery. Later, I came to realize that Richard wasn't exhibiting courage as much as pervasive lassitude.

I wakened at first light. Outside, the city had calmed; the storm was finally wrung out of the now freshened sky. After deciding it was Monday, I sorted through my upcoming day. There would be Meg, the hospital, the office, Ballistics, then the receipt of my new prosthesis. Finally, I remembered Melchior. Only half in jest, I prayed: "Please, dear God, don't make me face Smilin' Ray today." My request to the Almighty finished, I got out of bed and showered.

"You have to eat," I said.

We were at the kitchen table, quiet Meg across from me. A glass of orange juice stood in front of her. Her long blond hair—my color, but lighter—was still wet from her shower. Outside the window, a few puffs of cloud drifted against a brilliant blue sky.

"Did you hear me, Meg? Now, eat."

"Why?"

"Because you need brain food for school. It's energy."

I finished my coffee, then adjusted the collar of my blouse. I had gone back to a woolen suit—it was gray and pinstriped, more fashionably tailored than what I was comfortable with—when the radio said the temperature had dropped into the thirties.

"You can't think all day on a glass of juice," I said.

"I'll have a hot lunch at school."

"Hot lunch? C'mon, I've seen that stuff you kids get for lunch. Somebody at the Health Department must be on the take."

"What?"

"Never mind."

"If you'd get some decent food, Mom, I'd eat."

"Decent food?"

"Yeah, like some of that cereal with the pink marshmallows in it."

I *had* bought that cereal for Meg once—yes, there was a fleet of pink marshmallows that floated in the milk—and I had decided that feeding it to one's child was a crime against nature.

"No cereal with marshmallows, Meg. End of discussion."

Before heading downtown, I dropped Meg off at Anna's. We

kissed goodbye, our tiff at breakfast already forgotten. At eight o'clock, Anna would walk her to school, then pick her up at three, and keep her until I returned home from work.

Like Sunday, my first stop was the hospital. I found Eva sitting uncomfortably in a straight-backed chair. The tube was out of her nose. Although her face was still pale, it was less swollen. Her dark hair had been neatly combed by the nurse.

I stayed for thirty minutes, going over the same ground I had the afternoon before. In spite of feeling poorly, Eva gave the same answers to the same questions, never mixing up any details. I walked away as confused as ever.

His staff called him "Smilin' Ray," but only behind his back. To the unknowing, the nickname portrayed a buoyant, playful sort of man, an affectionate boss, this sixty-year-old Raymond Melchior, a Deputy Chief and the man in charge of Area Six detectives. The truth, however, lay to the contrary.

Melchior's moniker was born in derision at the Eighteenth District station house on West Chicago Avenue several years before my first assignment there as a patrol officer. Station lore had it that a long-retired, half-witted janitor named Marraway, who cleaned then Commander Melchior's office, had dreamed up the name in a moment of singular but utter brilliance. The name stuck because the source of the ridicule was plain enough: no one at the Eighteenth—and there were still a few troops around who had been there the full twenty years Melchior had— could recall a smile, even a tiny, evanescent grin, ever softening Smilin' Ray's stern face. Humorless and irascible, he honored his nickname in the fullest breach. Maybe, the staff tittered, he saved all his rollicking for home, for Mrs. Smilin' Ray. If not, she had our greatest sympathy.

My experience with Melchior's bad temper was firsthand. When I was still doing grunt work—working pickpocket details at downtown train stations and interviewing the victims of rape and illegal abortion—he was just an unpleasantness, a commander in his office who rarely spoke to me. By chance, we were promoted about the same time, me to detective and Melchior to Deputy Chief of Area Six, one of the home bases for the Department's Detective Division, and the Center where I was newly assigned. Soon after our promotions, things changed; Melchior went on the assault. Why should any woman be made detective? he said to my face. And why, for crissake, he said, does Downtown have to stick one in my Area? I had the good sense not to respond, except with a quick, upward flick of my head, a defiance Ray hadn't the insight to notice.

Melchior countered my promotion by teaming me with Jack Flaherty, a grizzled, thirty-year veteran who Melchior figured would grind me into Chicago's pavement. No such luck. Whether it was Flaherty's mellowing age or my unjaded nature was unclear, but within six months we were the most productive team in the Area. Flaherty hadn't shown so much energy since he had fought to make detective himself, and I steamed along on the happiest conjunction of events my thirty years had ever seen. I had made detective, I had a reasonably adequate husband, and a radiant two-year-old daughter. Moonwalkers had nothing on me.

Our Flaherty-Callum team blitzed the North Side's crime that first year. We brought in a dozen petty thieves, two rapists, a gang of car-strippers responsible for three years of auto thefts, and a Rush Street pimp who turned young, once-beautiful black women into desperate junkies spilling over with venereal disease.

All of this work gained Flaherty and me great distinction among our District peers, but not with Melchior. He said little or nothing to us, acting as if our successes were only luck: even a blind pig will occasionally root up an acorn. And Melchior never bothered to commend us on our biggest score, when we jailed the maniacal killer of two high-school girls.

It had gone like this. A murderer had stuffed his victims'

dismembered bodies into a steel waste can, then dumped the can in with the perch in Belmont Harbor. When a few of the gruesome remains—an arm and a pair of legs—floated from the can into the calm waters surrounding the harbor's luxury cruisers, a howl went up from the lakefront's well-to-do.

Flaherty and I were on the case by nightfall that day. Within a week we had recovered the can, traced it to a garbage pick-up company, then to one of its customers, and, finally, to a pitiful and hopelessly deranged employee. A confession poured out of the madman within an hour of his arrest. The city breathed its relief, and Jack and I hugged. Smilin' Ray never even called us into his office for a congratulatory cup of coffee.

Being ignored may have been insulting, but it wasn't the worst I was to see from Melchior. There was a time, after the loss of my leg, when he actively tried to have me thrown off the Force. Of course, he would have to grant me a full disability and pension, but he wanted me out nonetheless.

It began one midnight when Flaherty and I were the lead team on a drug raid that we had spent six months setting up. A million-dollar deal was going down in a stinking hellhole of a slum apartment when Jack and I burst through the door. Jack led the way in as he always did, not because he was the man but because of his experience. The three men who sat around a table froze in their chairs as Jack charged through the door into the smoky room, his gun bouncing in their faces. I followed, laying back several feet behind Jack, who stood close to the table.

Suddenly, from an adjoining bedroom, another man, a boozy, filthy vermin, appeared, his shotgun loaded and cocked. I was all he could see, and he fired at me in an instant. The shot drove me to the floor, my left thigh and knee taking its full force. Before my blood splattered, Jack had pumped two perfectly aimed bullets through my assailant's brain. The man was so dead so fast that he never even twitched.

I was taken, mute, in shock and stark terror, to the Northwestern Memorial emergency room. There I was matter-of-factly told that an amputation was all that could be done. Do you realize, the surgeon said, that this was a shotgun injury at point-blank range, and what did you expect, and would you like to see your x-rays? While a nurse, Mary Calder, bent over the cart and held me tenderly, I consented. In an hour, the exploded remains of my leg and half my thigh lay on a steel tray in the laboratory.

I was hospitalized for a week, then at home for the two months that Anna Skrabina mothered me through my horror. In the middle of my recuperation, Richard left me for California. I had noticed for some months before my injury that he and I had developed a slow leak: the pluck of our marriage was diffusing away like air. I had learned that early in a marriage spouses may be wonderful romantics, but when the romance inevitably went, that's when love had to become interesting. Ours never did.

A few weeks after Richard left, he wrote to say that he had become so financially involved in the wine country—as it turned out, he was picking grapes—that he couldn't return home. It was a divorce handled by the post office and two attorneys.

While I remained disabled, Melchior saw a chance to sack his one-legged detective: he asked Downtown to dismiss me from the Force. But he had underestimated me, the me who refused to wrap herself inside the warm blanket of her infirmity. Within weeks I had a prosthesis made for my stump, and by three months I was walking on it without crutches. The new leg hurt and didn't fit well, but I wore it anyway, even ran with it.

After a cursory review, Downtown did as Melchior had requested; their decision was an obvious one. But I protested—I was a fire-eater in those days—and I petitioned for an appeal. The administrators were forced to listen because I had a certain amount of notoriety just then: my injury had occurred soon after we had brought in the butcher who dumped the girls into Belmont Harbor. Besides, the newspapers had carried the story of my wounding and recovery as a human-interest piece. And, finally, I was not above involving certain women's and union organizations in my plight. After all, a woman—even a disabled woman—has a basic right to work, hasn't she?

When I was tested with my new leg, I proved I could do nearly everything I could before the injury, so Downtown cleared my return to duty. Jack Flaherty rejoiced. Melchior sulked bitterly, searching his soul for another bit of malice. And soon he found one.

Three weeks after I returned to work, Jack dropped dead of a brain aneurysm: our team seemed crossed by dark stars. When the pall of Jack's death cleared from the station house, I was left without a partner. Melchior decided my new mate would be Art Campbell, a fifty-year-old black man. Melchior's twisted logic went like this: he figured that as a white person, I would naturally despise blacks as much as he did, blacks being the only group in his command that he detested more than women. What better way to punish me than to team me with Campbell, one of the "night-warriors," as Melchior derisively called them. He thought Campbell would suffer too, for who in their right mind would want a one-legged female partner beside him when the proverbial chips were down?

Smilin' Ray's artless cunning failed again, and miserably. Art and I came together, I not caring if Art was black or green or mauve, and Art not counting legs. Art was satisfied to let me head the team; he didn't see me as one to try to shove him around. Within days we were motoring along in perfect harmony, and Melchior was left muttering to himself like a burlesque clown.

6

The lobby at Area Six was quiet when I arrived from the hospital. It's often that way after a busy weekend; the station seems to need a few hours of Monday morning to pass before the traffic begins again. Taking advantage of the lull, Frankie Luchinski stood alone at a corner inside the lobby's four-sided desk, his face buried in a newspaper. He didn't notice me until I sang out, "Frankie, oh, Frankie."

He looked up; his expression was flat, with none of the usual impertinence brightening his face. "Hi," he said.

"What's wrong, Frankie?"

He closed his paper, and we'd started toward each other when a cop summoned him to the phone in an adjoining office. Frankie nodded to me, then walked through a break in the counter, leaving the desk unattended for a minute. I turned toward the stairs, glancing at Frankie's paper as I passed. I was mildly surprised to see a sheet of yellow notepaper sticking out between pages of that day's *Racing Form*. Curious, I snatched the sheet: it was filled with a column of two- and three-digit numbers written in pencil. The words *quinella wheel* or *trifecta box* followed each set of numbers, then either the letters RJM or FGL.

I craned my neck toward the office and saw Frankie still on the phone, his back toward me. As in the hospital lab the morning before, I acted instinctively. I carried the sheet behind the desk to a copy machine, and in ten seconds had a duplicate for my purse. I returned to the desk and slid the original back between the pages of the *Form*, then left for my office.

Before saying "Good morning" or sitting down, I tossed the photocopy onto the desk and blurted, "Art, what the hell is this?"

Art was flipping through a computer printout. "There's no Eva Ramirez anywhere in the file," he said, ignoring my question, his eyes fixed on the printout. "The closest I can come is an Evita Ramirez ticketed for improper lane-changing six months ago, and she's eighty years old, probably half-blind." He looked up at my fancy suit. "You in court today, girl?"

"Did you hear anything I just said?"

"What?"

I pointed to the sheet, which he had noticed as soon as it hit his desktop.

Art dropped the printout to the desk. For a moment, he placed his large hands over his cheeks and eyes. Uncovering them, he looked squarely into my eyes and said, "Frankie's dirty laundry."

"This quinella wheel and trifecta box stuff—what is it?"

"Exotic bets," he said. "The numbers are post positions."

"Horses, dogs, what?"

"Probably thoroughbreds. Arlington Park opened last week, runs every afternoon."

"And the letters next to the bets?"

"Figure them out. It doesn't take a physicist."

I picked up the paper and looked again. "FGL is Frankie," I said, "and RJM is Melchior?"

"Congratulations."

I turned and stepped to my desk. Sitting, I plunked my baggy purse down in front of me. The pistol inside thumped on the steel desktop. "I haven't noticed Melchior or Frankie going to Arlington any afternoons."

"Me neither."

"Then where are their bets being placed?"

"A book on North Dearborn," he said. "He lives in a vintage condo. Very nice. You'd love the view of Lincoln Park."

"Why to a bookie?" I pressed. "If they can't go to the track, why not use an Off-Track Parlor? They're legal at least."

"Goddamn, you ask a lot of questions. Did your mother ever tell you you might be too curious?"

"Answer, Art."

In a voice as hard as granite, he said, "Because you can't bet off-track without physically being there, so it means leaving work. Because the parlors take a percentage of any winnings, and the book doesn't. He's overjoyed at just pocketing the losses. And then there's the big reason—they take only cash off-track. No credit."

"Okay," I said cynically. "Now here's a simple question. Why haven't you busted the book?"

"Are you kidding, Nora?" he snapped. "How long do you think I'd last after bringing in Ray's bookie?"

"It's him that wouldn't last, not you," I said. "Downtown couldn't let that go by."

"They'd take months to investigate it, and they wouldn't ever prove rat-shit. You think the bookie or Melchior's going to admit to it?"

"What about Frankie? He mules the money."

"Frankie wouldn't say a word. Now, there's something you can make book on."

"Did Jack know?" I asked.

"Flaherty?"

"Yes."

"Sure he knew," Art said, reaching for his coffee. "Have some coffee, Nora. Cool your jets, then let's get to work on this shooting."

I wasn't content to let it drop. "Why didn't Jack tell me?"

"Who knows? Maybe he didn't want to burden you. Consider yourself lucky."

"Goddammit," I said, "does everybody know around here but me?"

Art said, "It was just Jack and me, as far as I know. That's it, I'm sure. And now you, thanks to Frankie's carelessness. He's a stupid man, Frankie. Shit for brains. He's gonna get his ass in an auger someday."

I poured coffee from the pot on Art's desk. "I'm going to find this son of a bitch, Art," I said. "Melchior could be put away on this one."

"Forget you ever heard about it. Forget Melchior ever got on your case three years ago. Stop with that eye-for-an-eye shit, will you?"

Sipping coffee and hearing the traffic in the hallway outside, I said, "He couldn't touch me."

"Couldn't touch you?" Art said harshly. "Don't be so god-damned naïve, Nora. Melchior sets the schedule, he assigns the cases and tells us who he wants brought in and when. He could make it very dangerous for you. He could send you after people the cops aren't supposed to bother. You could get your brains shot out just like your leg was shot off."

He paused and glared down at his desk, looking embarrassed at the mention of my leg, something he hadn't ever done so directly before. More quietly, he continued: "And if you don't think he could do all that to you, then you're not as smart as I thought."

I slapped my desk. "Melchior supporting a bookie—dammit, Art, that gets me!"

"Then look at it this way," he said. "What do you think Melchior makes at the track? Hundreds? Thousands? Well, if you think about it for two seconds, you'll know he doesn't make shit. For every bet he wins, he's got to be losing on three others. The system's not built for the bettor to win—you know that. He's losing his fat ass."

A huge smile broke across Art's face. "Hey, make that the point," he said. "Enjoy the idea that Melchior's dropping a ton of money. Why, you'll never want to bring that bookie in. Pretty soon you'll be out there protecting him."

A young officer stepped into the office and delivered the bad news: "The Captain wants to see you both in his office. Now."

Solidarity between man and animals can occur to striking degrees. Dog owners, for instance, are frequently said to choose breeds that look uncommonly like themselves: the skinny, mean woman who favors Chihuahuas; the bearded and burly man who raises sheepdogs; the sag-face who wouldn't be without a slobbering bulldog.

If Smilin' Ray Melchior had a biological echo, then it was the walrus. Six feet three inches and nearly three hundred pounds, he was as neckless as a walrus, his head perched on declining shoulders, his chin doubled and tripled with rolls of blubber. His widely spaced, dark eyes and sloping forehead led to a skull so flat that one might logically ask, "Is there enough room inside for a braincase?"

Art and I entered Melchior's domain. I watched the paths of my crutches carefully, not wanting to create the slightest disturbance in that office.

Melchior was seated, his great girth forward over his desk; his dark jacket and tie were both police issue. He bit on a long black cigar with smoke curling from its end. He looked up and said, "Sit down, Lieutenants."

We took the only two chairs, both close to the front of the desk. Instinctively, we shoved our chairs farther back after sitting down, to distance ourselves from the storm we feared might break.

"I hear there was a shooting this weekend," Melchior said, "at

Holy Name Cathedral." He scanned our faces, peering over his half-rim glasses, comically small on his huge face.

I started. "A woman named Eva Ramirez was shot. She was in one of the confessionals."

"She dead?"

"No," I said, "I saw her this morning, and she's going to be okay. She was shot in the belly. Nothing vital hit, I guess."

Melchior dragged on the cigar and blew a column of blue-gray smoke into the air in front of him. "What was it? Drugs? Jealous lover? Family turmoil?"

"Doesn't seem to be any of those," I said, feeling good that Melchior still looked calm. "Eva's the young mother of what seems to be a good family. The shooting doesn't really make any sense yet."

"What have you got so far?"

"Not much," Art broke in. "A couple of witnesses, one a completely nuts old lady, and the other a priest who's probably still shaking in his boots. He was in the confessional box next to the one where Ramirez was kneeling." Art, looking relaxed, chuckled. "I think the gunplay scared the livin' shit out of him."

Melchior didn't share in Art's laughter. "Do we have anything from the witnesses?"

"The old lady was too far away to see much," Art said, "and the priest was closed inside his box. He saw nothing, only heard the shots."

Melchior puffed again, and another cloud of smoke oozed, corner to corner, from his mouth. "You get a description from the victim?"

"She never saw the shooter," I said. "She was inside the confessional."

"Shot through a closed door?"

"Yeah," Art said, "point-blank range through the door."

"Christ," Melchior said. "So what you're telling me is that we have an apparently innocent woman shot in church, at point-blank range, through a closed door, and you don't have a god-damned thing to go on."

"That's about it," I said.

"Yep," Art affirmed.

"Weapon?" Melchior said.

"None found," Art answered.

"No bullets recovered, either?"

I stayed quiet, remembering my trip to the hospital lab the day before and now sensing Melchior moving closer to home. I listened to Art fill the breach: "We recovered one bullet from the back of the church, and three from the confessional. Oh, and an empty casing from the center aisle. You know, Captain, the crazy old lady didn't know if it was a man or a woman she saw coming into the church."

"Any bullets recovered from the victim?"

A pause.

"There was one bullet pulled from Mrs. Ramirez," Art said.

Another large drag, then a moving funnel of smoke. "Pulled out during surgery?" Melchior asked.

Now I was sure somebody from the hospital had called. "Yes," I said, "it was recovered from her abdomen by her surgeon. We have it."

"The hospital's pathologist delivered it?" Melchior asked.

"No, I picked it up for us," I said. Smilin' Ray was proceeding step by step, eliciting testimony like a trial attorney.

"You picked it up?" Melchior said, pulling his cigar from his mouth and leaning his bulk toward me, "or did you steal it from the lab, Lieutenant—before the pathologist ever saw it?"

"I claimed it."

"Why, goddammit?"

"Because I thought we needed it sooner than we would get it," I said. "Sometimes it takes two or three days to get evidence back from the hospital. I didn't think we could afford to wait. The bullet is being checked in Ballistics this morning."

"Well, Lieutenant Callum," Melchior honked, "just who the fuck are you to decide hospital and police procedures? Tell me, who?"

There it was: *fuck*. I had been unruffled until I heard the word, but now I cringed. Unlike some policemen, Melchior didn't pepper his daily conversation with obscenities, saving them, rather, for reprimands—memorable reprimands, like this one.

My response to Melchior's question was a silent stare into his bottomless black eyes. I was trying to look more terrifying than he and his bluster were. I hoped to achieve in silence what he couldn't do with thunderclaps.

Melchior broke the quiet. "I'm asking you again, Callum, who the fuck do you think you are that you can steal evidence from the hospital laboratory? Would you like to fuckin' take over the work of the goddamned forensic pathologist?"

I made sure not to blink, trying to beat him with my eyes, as I had done to my father more than once.

Brave Art wiggled in again. "Captain, Nora saved a life in the Cathedral Saturday."

"What?" Melchior turned to look at Art.

"See, a couple of rookies were first on the scene, and they pegged it as a murder. When Nora came, she realized the Ramirez woman was still alive. Nora called the medics."

"Hot shit," Melchior barked derisively. "Callum gets the gold star."

He was puffing on his cigar two and three times after every sentence, the smoke rising through the room; we were losing him inside a boiling, blue-gray tent.

"I seem to remember, Callum, that you've done this before. Like when you stole a goddamned chopped-off hand from the hospital morgue," he bellowed. "You couldn't wait for that pathology report, either, could you?"

He was almost completely concealed by the smoke cloud; only the burning tip of his cigar was still plainly visible. "Well," he said, "you do this again, Callum, and you're fuckin' gone! Got it? Now, get the fuck out of my office!"

I stood and crutched my way out. In my soundless fury, I had considered charging him with betting the horses, but I decided to tuck that pearl away for better use on another day. Like Art, I had learned long ago that it was pointless to respond to Melchior. His venom was real enough to himself, but its lasting effect on me would be as airy as the smoke that filled his office.

I left the station for Ballistics after filing the required initial report on the Ramirez shooting. It was only three hours since Mount Melchior had blown its stack, but already it seemed like three days, with a new calm well in progress. I was back on track now, fully recovered from the shock waves, again more taken by the challenge of the investigation than by the repulsive and pitiable personality of my commander. While I was downtown, Art would interview employees of the shops and fast-food restaurants around the Cathedral to see if they had information on the Saturday shooting. I didn't expect enough from those people to fill the eye of a needle, but one never knew.

As I drove into the Loop, I heard church bells ringing, probably announcing the noon Mass at old St. Peter's on West Madison Street. The bells resonated majestically through the Loop's brick canyons, their sounds an unexpected pleasure in the middle of the traffic's mayhem. While waiting at a red light, I thought about attending the Mass, then chuckled to myself, remembering I had heard that the Police Commissioner was there frequently, always selecting a front pew for high visibility. It had been a long time since I had been to Mass, only once since my leg was shot off, and that at the funeral for a beat officer from the Eighteenth who had been killed on duty. I had attended for my friend the cop, not for God.

When the light went green, I didn't turn toward St. Peter's. Instead, I drove into an underground public garage, a dank, concrete tomb beneath the lawn at Grant Park. I parked, then rode an escalator back up to Michigan Avenue. A damp wind off the lake chilled the air.

Food was my only thought now. Except for a half-dozen cups of coffee, I hadn't put a thing in my stomach since the night before. Just north of Adams, I found a big, sprawling, brassy restaurant open for lunch. I entered and was granted a premium seat at a table next to a window facing the street. I knew my one-leggedness and crutches conceded me certain privileges in public places. But I would be off my crutches and back in a new prosthesis by day's end: the favors would stop soon enough.

The restaurant—Shenanigan's, it was called—was decorated to simulate a turn-of-the-century bar and eatery. Hundreds of antique memorabilia, from old Coke bottles to Norman Rockwell posters, littered the walls. A garden of leafy green plants cascaded from pots hung along the ceiling beams. The dark and highly polished wood floors resounded with the bang of silverware and the racket of boisterous conversation all through the room. Only the blind and deaf would be accorded any peace during a meal here.

I worked my way through the complicated menu, and decided on onion soup and a spinach salad. While I waited for the food, I found myself daydreaming about Meg, then Richard.

We had met as students during the time when my father was stuck in a bed or a chair, bitching his way through the last anguished remnants of his life. Richard, in contrast, was fresh to me, like new cream.

Beyond Richard's good looks, I was also attracted by his demeanor: he wasn't cut from the Albert Dybzewski pattern, which demanded every waking moment be spent producing, producing, producing. At first, I thought Richard was much like my mother, but I later came to realize my assessment was grievously wrong. What my mother wore as grace and *savoir vivre* was, in Richard, only languor. The man was perpetually adrift. With no career course in mind, he preferred simply to let things happen. Naïvely, I missed this red flag.

Maybe I stayed with Richard because I was angry at my father for dying and leaving me. At the end of my father's life, I managed to do everything he wouldn't have wanted: I quit school and married quickly. Three years later, after Meg was born, I painfully came to understand the insensitivity I had shown my father during his final months. That insight was a load I still hauled. Some mistakes will, and should, press like iron across our backs for as long as we draw breath.

Now, with a steaming bowl of soup in front of me, I was amused to recall Richard's final note about his "financial involvement" in the California wine industry. I doubted that he had two nickels to rub together. I knew his deeply ingrained laziness of spirit—I had loved him for a time in spite of it—would ultimately torpedo any early success he might fall into. Steady work was not a part of the man, although bombast was. Once, after a mildly successful first week of selling Bibles door-to-door, he returned home and proclaimed, "Nora, I've got this Bible-selling business by the balls!" Two weeks later, he mailed his samples back to the distributor, his net sales barely enough to pay the postage.

I was still surprised that Richard had left me, me with the regular paycheck. Maybe he was a nut for symmetry and just didn't wish to make love to a woman with only one leg. Who could know? I did know that I was better off with him gone, but sometimes I regretted it. I supposed my life was not so rife with intimacy that I could afford the loss of even a Richard.

Under the table, I squeezed the itching end of my thigh's stump, then turned my attention to the pigeons and sidewalk traffic outside the window. When my spinach salad finally came, I devoured it.

7

John Dover's office nestled in a corner of Ballistics. It was a distance away from the lab's bustle, but close enough to the back wall of the Headquarters Building that Dover could never forget the Englewood El trains that screeched along just outside. A comfortable clutter of folders and books filled his table and covered the edges of the desk where he worked. He turned away from his computer screen when I approached.

"Nora, sit down," he said, smiling. For a man who spent his days examining firearms used to kill and maim people, he was resiliently cheerful.

I sat, grateful for the rest after the eight-block walk from the restaurant.

Dover's thick mustache was as unkempt as usual. A scatter of too long hairs, some gray but most black, poked out here and there from his mustache, hairs that must have tickled, because Dover frequently licked them back into place, as dexterously as a lizard, with his tongue. A large nose and ancient, horn-rimmed glasses dominated the rest of his face. His teeth were perfectly arranged and remarkably pearly for a fifty-year-old. He wore a dark green sweater, white shirt, and striped tie.

"Now, I ask you, Nora," Dover said half-seriously, "are you *really* FBI or CIA? Tell me. And don't give me that Chicago Police detective crap anymore."

"What?"

"Are you FBI or CIA?"

"Make sense, John."

"These bullets and the casing you brought in yesterday— they're not from Saturday night specials, or police .38s, or any other guns we see in this city." His tone had turned serious. "Detectives don't bring in this kind of stuff. Maybe special agents don't even find it anymore."

I felt a small surge from his news. I took off my coat; the office was stuffy and I was still warm from my walk. "What did you find?"

Dover opened a drawer and pulled out a small plastic box, then flipped open its lid and dumped five bullets and a single empty casing onto the blotter on his desktop. Everything quickly rolled to a stop. "Tell me what you think, Nora."

I moved closer. "There were two guns," I said, "one, an automatic, took an isolated shot that didn't hurt anyone but left its casing behind. The other gun, the one responsible for the victim's injuries, should be a revolver—four shots fired, but no ejected casings found near the confessional."

Dover looked up, puzzled. "A confessional? In a church?"

"Holy Name Cathedral," I said. "The Cardinal's church."

"Where the hell are the sanctuaries in this city anymore?"

"Please go on about the bullets, John."

His fingers went for the most damaged slug. "This bullet's beat up, but it's still different enough from the others that I think it came from a different gun. Did it hit iron or stone?"

"Metal grillwork, then a metal bucket."

He nodded, his light gray eyes alive with excitement. He set the slug down and went for the brass casing. Holding it up into the space between himself and me, like a priest lifting a consecrated host, he said, "This is a rimless case, so you're right, it is from an automatic pistol. Its diameter and length make it from a Tokarev, a Russian Tokarev. The slug and its casing meet all the specs of a 7.62-millimeter Tokarev, a cartridge that would have been loaded into a gun also known as a TT-30. Tokarevs were the standard of the Soviet military during the thirties and forties, but have long since been replaced. They're still found in the Eastern Bloc countries, and in China."

"Have you ever seen one?"

"At gun shows, but never in this lab. I've never fired one. You didn't recover any weapons from this shooting, did you?"

"No. Tell me about the other bullets, John."

He gathered the four in his hand and shook them easily, like dice. "They're as strange as the Tokarev. They each weigh about a hundred grains, and their length is very near what the Tokarev slug would measure if it weren't so mashed. Now, there are several older guns that would fire bullets this size and weight, but they're all automatics except—"

"It has to be a revolver," I cut in. "Who would stop to pick up their ejected casings after a shooting like that? Hard to imagine."

"As I was about to say, Nora, all the guns are automatics except for one."

"And?"

"That one is a Nagant revolver. Another old gun, even older than the Tokarev, and also Russian."

"What?" I frowned in confusion.

Dover continued. "The Nagant was adopted by the Russian military before the turn of the century. They look more like something you'd see in a Western movie—a long barrel, big round chamber—than the revolvers of today." He shifted his weight against the back of his chair and clasped his hands behind his head. "So, Nora, who's shooting up Chicago? Some crazy old Bolsheviks?"

"I wish I knew."

He brought his hands back to the desk. As though talking to himself, he said, "Strange gun, the Nagant. Only revolver ever made whose cylinder moves forward when the gun is cocked, so that at the instant of firing, the chamber—"

"Is this gun available?" I interjected. I had no interest in technical ballistics.

"Just as a collector's item. It hasn't been manufactured for fifty years or so, not since World War II."

"Have you ever seen one?"

"Maybe at a show. I can't recall. Certainly not here in the lab."

"Back to the bullets, John. What's on them?"

"A couple have what looks like plaster of paris only. One has plaster and blood. The last has blood only. Oh, there were some tiny wood fragments found here and there also."

"Was the blood human?"

"Yes," he said, "AB negative. Does it match?"

"I didn't ask about the victim's blood type yet. The plaster and the wood fit. The gunman fired through a door into the victim. I think a couple of bullets missed completely, went right into a plaster wall. Another probably passed through her into the wall, and the last one was recovered from her belly during surgery."

"It was a woman?"

"A young Hispanic mother."

"Still alive?"

"Yes—doing pretty well, in fact."

Dover collected the bullets and casing and gently placed them back in the box. "Oh, one more thing," he said. "I think that all I've told you is accurate, but I'm sending this evidence to the FBI lab in Washington. They'll have both of these guns on the shelf, and they can do some test firings if need be. That might help, but, as always, what we really need are the actual weapons."

"We're looking, we're trying."

"I know. Who are you with now, Nora?"

"Art Campbell."

"The black guy?"

"Yes."

"I know him," Dover said, "good man." He paused, fingering his bullet box nervously. "I still miss Jack Flaherty."

"Jack was very good to me." I smiled thinly and looked down at my lap.

Moving from the uncomfortable subject, Dover asked, "Say, Nora, what do you think is going on in this case?"

Not answering for a moment, I finally said, "John, which are the Eastern Bloc countries?"

"Trouble is relative"—that was something Anna Skrabina had told me one day when she was nursing me after my amputation. At the time, I regarded the comment as a piece of pop religion, something Anna might have heard from a television evangelist early one Sunday morning. I let her remark pass without objection, but I wondered what Anna knew about trouble. She who stood on two solid legs; she who lived fifty years with a wonderful husband. What could she know?

Now I sat in the waiting room of Maytower Prosthetics, the shop on West Erie Street where my new leg was being built, the place where I could always come to recognize the force of Anna's wisdom. It was four in the afternoon. I had already been waiting an hour; Fred Maytower's appointment schedule was a farce, as usual. If he just wouldn't talk so goddamn long to every patient, I thought, then realized that was exactly how I wanted him to treat me.

The waiting-room furniture was sparse: a couple of uncomfortable, wooden-armed couches; three padded, upright chairs, all hopelessly stained; and, between the couches, a battered end table piled with old magazines. The walls were beige and bare. The only light in the room leaked from a floor lamp that Maytower must have found in the Maxwell Street flea market. It stood behind the table at attention, a weary old soldier praying for retirement.

That day, those who waited with me—a young black mother and her daughter—like those who waited there every day, gave no notice to the furniture. Their lives had taken them past stains and scratches and triviality. Standing, walking, grasping—these were the important things.

The child was a handsome, square-faced girl, two or three years of age. Down on the floor, she giggled as she scooted around in a kind of bucket with wheels, propelling herself with her tiny hands on the carpet. She went a few feet, then looked back and laughed wildly at her mother on the couch. The mother walked across the room and bent over the child. She said, "Let's change those diapers now, girl. You want to be smelling real nice when Mr. Maytower checks you, don't you?"

As the mother lifted the child from the bucket, I was stunned to see she had no legs. Her tiny body ended at the roundness of her buttocks, at her diapers. The bucket was her legs, her prosthesis, the way she moved about.

Yes, Anna, trouble is relative.

Mr. Maytower's assistant, an elderly woman, opened a door and called for me. I crutched my way into a back room, into one of the two labs where the fittings were done. Brightly lit and smelling of rubber and molten plastic, the room was familiar to me, even comfortable. On a long table was a prosthetic leg, flesh-colored and shapely, its knee joint made of two shiny steel hinges. I looked at it cautiously, as I might eye a new acquaintance. Not certain it was mine, I didn't touch it.

In a minute, Fred Maytower, a tall, stooped-shouldered, skinny sixty-year-old, came into the room. His face had no hardness anywhere. His skull was nearly bald; only a few short black hairs around the edges had yet to give up the fight. He wore a wrinkled white shirt with a dirty orange tie. As always, the tie was loosened and his collar button was opened. He might have slept in his gray slacks.

"What do you think of it, Nora?" he said, gesturing at the leg.

"I don't know. I haven't touched it yet."

He picked it off the table. "C'mon, let's try it. I think you'll like it. How's the stump?"

"A little itchy," I said, "but all healed."

"No more drainage?"

"No."

I had used my last leg hard, tearing the soft liner inside its socket, and the torn fabric had rubbed incessantly on my stump's skin. Because the skin there is scarred and insensitive, I had felt no pain, even as I wore a deep ulcer through a patch of skin. When the ulcer finally drained pus and blood, I returned to Maytower, who examined the leg and stump and decided the fit was wrong; a new leg had to be built. It was a month in the making, but a month necessary to heal over the stump.

I sat on a steel chair and Maytower carried the leg to me. I pulled my skirt up past the end of my lumpy and irregular thigh. I had no embarrassment when I did this, but only because it was Fred. No other man had seen my stump—except for Richard, and he had left.

"The skin looks good, Nora," Maytower said.

He slid a tan cotton sock snugly over the stump, then held the prosthetic leg while I slid my stump firmly inside. The plastic socket went well up onto my thigh, covering me nearly to the hip.

"It feels good, Fred . . . but maybe just a little tight."

Maytower pushed and twisted the leg to test it. "I think it's okay. The stump has to reshape a little after being out of a leg for a month. I think it'll be fine. Try it."

I dropped my skirt down and stood. The stability of two legs under me again felt wonderful. I took a few cautious steps. "Fine, Fred, very good." I smiled, thrilled to be crutch-free. I felt a catch in my throat, and my eyes welled. Stupid, I thought, such a reaction over a new fake leg.

"How's the knee's action?" Maytower asked.

"Nice. Smooth."

"Well, use it for a week before you decide for sure. Let me know if there's any trouble."

"I will. And thank you for this." I rapped the plastic leg with my knuckles and smiled again.

8

Tuesday's shift had been a washout, Art and I going over the little evidence we had, nothing rising from the muddle to tweak us. Discouraged, I headed home at six o'clock.

Traffic choked Lake Shore Drive: it was a rush hour of boorish speeders and lane-changers, nobody lamblike. Not needing the complications of an accident, I moved into the far right-hand lane and stayed there, meek and defensive. I tuned the radio to an oldies' station and let an Everly Brothers ballad lift my spirits. A low sun warmed my face through the Fury's window.

At home, I took the easy way out: chicken pot pies. Meg and I ate in virtual silence, did the dishes, then vegetated together in front of television sitcoms. Meg was in bed by nine. An hour later, as I started for bed, the phone rang. It was Steve Schwartz, a detective colleague on the night shift, calling from the Eighteenth District station on West Chicago Avenue.

"Can you come down?" Schwartz said. "I've got something for you on the Cathedral shooting."

"It's ten o'clock, Steve. And what are you doing at the Eighteenth?"

"They called me from Area Six to interrogate . . . look, I've got a guy sitting here—a big, twitchy guy who says someone's trying to kill him. He says it's the same person who shot the Ramirez woman."

"Where'd your guy come from?"

"From the street, I guess. Shit, I don't know. He just walks into the station and they phone me an hour ago."

"Where is he now?" I asked.

"In one of the back offices."

"Where are you?"

"Front desk. I stepped out here to call you. Can you come?"

As he spoke, I thought of waking Meg and taking her with me, but decided against it. Meg couldn't get by with a half-night's sleep and still survive the next school day. She sat next to a boy for whom the description "hyperactive" was a refined understatement, the kind of child who drives the ablest, bravest teachers to the rail of the Michigan Avenue bridge. Meg needed her full wits about her every morning.

I said to Schwartz, "It's late. I want to know—is this worth my trip?"

"This is a live one, Nora. I wouldn't call you if he wasn't. I figured you'd want to question him yourself."

"Okay, I'll be down. If I can get my sitter for my daughter."

"Good," Schwartz said. "I'll hold the guy."

I clicked off Schwartz's call, but when I dialed Anna, I heard a busy signal. I hung up and sat wondering why she was so unusually occupied with the phone lately. A love interest for a woman in her seventies?

I dialed back in another minute and found the line clear. Anna agreed to come down and stay with Meg. I strapped my new leg on, then threw on a pink sweat suit and a nylon jacket. I was careening south on Lake Shore Drive by ten-thirty.

As I passed the Foster Avenue ramp, a call from the dispatcher at the Eighteenth broke through the usual chatter on my scanner. Urgently, the man said, "I need people to Rush Street . . . I need them now . . . Rush and Oak . . . anyone nearby, proceed there . . . we've got a wrecked car on the sidewalk . . . lots down d it sounds like holy hell."

The scanner prattled on, but I didn't need to hear any more. Deciding that Schwartz would have to wait, I planned the quickest way to Rush. North Avenue would be the surest, North to State Parkway, then south to where Rush ended at State.

I spun from an inside lane to a clearer, middle lane, my foot leaning hard on the accelerator, and passed one set of glowing red taillights after another. My neck muscles tensed from that first surge of adrenaline, the seductive rush that detectives experience only occasionally, but beat cops feel all the time. Working the street nourishes one with a raw energy that disappears with promotion out of a squad car.

Traffic lightened when I left the Drive. I squealed around the corner at North and State, hoping my noise didn't wake the sleeping Cardinal in his corner mansion. I blew through a red light at Division and picked up the top end of Rush. Now traffic thickened. Three blocks ahead, a squad car's twirling red and blue roof lights sliced the black night. I wished I was in uniform instead of pink sweats.

Rush and Maple was as close as I could get: from there south, it was gridlock. I pulled the Fury in front of a fireplug and shut her down, then started walking in the street, between the lanes of jammed cars. Sirens whined from the south and west, closing. Buzzing with confusion, people on the sidewalks hurried ahead to the action. Rush Street was offering a bonus this night, something more than dinner and a nightclub, or a few beers in a strip joint.

At Bellevue and Rush, I came on the first squad, its lights spinning, both its front doors open. Two cops from the Eighteenth—Johnny Colles and Melissa St. John—were some twenty feet ahead, Johnny on the sidewalk. He knelt over a victim whose skirt was up to her underwear, her bloody legs crumpled grotesquely to one side. Melissa stood inside the shattered panel of glass that had been the east wall of Sweetwater's restaurant.

"Johnny!" I yelled. "What the hell's going on?"

He looked back at me. "Who is it?"

"Nora Callum."

"Oh, Nora. Car got loose, up ahead. Two hit here and more down the line. This lady's dead. I'm sure of it." His warm breath broke into the cool night air, in quick gray bursts.

Melissa stepped over a low brick wall layered with broken glass. A lean woman topped with a shock of curly brown hair, she wore her leather police jacket open in front. We had been classmates at the Police Academy. She said to Johnny, "The guy that went through the window is still alive somehow, but his head and face are bad. We need medics." When she saw me, she said, "Nora? Is that you?"

"Yes."

"Nice sweats."

"I'm not supposed to be here."

"Just kidding. Jump in, we need the help. And, hey, take a check where you're standing."

I glanced down and saw the thick black rubber tire marks of a braking car. "Skid marks," I said.

"See how long?"

"Three, maybe four feet."

"Yeah," Melissa said. "Pretty half-assed try at not mounting the curb. Wouldn't you say?"

"Have you had time to call an evidence team?"

"Not yet."

"I'll do it."

The casualties needed attention, but so did the accident scene. With dead and injured and three-foot skid marks, the charges could be criminal. Confusion on the street was growing, and this would be an easy crime scene to botch.

I hurried back to the squad and called Area Six for a team. Finished, I started south on Rush. It looked like a battlefield for a full block: most victims had been downed in pairs; fourteen the total, including the two near Sweetwater's. The carnage didn't end till Oak Street where the killer silver Cadillac had crossed traffic and buried its nose in the brick wall of an ice-cream shop.

I started back up Rush, looking to help the wounded but knowing I offered no more than the citizens who huddled to attend them. By now, the siren screams were nearly on top of me. A few of the injured were crying out; horns honked from blocks away. Gangs of flashing red and blue lights danced in the darkness. I saw several ambulances and squad cars jolting to a stop almost simultaneously. The medics and beat cops were here; my energy would be put to better use at the Cadillac. I hustled toward the battered ice-cream shop.

The Cadillac was a new model, long and sleek. Steam seeped from its crushed front end. Inside, a black male driver and a white female passenger sat unmoving, as though in a museum painting. The man was slumped forward over the steering wheel. The woman, a platinum blonde dressed in dark fur, reposed with her chin tipped up, her head against the leather rest behind her. The license plate on the rear bumper read WATS I.

A car squealed to a stop on the sidewalk behind me. Startled, I turned and saw a cop exiting his squad. He was one of the officers who had stood over Eva Ramirez in the Cathedral last Saturday. Before he had a chance to recognize me, I said, "I'm Lieutenant Callum. What's your name, Officer?"

Surprised, he said, "Jim Klipstein."

"Jim," I said, "get back in your car and run this plate number— WATS I."

Klipstein returned to his car.

I went to the left side of the Cadillac and opened the door. When I touched the driver on his arm, he straightened his broad shoulders and twisted his face toward me. A pencil-thin line of blood trailed from a cracked lip. His eyes were bulbous and pleading, their whites marred by a lacework of blood vessels. When he opened his mouth, the stench of alcohol washed over my face.

"I'm police," I said. "What's your name?"

His pink lips opened, and he seemed to want to speak, but instead he gently shook his head once.

"Are you hurt?" I said.

He closed his eyes and set his forehead back on the steering wheel.

Jim Klipstein tapped me on the shoulder. "Can I talk to you, Lieutenant?"

I turned away from the driver and saw Klipstein's fresh young face.

"Better close the door, ma'am," Klipstein said.

Puzzled, I did as he asked.

"Lieutenant, WATS I is the license registered to a 1988 Cadillac owned by Samuel Watson."

"Say again?"

"Samuel Watson."

Looking back through the car window, I said, "The alderman?"

"I dunno," Klipstein said. "I suppose."

Samuel Watson was the Honorable Samuel Watson, the city's most prominent black alderman and chairman of the City Council's Finance Committee. There was no politician closer or more important to the political health of Chicago's mayors than Samuel Watson.

I said to Klipstein, "He's drunk as a goddamn skunk."

"Yes, ma'am."

I pointed north on Rush. "And do you know that this son of a bitch has just run over fourteen people and at least one of them is dead?"

Klipstein nodded. "Does he need to be checked by a doctor, Lieutenant? Want me to take him to the emergency room?"

"You're damn right I do. And tell the nurses you need a blood alcohol because there's been a death in this accident."

"I will."

"And, Jim, don't take him to Northwestern, the place will be crawling with these injured. It could take hours for them to get to him. We need a blood alcohol *now*, not when it's had time to level off. Drive him up to Edgewater Hospital. It'll be quiet there."

Together, we hauled Samuel Watson from his car, Klipstein doing most of the work. Too drunk to know the slaughter he had just engineered, Watson slobbered, "The lady is . . . ahh . . . my administrative assistant. We were working late . . . city business—pressing city business, all of it pressing. She was very generous to do that . . . I mean, for the sake of the city."

We dumped Watson onto the backseat of the squad and slammed the door shut. Klipstein pointed to the Cadillac and said, "Need some help with the woman?"

"I'll manage her," I said. "It's more important for you to get Watson's blood drawn. I want the test results when you know them. Call me at the Eighteenth."

Klipstein drove off, easing his way off the sidewalk, then snaking through traffic. I returned to the Cadillac. By now, Melissa St. John was there and the passenger door was already open. "I think the seat belt's holding her up," Melissa said.

I leaned into the car. Mute, the woman still sat bolt upright, shoeless and hoseless in her thick fur coat, a leather briefcase on her lap. Alcohol fumes soaked the air around her. When I reached across her waist and released the belt, she fell forward in a dead drunk, cracking her forehead on the dashboard. Melissa and I dragged her from the car to witness her final disgrace: her fur coat gaped open and showed her sagging, milky-colored body to be without a thread of clothing—not a thread.

Later, at the station, we would find the woman's name was

Mitzi Williamson. We would also open her briefcase and discover not the documents of city business, but a pint of peach brandy and her wadded-up green underwear. The whereabouts of her other clothing remained obscure.

I was another half hour on Rush Street, time used to help the evidence team measure, photograph, and sample the skid marks near the dead woman at Sweetwater's, then photograph every site where victims fell. I asked that the Cadillac be towed to the garage at the Eighteenth, not to a local tow yard. Blood on the car's front end needed to be typed; the mechanics of the car itself required examination.

By the time I left, all the living, twelve, had been transported to hospitals. The coroner declared two people dead at the scene, and I heard a paramedic speak gloomily of the chances of three of the live ones. As the ambulances and squads began to disperse, the street quieted, but the horror of what had happened was still barely upon us. Somehow I remembered my appointment with Steve Schwartz.

I drove south on La Salle—a wide, tranquil boulevard bordered by young locusts—to Chicago Avenue. Nearing the Eighteenth, I saw a plug of vehicles three deep off the curb and blocking the street. I parked and left the car to walk the last block along the sidewalk. Ahead of me were civilians and uniformed police, men and women, some alone, some in chattering groups, others traipsing in and out of the station's front doors. A few men hauled videocam equipment into the station.

The Eighteenth District, the station house of my first police assignment, was plain and humdrum. Two stories of washed-out, dull beige brick, it sat sandwiched between an oily, littered alley and a fish store. The windows on its front face and sides came in squarish pairs, each pair signifying an office; the favored ones had air conditioners hanging from their sills on rusty brackets. The back of the building made a small, grimy garage for squad cars and paddy wagons. Not a jot of trimwork could be found on the Eighteenth's surface, not a brick, or turn of concrete, or change of color or angle. It was a monolith built during the nineteen-fifties when solidity and function and budget meant everything, and imagination nothing.

I followed a burly cameraman up three steps into the station lobby, and once inside I worked my way through a noisy congestion of people to the front desk. A young female officer, a thin, freckled redhead who looked too weak to have passed the endurance test, came over to me from behind the desk. Her chrome nameplate read "A. Reilly." I hadn't seen her before.

"Are you with the accident?" Reilly asked me while sorting through a sheaf of papers in her hands.

"What?" I said.

"The accident on Rush."

"Yes, I know about the accident," I said more gently than I needed to. "I've just come from there. I'm Lieutenant Callum. From Area Six."

Reilly, whose eyes were deep blue and just the tiniest bit out of sync, looked quickly up at me. "Oh," she said with embarrassment. "Sorry, Lieutenant."

"Forget it," I said. "Tell me, what the hell's going on here?"

Her eyes moving excitedly, Reilly said, "The accident's hit the news wires. I mean, that it was Alderman Watson who did it."

"So why did all the reporters come to the station?"

"Because they want to see Watson. He's here."

"Already?"

"Jim Klipstein brought him in twenty minutes ago. Captain Melchior came in personally to wait for Watson. They're alone in an office down the hall."

Melchior didn't come out near midnight without a personal reason. I could bet what was up: Ray and Watson squirreled away, and Ray pouring coffee into Watson to negotiate a statement.

"Have you seen Steve Schwartz?" I asked Reilly.

"Earlier. He was out here when the commotion started, about a half hour ago."

"I'm going back to find Schwartz. If you see Klipstein come by, don't let him out without sending him back to me."

The crush of people pushed my belly up against the edge of Reilly's desk. I turned and started for the corridor off the lobby, kicking shins when I had to to clear my way.

9

Schwartz, a young, thick-haired detective, sat at a desk that gobbled a third of the room. He was neatly dressed in a starched shirt and a plaid tie; he smoked a filtered cigarette. His desk was a clutter: dog-eared files, two half-filled coffee cups, the *Wall Street Journal*, and his holstered .38 special.

"Nora!" Schwartz said, and gestured me to an empty chair. "I knew you'd come. What took you so long?"

"I've been on Rush Street."

"At the massacre?"

"Yes." Before sitting, I said, "Where is he, Steve? This is an awfully small room, and I don't see anybody but you. Where the hell is this man you called about?"

"He left."

"Shit." I plunked into the chair. "Why?"

"Who knows? Afraid, maybe."

I sighed in exasperation.

Schwartz deflected me with run-on: "Tell me about Rush Street. You know that Sam Watson's in with Melchior right now? Can you beat that? Melchior in here at this time of night? God, the mayor must be pissed!"

My eyes burned from fatigue and Schwartz's cigarette smoke. "To hell with Watson, Steve. What happened to your guy, the *live one?*"

"Like I said, he bolted. About an hour and a half ago. I had nothing to hold him on, the guy's a walk-in. He must've left when I was phoning you from the lobby desk. It was just after the accident happened on Rush, when I got stuck in the confusion for a while."

"Any ideas where he might have gone?"

"No."

"Where does he live?"

"I dunno."

My watch read eleven-forty-five. "Okay, then here's an easy one," I said sharply, exaggerating the motion of my lips as I spoke. "What's his name?"

"Name? I don't know, Nora."

I stepped to the desk and gripped its front edge. Leaning toward Schwartz, I felt the pulse in my neck. "Goddammit, Steve!" I barked. "It's near midnight! Now, please tell me, what the shit am I doing down here? I mean, I've got an exhausted old lady watching my kid and—"

"Hey!" Schwartz shot back. "Sit down! Relax and shut up. Give me five minutes, will you? Huh?"

I sat down. I had gone to assault mode without giving him a chance. "Sorry," I said. "It's fatigue, I guess, or the accident on Rush. Or maybe, just maybe, it's the absence of even one goddamned decent lead in this shitbag case."

"I understand," he said. "Let me tell you about this guy."

Schwartz mashed his cigarette into a filthy ashtray.

He said, "Look, it's a quiet p.m. shift in here, maybe an hour before the Watson thing hit. Okay, from nowhere this guy walks up to the front desk. He tells the redhead—you know, Reilly—tells her someone's trying to kill him. Not knowing what to do with the guy, they call me at Area Six and I come down."

I rubbed my tired eyes. "Okay. Yeah."

"Well, I start by asking him his name and he doesn't answer. Instead, he starts right into this story, jabbering, nervous-like.

I didn't ask him his name again because I was afraid I'd stop his flow. Know what I mean?"

I did, but I didn't bother to answer. Instead, I asked, "How old was the guy? What'd he look like?"

"Big and tall. Well-built, but at least sixty—maybe seventy—years old. Common-looking face, really, except for a scraggly beard and a sort of a spot on his cheek."

"A spot like what?"

"I'm not sure. Maybe a bruise."

Reilly came into the room with hot coffee for me—a peace offering, I figured, for not knowing me earlier.

I took the cup she handed me. "Does the 'A' stand for Ann?" I asked her.

"Yes," she said.

"Thanks for the coffee, Ann," I said.

Schwartz watched Reilly's backside disappear into the hallway. I said, "Go on with the story, Steve."

"Well, our guy claims a man has been following him for the past two weeks, popping up here and there, driving a small red car, just sort of stalking him. Nearly every day, here and there, here and there. Then, last Saturday afternoon, our man—"

"Wait," I interrupted, "I'm getting these two mixed up. Let's give them some names."

"Name your poison."

I thought for a moment. "How's Homer for the guy who came in here tonight?"

"Homer?" Schwartz spoke slowly, his lips rounding on the name's first syllable. "I like it. Homer's perfect. Hey, then it's Fat Man for the chaser man. Homer said the guy was short and fat."

I smiled at Schwartz, and felt better. I moved my chair a few inches closer to the desk.

"Okay, fine," Schwartz said. "Now, Homer claims that last Saturday he's in a grocery store on Addison Avenue when Fat

Man shows up again. But this time Fat Man's not watching from the car, he's actually *in* the store with Homer, right there. And looking more menacing than ever, Homer says."

"Fat Man have a gun?"

"Dunno," Schwartz said.

"Doesn't matter."

"No, uh-uh. Anyway, when Homer looks up and sees Fat Man in the same aisle as he is, Homer's had it. He splits. I mean, splits right now, leaving his cart in the middle of the aisle. Fat Man takes after him.

"Outside, Homer runs along the sidewalk, trying to get away, but when he looks back he sees Fat Man following in his car. Homer doesn't know where the hell to go, sounds like he's panicked. Nora, this is a guy ready to shit in his drawers, huh?" Schwartz's dark eyebrows lifted for emphasis. "Huh?"

"Yes. Gotcha, Steve."

"Now, when Homer gets under the Addison Avenue El tracks, he runs into the station. Figures he'll pay a buck, jump a train, and get away."

"But no such luck," I forecast, my coffee cup halfway to my mouth.

"Exactly, no such luck. See, the Saturday afternoon trains don't run very often, so while Homer waits, Fat Man apparently has time to ditch his car. In a few minutes, he's hauling ass up the steps to the tracks himself, puffing to beat hell, I guess. He just makes it into the same car that Homer's on."

"North or southbound train?"

"Southbound," Schwartz said, "and don't ask me why I asked him that, because I don't have the foggiest."

"Okay, they're headed south. Then what?"

Sliding back against his chair, Schwartz spread his hands open as if in apology. "That's it, that's all I have. See, that was the point in our conversation when I heard a commotion in the hallway, so I went out to see what was up. It was the first reports on the Watson thing, and I got distracted. Then, before I went back to Homer, I decided to call you from the front desk, from a phone where Homer wouldn't hear me. The whole thing took about ten minutes. When I came back here, Homer was gone."

"Didn't stop at the desk to leave any messages?" I asked.

"Gone, no trace. Reilly never saw him leave."

"Does Homer know Fat Man?" I asked.

"No, not at all. Claims the guy's a complete stranger to him."

"Why does Homer run?" I said. "Sounds like he's in a helluva lot better shape than Fat Man. Why doesn't Homer stop and deal with the guy?"

"Beats me," Schwartz said. "Maybe Homer's a lot older or something."

I nodded. "Okay, you said Homer came in telling Reilly someone was trying to kill him. When was the murder attempt?"

"We never got that far. I've got him on the southbound train toward the Loop, no further. As far as I know, there never was a murder attempt."

I set my coffee on the desk, then stood and walked the few steps to the room's only window. The view, familiar to me from my days at the Eighteenth, was into an alley, and beyond that, across a vacant gravel lot, to a short row of one-story businesses: Prince's 6 Hour Cleaners; a currency exchange whose windows were meshed with iron bars; and a small, dark, bleak building identified only by the word "NUDES" glowing blinking red over its door. "Does Homer have a wife or children?" I asked.

"Neither," Schwartz said. "I found that out when I managed to ask him if he was worried about the safety of his family."

Turning back, my arms folded in front of me, I said, "Steve . . ."

"Yeah?"

"How could Homer have know it was Fat Man who shot Eva Ramirez in the Cathedral?"

Schwartz sat quietly for a minute, then said, "I suppose from the news. The Ramirez shooting was all over the news."

"So what? Lots of people saw it on the news—even Anna, my baby-sitter. But none of them claimed it was Fat Man who did it."

Schwartz sucked at a thumbnail. "You're right."

"Does Homer know Eva Ramirez?" I said. "Was Homer in the Cathedral? Did he actually see who shot Eva? Maybe Homer shot Eva. Or maybe Homer's a nutcase and his story's all bullshit—ever think of that?"

Schwartz shrugged his ignorance on all counts.

"And another thing," I said, "why would Fat Man be trying to kill Homer in such a risky way? I mean, this following the guy all the time. That shows either great confidence or great stupidity."

"Who knows?" Schwartz said blandly, his chin resting on his hand. "I never got near those questions with him. You've got to find him, or he has to walk back in here."

I said nothing, just quietly drummed my fingers against the hard plastic of my prosthesis. After a long pause, I said softly, "Shit, Mother, I can't dance."

"What?"

"Nothing." I returned to my chair but didn't sit. "I wish I knew why he picked tonight to come. . . . Well, whatever it is, I can't see anything to do now. I guess I'm outa here."

"I'm sorry I didn't do better hanging on to the guy."

"Forget it, Steve," I said as I noticed Jim Klipstein at the door, "I'm blaming Watson. What is it, Jim?"

"It was 0.32, Lieutenant."

"What?"

"Watson's blood alcohol."

"Did you say 0.32? Jesus, how was he still breathing?"

"High tolerance," Schwartz said.

"Must be," Klipstein said, "because he looks like the bloom's back on him already."

"Where is he now?" I asked.

"He just left the office he and Melchior were using. He's out back, and I'm supposed to drive him home. Melchior's finishing with the TV and press, then he wants you."

Schwartz winced and said, "Good luck, Frank Buck."

The District Commander's office, Melchior's old office when he was at the Eighteenth, was empty when I arrived; our chief was still in the lobby taking reporters' questions. A large, ridiculous desk lamp—a light bulb and shade sticking up from the horn of a saddle—lit the room. I sat, putting my purse on the floor.

Melchior walked through the open door wearing a white shirt, a yellow tie, and a black V-neck sweater that stretched over his paunch. He went to the desk chair without saying hello.

"Shut the door, Callum," he said rudely.

Already angry, I stood and shut it firmly, then crossed my arms and waited. Melchior fingered some papers on the desk, and finally said, "I heard you were on Rush Street."

"Yes."

"What do you think?"

"It was awful. Two are already dead. The paramedics said others won't make it."

Melchior shook his head. "That's not what I meant. I'm talking about the cause of the accident. Sounds like a car problem to me."

"Car problem?"

"Something mechanical. That's what I told the press." He wiped a hand across his wet lips.

"Watson breathed on me and I withered," I said sharply. "He was stinking drunk, Captain."

"That's opinion. Subjective."

"No," I retorted, "it's objective. I sent him for a blood alcohol, and it was 0.32. That's three times the legal limit." I kept my eyes steady on him, not wanting to look away and seem vulnerable.

"Tests can be mistaken," he said. "The lab might've fucked up."

"Possible, but Klipstein and I would testify that Watson was too impaired to walk." I paused, then added, "Walk? The guy couldn't stand, for crissake. This is manslaughter, vehicular homicide, take your pick."

Veering from the obvious, Melchior said, "Where's the car now?"

"Impounded in our garage."

"I want you and Campbell to talk with the boys in the garage in the morning. I still think it was a defective car, bad brakes, stuck accelerator, something like that. Look, Watson's been drinking for years. He can hold his liquor—everybody around City Hall knows that, including the press. I'm not impressed by one lousy fucking blood test."

I said nothing.

Melchior pushed away his chair and stood. The bottom of his sweater had half rolled up over his belly. "You and Campbell will talk to the mechanics in the morning," he said. "Right?"

"Right," I mimicked, wondering why he was standing.

He walked toward me, a leering smile unsticking his lips from his teeth. He stopped in front of me, so near that I could smell his greasy skin. I stood my ground.

He lifted his hands into the air, and I felt the first lick of peril. Grinning, he said, "Handsome pink sweatshirt, Callum. Police issue?"

"No. I didn't—"

"Very nice," he said. Then, suddenly, he dropped both his fat, open hands onto my breasts and squeezed firmly.

Stunned, I shoved him away, hard enough to make him stumble backward.

Fear engulfed me, but somehow disappeared as quickly as it came. In its place, rage bloomed and hardened. I started for my chair: I wanted my purse, my gun.

I reached into the purse and yanked out the .38, then pointed it at Melchior's waist. When he lurched, I hissed, "You dirty son of a bitch!"

I pointed the gun at his crotch. "Do that again, mister, and I'll shoot a round into that thing hanging between your legs. I'll blow your pecker so far apart that Mrs. Ray'll think she found the remains of a goddamn Roman candle after the Fourth of July."

Melchior's face whitened to talcum color.

I stepped to the edge of the desk. I waved the gun at him recklessly. "And if you go out of here and tell anyone that I pointed a gun at you, then you'll pay worse. See, I'll tell them I had to draw in self-defense because you jerked your pud out of your pants and stuck it in my face. And do you honestly think that anyone in this District will believe you instead of me? Do you?"

His eyes widened into black circles.

Shaking, I pushed my way through the still-crowded lobby and into the south hallway. In a far, deserted corner, I leaned my head against a wall. I wrapped my hands around my stomach, and felt a confusion of enmity and sorrow overwhelm me.

When Schwartz touched my shoulder from behind, I jumped as if it had been Melchior. "Wow," Schwartz said. "What's the matter, Nora?"

I smiled weakly, unable to form words, my eyes brimming with tears, my cheeks hot.

"Tell me," he said gently. "Please, let me help you."

I drew in a breath and managed to lie: "I think it's the accident on Rush. All the blood and guts, I mean."

"Want me to call Art?" he said.

"Oh, no, no. I'll be all right. Let me stay here for a minute, then I'll go home."

"I'll drive you."

"No. It's okay. Really. Thanks, Steve."

"Sure. Stay as long as you want. I'll keep the hall clear for you."

Schwartz left. Alone again, I pressed my forehead to the wall, then closed my eyes. The thought of Melchior's filthy hands rushed over me, and I saw myself waving my .38 in his ashen face.

By terrorizing him, I showed I was no better than he; that taste in my mouth sickened me.

There's a time when sleep is so deep that any sudden interruption feels like an ax halving your brain. You wake up, but nothing—who you are, where you are—makes any sense. All your usual connections to yourself are severed. It was that way for me when my bedside phone rang in the middle of that night. I know I grunted. I may or may not have said hello.

At the other end, a voice pleaded, "Nora? Is that you?"

"Who is this?" I pushed out.

"Steve."

Finally, I felt a few synapses working: I realized it was Schwartz. "What time is it?"

"Four-thirty in the morning."

I slid closer to the phone and propped my upper body on an elbow. I was nearly ready to hit on all cylinders. "Where are you calling from, Steve?"

"From an apartment on Eddy Street. Just west of Clark."

"What's the deal?"

"The guy was right," Schwartz said.

"What guy?"

"The guy I'm looking at right now."

"Stop the cat-and-mouse shit, Steve."

"He's lying in front of me on the floor. He's dead. It's goddamn Homer."

10

showered and was back on the street by five, Saint Anna again having come to my rescue to watch Meg. I drove south on Clark. The morning rush hour was already budding, even before the sun had cracked open the eastern sky.

Clark Street had been built to accommodate the horse-and-buggy days of 1900, and dilettantes still thought its pinched narrowness was quaint. History aside, the street was acknowledged as one of the city's rush-hour nightmares. But the weather was warm and calm that morning, so I decided not to push through the snarls as I sometimes did. Besides, I was jangled from thoughts of Melchior and my having had only three hours of sleep. It was no time to test the exquisite reflexes needed for speeding and improper lane-changing. There was nothing to hurry for: we had already blown our chance with Homer.

I turned off my scanner and flipped the radio to an all-night classical-music station. I was at the Eddy Street address by five-thirty. It was a narrow, yellow-brick three-flat. Four squad cars and an ambulance crowded the quiet street out front.

An officer at the lobby entrance told me I'd find the action on the third floor. He said the call had come in an hour before.

I trudged up a musty staircase. The grade of the stairs tested my new leg, and it felt snug and comfortable. At the next-to-last landing, I glanced up the final dozen stairs and saw several

people from one of Area Six's homicide teams. Steve Schwartz
stood in the apartment doorway. Schwartz and I glanced at each
other when I hit the last step. Looking shaken, he said nothing,
only pointed to the floor just inside the apartment.

The sight of Homer's dead hulk sucked the wind from my
lungs, and I gasped. I walked to the body, crouched slightly,
and whispered, "Son-of-a-bitch."

Behind me, Schwartz muttered, "Talk about fucking up . . ."

Not looking back, I said, "Twenty screwballs in a row will
come in with a story like his before one means anything. How
in hell can we know?"

I turned to Schwartz. His frown had made a deep cleft between
his eyebrows. "Steve, look, he beat it out of the station. He wasn't
pushed. If you want to eat your stomach lining away over that,
go ahead. We couldn't have done squat. Think about it."

I looked back to the body. Big and peaceful, the man gripped
an automatic pistol in the stiffened fingers of his right hand. He
was dressed in rumpled trousers and a bullet-torn gray undershirt. Dark blood soaked the front of the shirt, and a shallow
pool of more blood lay clotted under his back. His half-shut eyes
had the sheen of raw egg white.

His beard was as scraggly as Schwartz had said, the ratty
growth helping to hide a large purple blemish on his left cheek.
Probably a birthmark, not a bruise. The part of the blemish that
lay beyond the beard and near his eye had an edge as irregular
as a complicated coastline.

I knelt close to him, smelling a mixture of alcohol and blood.
When I touched him, I found the skin of his forehead cold and
dry; his neck and wrist were pulseless. He wasn't going to get
the second chance that Eva Ramirez had.

I lifted the bottom edge of his bloody undershirt. Four oval
bullet holes marked the hairy white skin of his belly, the entry
wounds black and scattered, nothing lined up. I laid the sticky
shirt back down gently, as if it mattered how I handled it.

I stood and faced Schwartz. "Who is he?" I asked.

"I dunno," Schwartz said as he lit a cigarette. "He's still Homer to me."

"Who found him?"

"The landlady on the first floor. Several shots woke her. Steiner's downstairs taking her statement."

I took a step closer to Schwartz and said, "I want the lead on this one, Steve. I know it's your shift, but I want it. Because of the Cathedral tie-in. Okay?"

"Sure," Schwartz said, "that's why I called."

I looked at the door. Its surface and lock showed no obvious damage. "Door found open?" I asked.

"Yes," Schwartz said.

"Blown backwards, I guess."

"What?"

I said, "The shooter must have been in the hall and poured the shots in when Homer opened the door. The force blew the body back onto the floor."

"Think he got a volley off?" Schwartz said. "Homer, I mean."

"His gun is an automatic, and there aren't any ejected casings. Let's check outside."

I stepped into the hallway and found no damage to any wall. The carpet was too dark a color to see wetness, so I knelt and brushed my hands across it. "Carpet's dry," I said, "no blood from the killer. Homer never fired a shot."

As I stood, a glint of metal caught my eye. A few feet away, where the carpet joined the base of the wall, a small brass key shined. I picked up the key, touching it only by its edges. It was simple, generic-looking, with a thin shank. Its pattern was so rudimentary that it might have opened any one of a thousand different satchels or briefcases.

"Make anything from this?" I said. Schwartz stood at Homer's feet.

"Looks like something from any hardware store," he said. "It might've been there six months."

"Pretty clean for that long."

"Run it by Hugh when we get back," he said. Hugh Thomas was Area Six's resident expert on key locks.

Carefully, I stowed the key in the pocket in my purse, then re-entered the apartment where the photographers, the evidence people, and the coroner were all at work. The morning's first sunlight now brightened the living room, which contained only a few furnishings, all of them badly worn. A lumpy easy chair and its footstool stood in the center of the room. The chair was aimed at a television on the wall in front of it.

Alice Adams, an evidence woman, called me over toward the chair. Alice was twenty-nine years old and tall, as tall as I am. She wore a long, flowered dress and Jesus sandals with white cotton socks. She preferred her hair pulled even more tightly to her skull than I did. Round wire glasses framed her busy eyes. Alice was pure granola, but meticulous and tireless and still unjaded by her job.

"This table's loaded, Nora," she said. "Start with the box. Don't worry, any prints have been lifted."

I scanned the table, where an empty gin bottle and a drinking glass stood next to a small box made of oily cardboard deeply browned by age. A dozen or more cartridges—presumably for the gun Homer clutched in his hand—nestled inside the box. I fingered them, then lifted the box from an envelope it rested on.

"Have you checked inside the envelope?" I said.

"No," Alice said.

"Any ID on this guy?"

She shook her head. "The envelope doesn't help, but I haven't swept the bedroom yet," she said. "I'm going there now."

I picked up the envelope. It was plain white and ripped open along its upper edge. Half of it had been stained by what I assumed was spilled gin. The envelope bore a canceled stamp, Homer's Eddy Street address and apartment number, but not Homer's name, and no return address. The postmark showed the envelope had been mailed from somewhere within the city the week before.

I opened the torn edge and pulled out two folded sheets of paper. The first was a Xerox copy of a faded, barely readable map, a map that diagramed a city's streets. At the center of the map, an "X" had been drawn in red ink. I found nothing about the map or the position of the X recognizable.

Next, I opened the second sheet of paper, this a photocopy of a typewritten letter dated several weeks before. The type was filthy, the loops of letters such as "e" and "a" smudged with ink. Like the envelope, the letter bore no sign of its origin.

April 23

My dearest Nikki,

I am writing tonight because I am thinking of you and I miss you. Today I attended a lecture that brought many things back to me. You are strong in my thoughts now.

I am sad tonight, Nikki, and I needed to tell that to someone who would understand. I am thinking constantly of those who were with us through our worst months, those I cannot even bear to mention.

I would love to see you sometime, if there is a way we could do that. For now, with my love,

Talitha

PS—Today, at the lecture, I saw a man who seemed to know me, I mean, know me from our Vyborg district. When he looked at me and I saw his face, it put a fear in me and I don't know why. He looked your age, and he had a large spot on his cheek. My brain is rusty. Would you remember him, Nikki? Write if you can. Love, T.

Neither the map nor the letter made any sense to me, although it seemed Homer's cheek had somehow marked him for death. I refolded both sheets of paper, stuffed them in the envelope, and dropped it into my purse.

Alice returned. "The bedroom gave up a wallet." She handed it to me.

"Find a name?" I said.

"Yes."

"On a driver's license? Social Security card?"

"Neither," Alice said, "but it's a start."

The worn leather wallet held fifty dollars, and three cards: one for the Chicago Public Library, another for a printer's-union local, and the last from the Fed, the Department of Immigration. The cards had all been issued to a Semyon Lugotov.

I walked to a phone parked on top of the television, dialed information, and asked for the number of Immigration Services.

While the phone rang, I said to Alice, "I saw you walking on North Michigan the other day. Who's Mr. America?"

She grinned with her lips closed. "My roommate fixed me up. We spent the afternoon shopping for muscle shirts and elastic wrist supports for him. Four hours of that and I'd made my decision. I told the guy to take me home because I was feeling *biological.*"

"What the hell's that?"

Alice laughed and said, "Who knows, but it scared the bejesus out of him. Had me home in fifteen minutes."

As the phone continued to ring, I asked, "Where are they?"

"Who you calling?" Alice said.

"Department of Immigration."

"Nora," Alice said gently, "it's five-thirty in the morning."

Embarrassed, I took the phone from my ear. "Oh, yeah. Maybe you'd better run this case, Alice."

"No, thanks."

Our tour of the apartment was brief because there was so little to see. Lugotov had lived with a small table and a few chairs; a bed and a dresser; a television and a portable radio; and a scavenged-looking collection of dishes, half of them dirty and stacked, in his tiny kitchen. There were no paintings or prints on the walls, not a likeness or photograph of a single human form anywhere. There was nothing personal, nothing of substance or warmth about the place, only the profound feeling of emptiness that must have permeated Lugotov's life.

At the end of the tour, Alice turned to me and simply said, "Strange."

"This place makes me wonder who could have cared enough about the man to shoot him," I said.

John Steiner, a twenty-year man with the Force, worked the Department's new bridge-shift hours of 4 a.m. to 2 p.m. I met him in the first-floor apartment of Mrs. Miklewicz, the building's owner and manager. Steiner and I sat with her in her living room for half an hour. Together, we assembled a fragmentary sketch of Semyon Lugotov.

When Mrs. Miklewicz and her now dead husband had purchased the three-flat thirty years before, Lugotov was the only tenant who stayed through the change of ownership. During the Miklewiczes' first year on Eddy Street, Lugotov married, but briefly and unsuccessfully; the woman was gone in six months. Since then, he scarcely ever had a visitor. Except for work, he went out only for groceries or liquor, or, in good weather, for an occasional walk to the lakefront. He paid his rent on time, never made a decibel of noise, and always refused, although politely, Mrs. Miklewicz's invitations for coffee, even after her husband died. Mrs. Miklewicz saw Lugotov as a member of the human species who was doomed to be permanently and joylessly alone. To his gregarious landlady, Lugotov's cloistered habits had become one of her life's great mysteries. She said she had never been rude enough to ask questions, but she always wondered if someone had hurt him deeply long ago.

An hour later, at Area Six, I sat at my desk across from Art. The same sun that had brightened Lugotov's apartment also nursed our office. I briefed Art on my visit with Steve Schwartz the midnight before and on the Eddy Street killing. Art, of course, already knew of the Samuel Watson massacre. The scene with Melchior had stayed with me like a deep, painful wound, but I couldn't bring myself to say anything about it.

When I showed Art the brass key from the hallway, he made no more of it than I had. Like Schwartz, he suggested Hugh Thomas. When Art finished with the key, I slid him the letter and the map. He scanned both.

"What do you think?" I asked.

He said, "I think Semyon Lugotov was right about somebody trying to whack him."

"Brilliant. Keep going. What do you think of the papers?"

"Which?"

"The letter first."

"Doesn't mean shit to me," he said. "Who's Talitha?"

"I'm clueless."

"Lugotov's got something on his cheek?"

"A purple thing," I said.

"I figured. Say, did you notice the typewriter? Types dirtier than the pieces of shit we bang at around here."

"What about the other paper?"

"What is it?" he asked.

"A map."

"Yes, I realize it's a map, Nora. Thank you."

"I didn't mean it that way, Arthur."

"Just kidding," he said. He swigged from the cup of coffee on his desk. "Is it part of Chicago?"

"It's such a lousy copy that it's tough to read. But, you know, I thought I saw something that looked like a river." I stood and walked next to Art's chair. Pointing at a faint, wavy line on the map, I said, "Chicago River? Do you think?"

Art took the sheet close to his face and squinted at it. In a moment, he said, "Two things against it being the Chicago."

"Yes?"

"First, there isn't the ninety-degree split where the Chicago's North Branch and South Branch fork off the main trunk. And second, if you look real close, you can see the map says this river is named the Neva."

I grabbed the map from Art's hands. He chuckled.

"Lemme see that," I said, scowling. I brought the map close enough to my eyes to see the print I hadn't noticed before. Art was right.

"Nora," he said, "you look so goddamned good in your new leg that you don't have to read to be on this team."

"Thanks. I thought you'd never notice."

"I noticed, I noticed. Good for you, girl," he said, with the tender inflection of dialect he knew I enjoyed. He reached for my hand and squeezed it. "So where's this Neva?"

"Poland?" I guessed.

"I should know? Do I look Polish? We'll ask Frankie."

"What do you make of the red X?"

"It was drawn after it was photocopied. Other than that, I've no idea."

I walked back to my desk and sat. "We need a trip to the library, Arthur. You or me?"

"I dunno. Who's doing Melchior?"

"Melchior?"

"He had me into his office earlier this morning," Art said.

"He gave me the same *directions* about Watson's car that he said he gave you last night."

"I'm surprised he mentioned me."

"Why?"

"General principles," I muttered.

The vision of Melchior and that half-lit office at the Eighteenth swirled in front of me; Art now looked blurry to me. I jerked my head slightly and it cleared.

Art, noticing something, said, "Nora? Are you still with me?"

"Yeah, sure. I was thinking about my meeting with Melchior last night. I'm sure he gave you the same pitch."

"He's looking for some creative detection on this thing."

"Do you know how drunk Watson was, Art?"

"I heard over 0.3." He chuckled and said, "I also heard Watson's bimbo wasn't dressed for the weather."

"She decided to go with antifreeze instead of clothes."

"Back to reality," Art said. "Now it's our job to make a nice, polite story for the benefit of the media and the mayor. Like a Christmas package wrapped in tissue paper. Pleasant."

"Shit." I shook my head.

Suddenly, Art shifted gears and slapped his desk with the flat of his hand. "That dirty son-of-a-bitch Watson!" he barked. "And he's black, too. We don't have enough trouble in this city already?"

I hadn't anything to say.

"You do the library," Art said. "Chase down this Neva River thing. I'll talk to Smilin' Ray."

"Sure?" I was thrilled not to have to face Melchior that day.

"Positive."

I stood and started out of the office, then turned back. "Art, why's Melchior trying to protect Watson if Watson's black? Melchior hates blacks. I don't know why he—"

"Because Melchior's in the mayor's pocket somehow," Art

broke in. "The mayor can't afford to have his main black in the city council doing time for drunken driving and vehicular homicide. You think a whitey like the mayor could win again in this town without Watson?"

"No."

Art smiled wryly. "And I haven't even mentioned what black voters might think of Miss Mitzi with the creamy-white skin."

"Mitzi Williamson?"

"The same."

I found Hugh Thomas before I left the station. Hugh was fifty, a career officer who could have made detective years before but preferred the steadier action of the beat cop. He liked working the street where anything could happen at any moment, where you swooshed through some shifts on a river of straight adrenaline. Hugh was also the son of a locksmith. The man could pick any key lock in Cook County.

In the narrow corridor off the lobby, Hugh studied the key I had handed him. His face was long and slack, his eyes puffy.

"It's a double-bitted key," he said, "probably for a lever tumbler lock."

"Want to try that in English?"

He pursed his lips with a hint of impatience. "Nora, do you know how essential locksmithing is to a detective's work? You young detectives skip half the damn fundamentals."

I smiled him down and said, "Don't hand me that Arthur-type bullshit. Just enlighten me on the key. That's enough."

"If you want to be spoon-fed, then okay."

I nodded graciously.

Loving every second of his time on stage, he smacked his lips and started. "Lever tumblers are simple locks, really, but locks that still give a degree of security. See, a lever tumbler makes it impossible to remove the key while the lock is open. You can't get the key out until the door is safely locked again. You with me so far, Nora?"

"A lever tumbler would prevent you from leaving an unlocked door behind. You must lock the door to get your key back."

He smiled benignly. "I'm proud of you, Nora. As a reward, I'm going to invite you to ride with us this afternoon. Into the war zone on West Division. Got a flak jacket?"

"Sorry, gotta spend some time at the public library."

"And I suppose you're paid for that duty?"

"Hugh, seriously, where are these kinds of locks most used?"

"These days?" he said. "Probably safe-deposit boxes, although this key looks a little weak for that. Many old mailboxes also used lever tumblers so the mailman didn't pull his key without locking up the mail he just delivered."

Inexplicably, something made me say, "Do you ever read Plato?"

"Well, as a matter of fact—"

"I knew it!" I said. "You and my father would have loved each other."

"He enjoyed philosophy?"

"And front-end alignments. Thanks."

11

Mrs. Caverretta's Loop office was on the fifteenth floor, east side of the Federal Building. Her window looked out to a jumble of buildings, a narrow slice of Lake Michigan showing between two of them. It wasn't much, but on mornings like this, when spotty sunshine constantly changed the colors and moods of the water, the view was intriguing.

I explained who I was and what I needed. While I waited in a chair next to her desk, she fetched the Lugotov folder from another office. She spread the file out on the desk in front of us, and we leaned over it. Her white sweater emitted a penetrating smell of evergreen: Christmas in May.

"See, he was born in 1923," she said. "That makes him sixty-five." Mrs. Caverretta looked to be as old.

"Why was he carrying an immigration card?" I asked.

"He was required to. He wasn't a citizen."

"When did he come to this country?"

She flipped a page and pointed. "It says 1947."

"He could stay forty years and not become a citizen?"

"Oh, sure," she chirped. "He had permanent visa status. As a resident alien, all he had to do was report in annually, then just obey the laws and pay his taxes."

"Do you know where Lugotov came from?"

She scratched her gray, close-cropped hair, then turned to another page. "Looks like he deserted the Russian Army after the liberation of Berlin in 1945. Then he went from free Germany to France to the States. In the States, it was New York City for a year, then Chicago."

"Where was he born?" I asked.

Back to the first page. "Russia," she said, "Kiev."

"Kiev," I said slowly, thinking. "Mrs. Caverretta, have you ever heard of a river called the Neva?"

"It's Russian. I'm sure of it."

"Where?"

She touched the dry skin of her cheek. "I would guess Moscow or Leningrad. I don't know."

"Do you see either of those cities mentioned anywhere in the file?"

She rustled through more papers. "I guess not. Neither."

"Any family mentioned? Anyone named Nikki or Talitha?"

"No, just something about a brother named Josef Lugotov. He's also listed as living in Kiev."

She looked up from the file. "That's all I have, Lieutenant. Not much, I know. These old files have been purged of so much outdated paperwork, especially in people with whom we've never had any problems."

"Do you know that he married?"

"Marriage, you say . . . um . . ." Her fingers went back to the pages. "All right, I do have a marriage here. He reported marrying a Polish immigrant, Mary Klivka, in 1960. Oh, look, divorced in less than a year. Too bad. I always hate to see that, don't you?"

I ignored the question. "Any trace on Mary Klivka?"

She turned and punched the name into a computer keyboard to her left. After lists of names scrolled quickly across the screen, she said, "Neither Mary Klivka nor Mary Lugotov is in our files."

"Would that mean anything? Could she be an immigrant and still not have a current file?"

"Yes, if she either became a citizen, or else died. In either case, her file would then be dumped."

I knew there were more questions to ask, but I couldn't think of them. I thanked Mrs. Caverretta and left. She promised to review the file from scratch again, and call if she found anything of interest.

I sat at a walnut table, decades old and as sturdy as a vintage whaler, in a reading room at the downtown public library. The room boasted a long wall of magnificent arched windows, two-story glass portals opening onto Grant Park and, beyond that, to the flat gray-blueness of Lake Michigan. Except for the windows, the room was nondescript, another of the large, general reading areas on the library's first floor. Other, more specialized rooms that still wore the dark wood-paneled walls of the original construction could be found on the upper floors. But sadly, on the first floor, where traffic was heaviest, the walls had been skinned of their shiny wood. Only so many sets of initials, Cupid's hearts, and base obscenities could be carved into a wall's surface before it became too blighted to be tolerated. The new walls—dull gray slabs of granite composite—were more functional, impervious to the tips of teen-agers' knife blades.

An encyclopedia told me that the Neva was a river that flowed through northern Russia and Leningrad and emptied into the Gulf of Finland. Lugotov's map was of Leningrad, a city I had known of but never given a moment's thought to.

With the help of a librarian, I had built a stack of books on the table. They all told of the history and culture of Leningrad. Several were heavy and full of dense text printed on musty, yellowing pages. The others were newer, notably less scholarly,

and eminently more interesting. These were crammed with photographs and maps, visual concepts that easily grabbed my
attention.

The *Pictorial History of Russia in World War II* was the volume
that now held me riveted. The book's largest and most dramatic
chapter told of the winter of 1941–42 and the siege of Leningrad
by the German Army. What I saw in dozens of grainy, black-
and-white photographs astonished me. Roiling flames from the
Nazis' nighttime bombing raids. Knots of evacuees in turmoil
at railroad stations. Bombed-out apartment buildings, their
broken and frozen water pipes sticking into the air. Sheet-
wrapped corpses being pulled on sleds through streets of ice.
Snowy piles of Leningrad's starved dead, many wrapped in rags
or newspaper and stacked like firewood outside the gates of a
cemetery named Piskarevsky. The scribbled diary pages of an
eleven-year-old girl—a diary that recorded, one by one, the
deaths of all eight members of her family during the course of
two months.

I studied the Leningrad photographs for an hour before closing
the book and pushing it aside. I stretched my arms into a circle
on the table in front of me, then laid my cheek into their hollow.
Exhausted, I fell into a quick, deep sleep.

Thirty minutes later, I awoke, straightened my blouse, and
fluffed my hair. I picked up the book of photographs and left
the others in a neat pile. I would check the book out to take
home. I wanted to show this to Meg.

Before leaving the library, I made a series of phone calls from a
dingy booth in the lobby; my first call was to the city morgue
at Cook County Hospital. The secretary to the forensic pathologist, Dr. Vincent Dorner, said Dorner would not be doing the
Lugotov autopsy before the following morning. He would be in
court giving testimony all afternoon.

Next, I called John Dover at Ballistics.

"Did you get the gun, John, and the cartridges?" I said.

Taken by surprise, Dover said, "What gun? What cartridges?"

"From this morning's murder on Eddy Street."

"Never heard of it."

"Goddammit!" I snapped.

"Easy, Nora. Hey."

"Sorry. I thought you might have already done some test firings and could tell me something."

"I don't know anything about it. What's the rush on this?"

"John, a man named Semyon Lugotov was murdered early this morning on the North Side. Last night, maybe five or six hours before he was found dead, Lugotov came to the Eighteenth. He told Steve Schwartz that he was being stalked by the same man responsible for the Cathedral shooting last Saturday."

"So?"

"So remember those bullets and the casing I brought you from the Cathedral? The ones from the Russian pistols?"

"Of course."

"Well, a gun was stuck in Lugotov's hand," I said, "an unfired automatic. It's an old, funny-looking thing. We also found a box of cartridges."

"Anything from the killing itself?"

"Two slugs dug out of a wall," I said. "Both probably went through Lugotov's gut. But he's got at least four holes in him, so two more slugs are still unaccounted for. Maybe they're inside the guy. Dorner can't post him till tomorrow."

"And your hunch?" Dover asked.

"The slugs that killed Lugotov will match up with those from the confessional. And Lugotov's box of cartridges should fit with the single casing and the bullet that struck the metal grillwork."

Quiet for a moment, Dover then said, "Okay, don't worry about it. I'll find the automatic and its cartridges, and the slugs that killed your Mr. Lugotov. I'll call around—they have to have reached here by now. They're somewhere close."

"Can you do any firings yet today?" I asked impatiently. "You have time?"

"I'll make time. Call me later."

My next call was to Steve Schwartz. It was three in the afternoon, and I decided he'd have had enough sleep by then.

He didn't answer until the eighth or ninth ring, and his voice sounded thick and groggy. "What is this, Nora, revenge?"

"What?"

"A payback for me waking you at four this morning?"

"No, no," I said apologetically. "I need to talk with you more about Lugotov. Go over some things he might have said to you. Okay?"

"Give me half an hour to get my brain engaged," he said. "I'll meet you at the station about four. Okay?"

"Not okay. I'm not going back there before Melchior goes home. I'm avoiding the guy. He's after Art and me to glaze over the Watson thing."

"C'mon, Ray's trying to fix up the Rush Street slaughter?"

"Maybe."

"Why you and Art? Melchior's got a dozen other detectives he could put on that."

"Maybe it's because of that evidence thing with the hospital," I said. "You know—"

"I heard about you yanking the slug from the path lab," Schwartz said.

"Melchior probably sees Art and me being a little more beholden to him than usual. Easier to manipulate."

"I'd stay away from the Watson thing if I were you," Schwartz said. "The walrus isn't going to be able to rig that one."

"You're awful cocksure."

"Just watch."

"Anyway, how about the Oak Tree in an hour? I'll buy your breakfast."

"You're on."

Before meeting Schwartz, I needed a break. I had saved my next call for last, the one call that always cleansed turmoil from my spirit. I dialed Caitlin, my sister.

Cait, who was born three years after me, lived in a small farming community—corn and hogs—an hour west of the city, with her husband, George, a kindly beanpole in dermatology practice. They had six children, all under the age of seven. I had decided one niece and two nephews ago that Cait either suffered from early dementia or had the patience of an Indian woman from the Illinois prairie. Naturally, I chose to believe the latter. And, rebounding from Richard, how could I not like a man with George's energy?

Cait and I had always been close. I was baptized Nora Joyce Dybzewski, and when the holy water dribbled over Cait's forehead, she was transformed into Caitlin Thomas Dybzewski. Both Cait and I happened to be born during our father's infatuation with European poetry and fiction: I was named for Nora Joyce, the wife of James; Cait for Caitlin Thomas, the wife of Dylan. The logic was indisputable.

I'm sure that all discussion of the names passed by our mother without her notice. She was not offended by Albert's methods and choices. Once, she said Caitlin and I could have been twins named Ivory and Ovary and the names wouldn't have mattered: by the age of six weeks, every baby's name fits perfectly. My mother was a saintly and long-suffering woman, and, better yet, she was never burdened by self-knowledge. Still, I always cringed when I thought that if it had been left to her, I might be tagged Lieutenant Ovary Dybzewski-Callum. There *were* fates worse than death.

———

"Hi, Cait," I said.

"Nora, where are you? Sound like you're calling from goddamn Africa."

"I'm at the public library, on Randolph. I've got the phone away from my lips because it stinks so bad."

She laughed. "I told you it's not healthy in that city."

"It smells about half as bad as the pigshit in your backyard."

"Very funny. I've told you, we don't have pigs. Hey, Tim, climb off me, will you? Sorry, Nora. What's up?"

"Just calling to say hello. I needed a lift. I'm stuck on a case."

"Guess what? *I'm* stuck with a broken clothes washer and about thirty pounds of dirty diapers. I'll do them by hand, I guess. George can cook tonight. How's Meg?"

"Good," I said.

"You know, I've been thinking, she should come out for a couple of weeks in the summer. The kids would love to have her."

"It sounds good," I said. "Let me ask her."

"So what case has you tied up?"

"There was a murder this morning, near Wrigley Field—"

"I hope it was a multiple murder," she interrupted, "and I hope it was the entire Cubs' pitching staff. You been watching them lately? Bums. Even the preschoolers around here are mad."

When I stopped laughing, I said, "Actually, the guy killed had something to do with the shooting in the Cathedral last Saturday."

"I did hear about that one," she said. "On the news. Isn't that the Cardinal's church?"

"I think so."

"No clues, huh?"

"I'm moving a few pieces around the board, but nothing fits."

"I know you'll figure it out, Nora," she said. "Really. Just don't try and be the hero."

"Yeah."

"Say, how about we go see the trotters some night soon? George has been working out a system, something about betting and permutation theory. He's working on it every night."

"Jesus, Cait, when does that man sleep?" I asked. My mood had lifted already.

12

The Oak Tree Grill stood at the corner of Rush and Oak Streets, half a block from the square of sidewalk where Samuel Watson's final victim had fallen the night before. The Grill was a brightly lit, high-energy, twenty-four-hour-a-day operation that served stumblebums and Gold Coast millionaires alike. It was also a favorite place of cops on and off duty: the greasy cheeseburgers were some of the city's best.

Schwartz and I sat across from each other in a window booth. Our seats were covered in garish Kelly-green leatherette that squeaked when we moved. Schwartz wore a dress shirt, starched and open-collared. His face was freshly shaven, and the faint smell of soap wafted off him. His hair still glistened from a wash.

"A diet Coke, please," I said to our waitress, with a small sigh, glad to be resting my leg.

"Diet?" Schwartz said. "Come off it, Nora. You need to fatten up."

"Diet," I repeated.

Schwartz ordered pancakes and bacon and coffee for the first meal of his day.

When the waitress left, I said, "If they ever put me back on the midnight shift, I'm quitting the goddamned Force."

"Ahhh, prefer your pancakes at six in the morning, do you?" Schwartz said.

"And with my daughter."

Schwartz rolled his head and said, "Midnights are definitely for singles or spouse-haters. What's your daughter's name?"

"Megan . . . Meg."

"Pretty."

"Thanks," I said.

"Her father's gone?"

"Long gone. He works in a vineyard in the Napa Valley, the last I heard."

"He left you to pick grapes?" Schwartz asked.

I sat quietly for a moment, thinking whether to say more or not. Why keep it inside all the time? I had always sensed that Schwartz, like Art, was somebody you could trust.

"Richard was a man who should have stayed twenty years old forever," I said. "He had trouble with personal growth."

"Meaning?"

"Meaning he didn't understand that life demands more of us at thirty than it does at twenty. Watching daytime TV nursing a beer doesn't cut it."

"So you tossed him out."

"Not really. I put up with it, hoping something would light a fire under his ass."

"I'm surprised he had the energy to leave," Schwartz said.

"In the end, I think it might have had something to do with me losing my leg," I said, my eyes fixed on the ridiculous pattern of Formica on the tabletop. I looked up with a self-conscious grin. "I don't know—maybe he disliked my lack of symmetry."

Schwartz straightened against the seat back. "Are you serious? He dusted you because of the leg?"

"I think so."

"What an asshole." Schwartz scowled.

I smiled. "Actually, he saved my life when he left."

Schwartz was five or ten years my junior, but for a moment I wanted to move to his side of the booth, just to sit against him:

a brush of contact would have satisfied me. Instead, I turned away and looked outside to Rush Street's crawling traffic.

I said, "Feel any better, about last night, Steve?"

"You mean, letting Lugotov slip through?"

"Yes."

"I guess," he said. "I know you're right about the someone's-trying-to-kill-me routine. Like the boy who cried wolf. You get so hard-assed you don't listen."

The waitress brought coffee for Schwartz and a Coke for me. I sucked a mouthful through the straw and felt the icy cold run down my throat. I hadn't had anything in my stomach since doughnuts at the Eighteenth that morning, and the fizzy, sweet drink tasted wonderful.

"Tell me," I said, "did Lugotov mention anything about the city of Leningrad?"

"No. Why?"

"That map in his apartment was of Leningrad."

"The guy never mentioned it."

"How about the name Talitha?" I asked. "Or Nikki? Did those names come up?"

"Never."

I took the Talitha letter from my purse and handed it across the table. Schwartz studied it for several minutes, then said, "Beats the shit out of me. We didn't talk long enough to get this far. Have you found out anything about the guy?"

"Virtually nothing," I said. "According to his landlady, he lived like a hermit. He worked as a printer somewhere, he was in a union. I have to check that out, probably tomorrow."

The waitress brought Schwartz's pancakes and bacon. I said no to his offer to share his food. "Did you think to ask Lugotov if he knew Eva Ramirez?"

"Never got to that either."

I sat quietly and allowed Schwartz to eat his meal. He wiped his lips of syrup and motioned to the waitress for a check. "You need the Fat Man, Nora," he said, "or at least a make on his car."

"Yeah," I said. "Dream on."

When the waitress brought the check, Schwartz beat me to it. "No, this is on me," I said, "remember?"

"And you have just a Coke? Are you kidding? No, I'm going to get to you for a meal at some fancy place, or maybe at your apartment even, but not here."

"That's a deal." I smiled. Some kind of crazy hope ballooned inside me.

Schwartz started out of the booth. "Need a lift?"

"I have my car," I said.

"What are you going to do now?"

"I don't know. I'm kind of stuck. I guess I'll have to go back to the station—Melchior should be gone. I'm waiting on John Dover at Ballistics. The autopsy isn't until tomorrow."

Schwartz stood, but I stayed seated, thinking while staring blankly at the procession of legs moving along the sidewalk outside.

"What's up?" Schwartz asked.

"Nothing, just that car. How to get a fix on the car that chased Lugotov down Addison Avenue."

"With him dead, we'll never get more than his rough description of the thing," Schwartz said. "Not enough even to check model types on ticket printouts."

I turned back to Schwartz. "What do you mean? Sit down a minute."

He did. "Look," he said, "if Lugotov had given me a passable description of the car, we could cross-check its model type against all recent traffic and parking tickets. We might hit a license number that way. It would be a long shot, but something."

I said, "If we can't check for model types, why can't we check for sites of tickets?"

"What site? Where's the car been ticketed?"

"At the Addison Avenue El stop," I said. "We know Fat Man left it there Saturday afternoon when he jumped on the train. Maybe it was ticketed for illegal parking."

Schwartz chuckled and said, "And maybe the Cubs are going to win the World Series this year."

Back at Area Six, I slouched in my office chair, stunned.

"You don't believe me, do you?" Art said. "Want me to show it to you? It's in the safe, I'll get it. Maybe you've never seen ten grand before. I hadn't."

I tossed the sheet of pale blue paper back to Art and said, "Jesus, forget it, will you please? I believe you, I believe you. Please."

"Then why you got on your shit face, Nora?"

" 'Cause by this time of day I'm tired of shitbird letters that don't mean a goddamned thing. Understand?"

"What I understand is that it's a clue," Art said, "and clues are what we don't have many of. Let's thank the guys from the Eighteenth for sending it over. Let's not be so fussy."

He lowered the tone of his voice and continued, "The bills are all brand new, just off the press, so fresh they crinkle when you touch them. I'll run a trace on their serial numbers. We can find the bank where they were distributed. Who knows? That might tell us something."

I said, "I talked to Hugh Thomas about the key. He said 'lever tumbler' or something like that. Safe-deposit boxes, mailboxes."

"You try it in Lugotov's mailbox?"

"Yes, on the way out of his building this morning," I said. "Didn't fit. Let me see that note again."

"Good girl," he said. He reached for the piece of paper Juan Ramirez had brought in to the Eighteenth that morning with the cash, and he passed it back to me.

The type was clean, obviously done on a different machine from that used for Lugotov's letter. The message read:

This payment is due you. Your troubles are mine,
mine yours. As you heal, I will heal.

A friend, not an enemy

Making no more from the mumbo jumbo than I had in my
first ten readings, I flipped the note back toward Art and sipped
at my cup, which was half full of cold coffee.

"Don't drink that crap," Art said. "Let me get you some hot."

"No, thanks. The cold stuff hits me with a better caffeine
jolt."

I felt a tiny smile loosen my scowl. "I didn't mean to jump at
you about the money, Art, really. I somehow thought—I mean,
I hoped the Ramirez family was clean. They seem nice, honest—
you know? This is a disappointment."

Art folded his hands in front of him prayerfully. "Maybe you're
still right about them."

"With ten big ones sitting in their mailbox this morning?" I
said. "C'mon, just an accident of time and place?"

"Then why does Ramirez bring the money and the note in to
the police? How can this guy be guilty of anything except profound honesty?"

I shook my head. "Jesus, he's got to be the only guy, rich or
poor, on North State Street who doesn't pocket found money."

Art said nothing.

I finished my coffee, and said, "He was probably raised by
penniless Mexican parents who scrubbed their children's con-
sciences scrupulously clean. The kind of people you meet once
in a blue moon in this job."

Art, his hands still folded, said, "Okay, girl, let's play it another
way. Maybe this means Eva was supposed to empty the mailbox.
Maybe Juan wasn't on the inside, but he winds up emptying the
box because Eva's in the hospital. Then, like a dummy, he brings
in the money thinking it will help us find out who shot Eva."

"You're implying the archangel with the big wallet doesn't know Eva's in the hospital. Doesn't make sense, partner."

Art said, "Shit, Mother, I can't dance—"

"Wake me up for the screwin'," I finished.

For the next few minutes, neither of us spoke, each content to glance around the office aimlessly, allowing our eyes to meet occasionally. I finally looked out the window and down the street at the adult video parlor, its normally crimson sign shimmering purple in the dying sun.

"Art," I said, "should we rent a triple-X movie from Sin City over there? You call Helen and tell her to come down, and we'll all take a break and grab a couple hours of gratuitous filth? You know, the kind the Supreme Court said we'd know was pornographic when we saw it?"

Art cracked a tired smile. "Can we invite Watson?"

"Oh, yes, and Mitzi, his bimbo. What a great fivesome we'd make!"

When we'd stopped laughing, Art said flatly, "Say, Nora, why don't you go check on that ticket stuff you were talking about when you came in here?"

I felt my smile fade. "Yes, fine," I said seriously. "Good idea."

"And another thing . . ."

"Yeah?"

"Next time you're on North State, stop and try that key of yours in the Ramirez mailbox."

"No way, Arthur. No way."

He lifted his eyebrows and bugged out his eyes at me until I giggled.

The cooling fan inside the computer terminal hummed monotonously. Nearly oblivious to the noise, I scanned screenful after screenful of traffic and parking tickets issued by the Police Department the previous Saturday, the day of Lugotov's chase and Eva's shooting. I found twenty-two tickets had been written within the Addison Avenue district, but none closer than three blocks from the El station. Strikeout.

I punched an access code into the keyboard and went on line to the State of Illinois's mainframe, then followed its menu into the driver's registration files. Semyon Lugotov did not possess a driver's license currently, nor had he for any of the previous ten years that the program could search.

I returned to my office, my eyes still burning from the hour at the computer screen. It was nearly five o'clock, so I called home. Anna told me she could stay longer with Meg, and I shouldn't hurry home if I had more work to do. I hung up the phone thinking, What would I do without that woman?

Art came back into the office. "Guess what happened with the Watson thing," he said.

"Gosh, I forgot about that," I said, embarrassed I hadn't remembered to ask.

Art plunked into his chair and lifted his feet up to his desk. The cuffs on his trousers begged for a pressing. "After you went to the library, Ray had me into his office. Remember?"

"Sure."

"Well, Melchior said he thought the alderman's brakes must have failed last night, and he said it without so much as a grin. He said it was probably a mechanical breakdown causing Watson to lose control of his car and mow down those poor bastards."

"Art, the guy was a gin mill. That brake stuff is bullshit."

"Of course it's bullshit."

"Melchior tried the same thing on me last night," I said. "He wanted a report before the guys even pulled a wheel off the car."

Art's feet came back to the floor, and he leaned his thick middle into the edge of his desk. "He told me to check the car's brakes and confirm their poor condition in writing. A full and official report, he said. And he wants it from me, not you."

"You? Did he say why?"

"No, but count your blessings."

"You going to do it?"

"Hell, no," he said, sweat popping out on his forehead. "Would you?"

"No."

"But it'll mean my ass. If I don't file that kind of report, I'm back on the street. You watch."

I turned to the window and looked out. My thoughts inevitably cycled back to those few minutes the night before in Melchior's office, and again I felt bankrupt to my marrow.

"What are you thinking?" Art said to my back.

I spun toward Art. "Play your trump card."

"What trump card?" he said.

Lips set, I whacked the metal desk with my open hand. "The ponies!"

"I've held that card for a long time, so long I tend to forget about it. But maybe this is it, isn't it? The time to cash it. But what about Frankie? I don't want to hurt Frankie."

"Forget Frankie," I said. "It'll never get as far as Frankie. Mayor or no mayor, you think Melchior's going to the barricades over Watson? Shit, no! Watson's a downed bird, as he should be. And watch, when this is over, you'll still be holding your card."

"And if it doesn't work?"

"Then I'll make him draw to *my* trump card," I said, thinking about Melchior harassing me.

"What's that?"

I paused before saying, "I don't know. I'll have to think about that."

Art's heavy features loosened. "Okay, tomorrow," he said. "I'll confront him tomorrow. Tonight, I marshal my courage."

"You'll do fine."

Art wiped his forehead dry with a handkerchief. "You're a goddamn good partner, Nora."

I smiled in embarrassment.

"Say," he said, "what did you come up with on the computer? Anything ticketed at the Addison El?"

"No. I'm skunked, out of ideas."

"Well, this old man has one more for you. A long shot, but who knows?"

Perked up again, I sat back against my chair and opened my arms as if I were going to catch a beach ball, not an idea. "Hit me with it, Arthur."

"Check the tow records for Saturday," he said. "If the car was parked in a no-parking—tow zone, it wouldn't have been issued a ticket. They just haul those cars away and collect the fines when the cars are released."

13

Bingo!

There it was, in black letters that nearly jumped at me from the pale green screen—like dumping a silver dollar into a slot machine in Las Vegas and watching the cherries and lemons spin to a quarter-million-dollar hit. I couldn't have felt any better if the computer had been filling the floor around me with a pool of clanging money.

The letters said:

/ Sat / 5-15 / Ford Escort / red / illegal park-tow zone
/ Add. Ave. El / 2:35 PM / Windy City Tow /
pickup: Sun, 5-16 / $75 pd /

Bubbling, I patted Art affectionately on his wiry scalp and told him my news.

"See what it means to spend time on a beat?" he said. "See what writing tickets and tow orders can mean to a detective someday? You young ones make promotions too damn fast, miss way too much on the way up."

"Sure, sure," I said, and reached for the city phone book. Windy City Towing was on North Elston Avenue. "They must keep a logbook with license numbers."

"They do."

A woman—at least I thought it was a woman—answered the Windy City phone. She told me that no information was given out by telephone, even if the caller did say she was police. Everybody's a cop, the lady complained.

I hung up the phone. "They won't do anything for me on the phone. I'm going there—it's not that far. Will you be here a while?"

"Sure, see you when you get back. If you get a license, we'll run it through the computer."

Finally tubeless and tapeless, Eva Ramirez sat in a window-side chair on the hospital's tenth floor; her view was eastward and down to the lake and the tiny, high-rise-shaded Ohio Street Beach. Without medical paraphernalia pasted to her face and arms, her simple beauty startled me.

I had delayed my visit to Windy City Towing to see Eva, to ask her about the windfall discovered in their mailbox.

When I entered her room, she straightened in her chair. "You're the lieutenant who asked me questions the other day. When I was in the intensive care unit."

I walked to a dresser and leaned my bottom against the edge. There was another chair near Eva, but I felt like an intruder with no license to sit. "Yes," I said, "that's me."

Smiling warmly, she said, "Come closer, please. Sit with me."

I moved into the empty chair.

"I don't know your name," she said.

"It's Nora."

A nod of her head in acknowledgment, then, "The Father was here to see me yesterday."

"From the Cathedral?" I asked. "Father Ritgen?"

"Yes."

"I'm glad he visited."

She looked away from me, down to where Lake Shore Drive

bustled next to the deserted, waveless beach. Her face toward the window, she said, "He told me what you did in the church, when I was shot and lying on the floor. He said he and the others assumed I was dead until you came and checked."

"You did look more dead than alive just then. Young officers will make some mistakes. We've all done it."

She turned back to me. "The doctors say I will be okay and can go home in a few days."

"That's fine, Eva."

"You are as responsible for that as the doctors and nurses." She started her right hand out of her lap and toward me, but she stopped short of touching me. "Thank you, Nora."

"You're welcome."

"Juan said God smiled on me that day."

"I guess He did," I said. Some smile—three bullet holes ripped through your belly and a half-gallon of your blood soaking the carpet.

"Eva," I said, "a man, an elderly man named Semyon Lugotov, was shot and killed on Eddy Street early this morning. We think the murder may have been committed by the same man who shot you."

She flinched—maybe it was the news of her assailant still out on the streets, still shooting. Her face and body suddenly grew taut, and she glanced toward the door as though she were expecting Lugotov's killer to jump through it and have another crack at her.

"Do you know a man with that name, Semyon Lugotov?" I asked.

"No. He's dead?"

"Yes. No smiles from God for him."

"Family?"

"Apparently not."

"Mmm."

I hesitated, preparing to begin my questions about the ten thousand dollars, when Eva surprised me with, "Juan told me he took that money in to your police station."

"He did, yes."

"When he found it, he called me, and we talked about what to do with it. We decided he should bring it to you—not that we couldn't use it, but it wasn't ours. And maybe it will tell you who shot me."

"You have no idea where the money came from?" I asked.

"No."

"And the note that came with it?"

"Juan read it to me over the phone. It means nothing to me."

"Not a thing?"

"Nothing," Eva said as sincerely as I had hoped she would.

For a couple of minutes, both of us were silent. Then she leaned forward from her chair, closing the gap between us. Her dark eyes searched my face, her hands curled into delicate, bird-like fists, and she said, "Do you believe me—about the money, I mean?"

Resolutely, meaning every syllable, I said, "Yes, I believe you."

She sat back, her fingers opening. She said, "Are you married, Nora?"

"Divorced."

Her eyes softened. "Sorry," she said. "Children?"

"A daughter. Megan."

"A beautiful name."

"Yes, thank you."

She smiled and said, "A beautiful name, but if ever I have a daughter, she will be a Nora."

The sun was low in the west as I headed toward Clark on Chicago Avenue. Rush hour was in full swing, every block a push. After missing a second light at State and Chicago, I suddenly remembered Art's prediction. I made a quick left turn, rudely cutting in front of an oncoming bus. The bus driver rightfully flipped me the bird.

Parking was wide open in front of the Ramirezes' building. I walked through a knot of children on the sidewalk and into the small lobby. Dim and cramped, it smelled like a wet basement. I located the Ramirez mailbox, an end one in a row of six. Each mailbox door had its own key slot. Over the Ramirez box, above the bank of doors, was another slot.

I reached into my purse for the brass key from Lugotov's hallway, tried the key in the slot above the Ramirez mailbox but was unable to seat it. Next, I pushed it into the slot in the Ramirez box door. The key's tip hung in the lock for a second, but a shove easily buried its shank to the hub. I turned the key and the door opened. The box was empty. I removed the key and started from the lobby, then turned back. I tried the key in each of the other five mailboxes. One opened and four wouldn't. I stood in puzzlement for a moment before I left.

Clark to Addison took fifteen minutes; then it was another ten minutes west to Elston. The short drive south on Elston took me through somber, treeless blocks dedicated to ancient factories and decrepit warehouses—and to Windy City Towing.

A high chain-link fence crowned with barbed wire surrounded the yard, and a sliding gate opened to the street. Dozens of cars, many of them abandoned heaps, but also a few shiny, newer models, rested peacefully on the gravel lot. A large German-shepherd dog, matted and filthy, meandered among the cars. No one in her right mind would be driving off without first paying the fine.

Praying I wouldn't catch the dog's notice, I drove slowly through the gate and up to a wooden hut labeled "Office." I hurried inside from the safety of the car. The stench of smoke and alcohol fouled the small, barren room. Ahead of me, an old woman with sad, still eyes slouched behind a pay window. Her

hair bore a remarkable resemblance to the dog outside. A cigarette hung from her loose lips.

I approached the window, which was inches thick and marred
at its center by a shallow crater. I decided a disconsolate car
owner must have vainly tried to penetrate the window with a
bullet or a rock or an ice pick. Windy City's collection system—
an old lady behind bulletproof glass and a ferocious German
shepherd in the yard—seemed simple but effective.

"I need some information," I said through the window. "I'm
the police detective who called you a short time ago." I opened
my wallet to my ID and held it to the window for the woman
to see.

She stirred. "It wasn't me you talked to," she said, her words
sloppy with saliva. "It musta been the other one. We just changed
shifts." She mashed out her cigarette in the overturned lid of a
coffee can. Dirt rimmed her fingernails. "I work the evening shift
and all day Sundays. That's the horseshit shift, that Sunday one."

"Yes, I imagine it would be," I said.

The woman rattled out a cough, then, "What you want from
me?"

"I need to see your logbook starting with last Saturday. I'm
tracing a car."

She reached into a drawer and produced a battered hard-cov-
ered book. She pushed it to me, through the pay slot at the
bottom of the window. "Thank you," I said.

The pages were ragged with use, but orderly enough, the
listings all logged by each car's time of arrival on the lot. It looked
as though thirty to forty cars per day were towed in by the
Windy City trucks, most of them under contract with the Traffic
Division of the Police Department; the offense was usually illegal
parking. A few cars, mostly accidents and breakdowns, came in
by private request.

The page for the previous Saturday's arrivals showed ten cars
had been brought in between noon and six o'clock. The pick-up

points were scattered all around the North Side, two from Addison Avenue. The first was a smashed Lincoln limousine hauled from Addison and Marine Drive, near the lakefront. The second was a Ford Escort brought from Addison near the corner of Sheffield Avenue, the east side of Wrigley Field, the Cubs' park. I knew the intersection well—I had crossed it a hundred times coming and going from Cubs baseball games. It was no more than twenty yards from the El station that Lugotov said he had run into while being chased.

The log also showed the same car had been retrieved from Windy City at 1:45 p.m. on Sunday, the next day, but I couldn't tell by whom: a scribbled signature was the person's only identification.

"Do you have a way of telling who picked up this car?" I asked the woman.

"They sign," she growled. "Look at the signature."

"I am. It's unreadable."

"Tough shit."

I decided not to respond in kind. Instead, I jotted down the car's license number—Illinois, AFS 697. "What was the charge for the tow?"

"Seventy-five," she said. "Fifty for the tow and twenty-five extra for Sunday pick-up."

"Paid by cash or check?"

"Can't tell."

I closed the book and shoved it back through the slot. "I have what I need," I said. Starting out of the room, I turned back and asked, "Oh, is the dog outside very dangerous?"

"Damn dangerous," the woman said, snickering.

"Any suggestions for getting back to my car?"

Still inordinately amused, she lifted her head to the ceiling and shouted, "Tyrone!" Suddenly, from nowhere, a scrawny black teenager appeared next to me. "Take her to her car, Tyrone. She don't think she can get past Dixie."

Outside, Tyrone walked me to my car, then held the panting dog by the throat while I entered and started the engine. Instinctively, before pulling away, I opened my glove compartment: it had been picked clean of loose change and several cassette tapes—the heist, no doubt, courtesy of Windy City Towing. I rolled down my window, just enough to talk to Tyrone and still be safe from drooling Dixie. "Tyrone," I said, "my glove compartment's been emptied."

His face flat, he shrugged his ignorance.

"Tyrone, I'm a police detective and this is my unmarked squad car. Now, if you go to the other side of the car and put back my money and tapes, then I'm going to forget about this."

Smiling at him, I continued, "And if you don't do that, Tyrone, if you don't put my things back, then I'm going to take you downtown and I'm gonna bust your skinny ass. Do you understand me?"

Tyrone spun and started for the other side of the car. I called after him, "And tie up the goddamn dog before opening the car door!"

Tyrone quickly obeyed, dumping more coins into the glove box than I thought I probably had there in the first place. When he shut the door, I dropped the Fury into Drive and rocketed off, my rear tires spewing two wide columns of gravel and dust behind me.

Back at Area Six by seven o'clock, I went directly to the computer room and called up the license-tracking program. When I typed in the Escort's license number, the screen read SYSTEM ERROR #4536. Two more attempts yielded the same message.

In my office, I plunked into my desk chair as Art told me the computer system had bombed out just after I had left for the tow yard. It would be down for several hours.

I still had one more thing to do before quitting time. I picked up the phone and dialed John Dover.

"You were right, Nora," Dover said. "The gun found in the Eddy Street victim's hand is a TT-30, a Tokarev automatic. It's the same gun that fired the bullet that bounced off the metallic thing in the back of the Cathedral. The test firings prove it."

"For sure?"

"Yes, and by the way, the gun probably wasn't fired last night."

"But the Tokarev was in the Cathedral last Saturday?"

"No question about it," Dover said. "Who fired it there is another matter."

"Of course, but the likely answer is that it was Lugotov."

"No comment. That's your job, not mine."

"Hold a minute, John." I took the phone from my mouth and said to Art, "Dover puts Lugotov's gun in the Cathedral last Saturday."

Art raised his fist at our first small triumph.

I returned to Dover. "Now, what about the bullets that killed Lugotov?"

"I don't have any that have been removed from the body itself," Dover said. "Nothing's been sent from Forensics yet. But I do have a couple of slugs the team dug out of a plaster wall. They both have traces of blood and presumably traveled through the victim. And guess what?"

"They could be from a Nagant revolver, the same gun that shot Eva Ramirez."

"Right."

"You're positive about this, John?"

"Well, I don't have the gun to test-fire, but how many Nagants do you think are floating around this town?"

"So the same person shot both victims?" I asked.

"The same gun shot both victims. Oh, one other thing, Nora."

"Yes?"

"The FBI called today from Washington. When they saw the stuff from the Cathedral that I sent them, they became interested. They're looking to horn in."

"Why? What's the big deal?"

"Well, how often do you think they're asked to do ballistics on a Tokarev and a Nagant from the same shooting?"

"I don't know."

"Try never," Dover said. "Not in this country, at least. So they're interested. I'm actually surprised they're not bothering you already. And wait'll they hear about this morning's murder, with the Tokarev itself showing up and more Nagant slugs being sprayed around to boot. Particularly when they find out the dead man is a Russian immigrant."

I didn't answer.

"Nora, are you still there?" Dover asked.

"Yes, yes, I am."

"You okay?"

"Yes," I said, doodling on a legal pad. "Just thinking."

"Do you have any idea who did all of this?" Dover asked. "Any names?"

Two old Russian guns, one old dead Russian, I thought.

"Nora?"

"Ah . . . no, I don't have much yet, John, not yet. Just a hunch. I think we can crack this, but we need a day or two. Can you get us that?"

"Maybe," Dover said. "I could hold up today's ballistics for a day or so. That wouldn't seem out of the ordinary to anybody."

"Would you mind?"

"No, it's okay."

"Thanks, John. I'll be in touch." I hung up the phone and laid my pencil down.

"FBI, huh?" Art said.

I rested my chin in my hands and said, "We have a couple of days before they're here."

"Then we could quit now," Art said, "put our feet up, wait for the big shots, see what else Melchior might have for us."

"You're kidding, right?"

"Of course. Look, Nora, we're on a little roll these past few hours. As soon as they fix the computer, we should have a license number. That should take us to the killer."

I sighed. "What the hell was Lugotov doing in the Cathedral when Eva was shot?"

Art didn't answer. "Go home, Nora. We'll never be able to run that car trace till after midnight. Go feed Meg, get some rest. Helen and I and the kids are going to the Sox game tonight." He chuckled. "We'll see if they can notch their first win in a week. I'll see you early tomorrow and we'll run the trace and talk more about Lugotov. Deal?"

"Deal."

"I have a good feeling about this one, girl. Tomorrow we break it!"

14

vening had cooled the city's air, and the threat of rain hung low and dark in the sky over the lake. My drive home was easy, but on Fargo Avenue not a parking spot had been left vacant. Three blocks away, on Sheridan, I wedged the Fury between two parked trucks, then lugged my purse and the heavy library book to my building. I found Meg and Anna in the living room, Meg belly-spread on the floor in front of the television, Anna drowsy on the couch, half reading the newspaper.

"What, no hugs?" I said when Meg didn't budge her eyes from the stream of color spilling from the television.

"Oh, sorry, Mom," Meg said. She ran across the room and hugged my waist tightly, pushed her nose into my belly. "It's a show about murder, Mom! It's exciting!" She returned to the floor and the tube.

I sat down in a chair. "How are you, Anna?"

"Good," Anna said, now fully awake. Her eyes, blue and steely, smiled in her wrinkled face. She wore a complicated, dark green paisley dress. "It was a long day, dearie?"

I put my purse and the book on the floor in front of me. "Not bad," I lied.

"Nora, my God, it was terrible what happened on Rush Street last night," Anna said, a sense of genuine indignation etched in her face.

I nodded. "It's in our district. Art, my partner, is working on it."

"He was drunk? The alderman?"

"Very drunk," I said. I slid my arms from the suit jacket, opened the top buttons of the blouse, and lay back against the chair's comfortable cushions. "You two eat yet?"

"Meg would not let me fix her something for supper," Anna said. "She says she's not hungry, she will wait for you."

"Good, I'd like someone to eat with. Anna, you stay and eat with us. That would be fun, wouldn't it, Meg?"

"Yeah, yeah!" Meg cried enthusiastically, never turning her face from the screen.

With only the moment of hesitation required by good manners, Anna said, "This is a nice offer, Nora. I will take it."

"You know we're talking frozen here, don't you?" I said, laughing.

"Fine, fine. I can help."

"No, you sit. I like doing this. It'll feel good to cook, even if it's just from the freezer."

Up from the chair, I settled my stump more firmly into its socket, then started for the kitchen. Remembering the book of war photographs on the floor, I said to Meg, "I brought home a book I want you to look at. Turn off the TV and come over here."

A groan eased from Meg, her body not stirring.

"Meg, move it. C'mon. Now."

Another groan, then she struggled from the floor to kill the TV.

"Maybe Anna will help you with the book," I said, and looked to Anna.

"Yes, oh sure, dearie," Anna said. She smiled and winked her collusion with me.

I picked up the book from the floor and gave it to Anna. Meg joined her on the couch. "I found this at the library, guys," I said. "It looked interesting."

In the kitchen, I scoured the freezer compartment for something, anything. Lasagna—no, too runny, Meg always said. Frozen omelettes? Never. Rummaging among the frosty boxes, I finally found two packages of fettuccine Alfredo. Easy: six minutes in the microwave, snip open the bags, and dump out the cheesy pasta wads.

As the oven hummed, Meg walked into the kitchen. "Can I have some peanuts, Mom? I can't wait. Really."

"It'll just be a few minutes, kiddo. Hang on."

"Aww."

Meg hopped up onto the countertop. She was dressed in black-and-white striped shorts and a simple white T-shirt. Her hair was back over her ears. As I went to the cupboard for plates and glasses, I asked, "How was school?"

"Sister Aletius said my drawing of the rain forest was pretty good. I didn't tell her you did the trees."

"That's okay. It's not cheating. Moms are allowed to help with big projects like that one."

"Yeah, I thought so."

I peeked from the kitchen to the living room. I saw Anna sitting with the big book cradled in her lap, staring at its pages, turning them slowly and deliberately, her head as still as the marble David's.

I pulled the cloudy pouches from the oven and split open the first bag. Hot melted cheese splashed onto my forearm, burning me. After rinsing my arm under the cold-water faucet, I opened the second bag: I would let the platefuls of pasta cool for a few minutes before serving.

"Meg, get your milk. Did you get a snack after school?"

"A doughnut."

"A doughnut?" I said, only half paying attention. "Where?"

"Up the street. You know, Sheridan. Anna and I took a long walk, and at a doughnut shop a man bought me a chocolate one."

I tuned the kitchen radio to a classical-music station and found Bach, solo violin, very austere. Outside the windows the lake looked as hard and choppy as the music.

"Who's the man, Meg?" I poured her milk and began opening a bottle of cheap white wine for Anna and me.

"I dunno. He talked with Anna. He bought her a doughnut, too."

I wondered crazily if the man was the love interest I had fantasized was keeping Anna's phone so busy lately. I promised myself to ask her discreetly at dinner.

I sliced a loaf of French bread, then hauled the hot plates to the dining room. I knew my effort at dinner had been meager, but I was proud of it nonetheless. I said, "C'mon, Meg," and walked to the living room to call Anna.

I found Anna with her back humping rhythmically, her fingers buried in the thickness of her hair. Her chin hung so low that it brushed her collar. Tears swept the wrinkled landscape of her cheeks, then dropped off her face to stain her dress's intricate green swirls. Her elbows rested on the open book.

Stunned, I moved quickly and sat on the couch next to her. "Anna," I said gently, "what's wrong?" I slid an arm across her back and cupped her bony shoulder in my hand.

She couldn't speak. The only noises she managed were faint sobs that she choked to suppress. I reached my other hand under her chin and brought it up out of her moist collar. The twisted ache on her face was an expression I hadn't seen on her before, never thought was possible from this woman of perpetual cheer. Even when Andrei, her husband, had died, she had shown an unnatural kind of strength that I was unaccustomed to seeing at funeral parlors and gravesides.

"Anna, dear, what is it?" I persisted.

Shaking her head in gentle arcs of no, no, no, she extracted her hands from her hair and folded them together over the book. When I slid the book from her lap, I recognized one of the photographs I had seen in the library. It was a picture of bodies, hundreds of dead bodies, stacked along the edges of the frozen Neva River. I knew the significance of the piled bodies, knew that evening what would have meant little to me that morning.

"Is it this picture that makes you sad, Anna?" I asked.

She looked at the book and nodded.

"Are you—do you know about Leningrad? Did you know somebody in Leningrad that winter?"

By this time, Meg was at Anna's other side. Anna placed a hand on Meg's knee, then turned her face toward me. She wiped a stream of tears from her face and, with a tone of profound dignity, said, "Nora . . . I was there that winter."

My eyes snapped wide open. "You were in Leningrad at the time of the Siege?"

Her chin lifted slightly, she said, "Yes."

"With Andrei? You were married then?"

"Yes, dearie."

"My God, Anna!"

She turned and offered a small smile to Meg. Meg, not understanding, laid her head on Anna's breast.

"Did you have family there?" I asked.

Her glistening eyes slid from Meg back to me. My left hand, still on her back, felt a deep, rippling sigh roll through her chest.

"My mother died of starvation in December, 1941," she said.

I opened my mouth, but was unable to speak.

Then, as a thin, ironic smile shored up her face, Anna said, "And I had Misha and Merusha there. Misha and Merusha. Andrei and I buried them in ground like frozen tundra in the place called Piskarevsky Cemetery. At night, in January, 1942."

"Misha?" I said.

"Misha was our son, four years old—"

"Jesus, God!"

"A beautiful boy." She wiped her eyes and went on, no stagger in her voice: "Merusha was our daughter, Nora. She was one month old when she died, when she starved to death because I was starving and could not make any more milk to feed her. She was born on Christmas. Can you imagine that?"

"Oh, Anna, dear Anna," I said and wrapped my arms tightly around her, pulling her to me, embracing her. "I'm sorry I didn't know, Anna," I whispered. "I'm so sorry." My tears came before I realized it.

Confused, Meg searched my face and said, "I'm not sure I get it, Mom."

Anna poured out the torrent of her Leningrad horrors—the bombings, the fires, the starvation and death, the unbearable cold—with only the slightest encumbrances. My interest in her story wasn't self-serving or professional; indeed, I had all but forgotten my morning of murder, my afternoon of library books, computer scans, Eva Ramirez, and Windy City Towing. My concern was the interest a younger generation has in the torments of an older one; the interest one mother has in knowing, somehow sharing, the pain of another mother's greatest possible loss: the lives of her children. I had lost a leg to a crazy, drunken gunman and a husband to capriciousness, but never a child to starvation.

It wasn't long before hungry Meg, drawn by the rich smell of the food, wandered to the dining-room table. "You go ahead and eat, honey," I said, "but first will you bring us that bottle of wine and the glasses?"

For the next two hours, Anna and I, neither hungry, drank the pungent yellow table wine and talked of Anna's brief and troubled motherhood. We stayed on the couch, close, side by side, mother and adopted daughter, our wineglasses on a table in front of us, our hair lifted occasionally by chilly lake breezes from opened windows across the room.

After we had talked for some time about Misha, I asked her about the baby, Merusha.

"I told you? Yes, I told you, Merusha was born on Christmas night," Anna said, her memory now relaxed by the wine, her body settled back into the hollow of the couch. "Andrei was gone, working on the city's defenses, I suppose—I don't know. But I had Misha to help me."

She smiled at the mention of Misha. "He brought some towels to me in the bedroom," she said, "and a candle because we had no electricity. Then he fell asleep next to me. There was no heat, so we both wore our heavy coats under the blankets. It was after midnight by then, and the moon was very strong. When my pains became worse, the baby's water bag broke open and ran all over the bed. Misha woke up in the wet, in the commotion. He was frightened at the water, and he shouted, 'Mama, you peed in the bed!' "

Our swollen faces softened with laughter at Misha's remark. After that minute of relief, Anna continued. "Finally, the baby slid out of me onto the sheets. She was like a tiny bird steaming and squawking in the cold. I picked her up and brought her under my coat to my chest. I kissed the waxy slime off her cheeks. Sometimes I can taste it even now. It was the beginning of her only month, dearie. I loved her as strong as I could."

I refilled the wineglasses. "Anna, do you want to stop now? Maybe go up and go to bed, or sleep here if you wish? That would be okay. We can talk more tomorrow."

"No," she said firmly. "It has taken so long for this to come out of me. I want to tell you more. Now, if I can."

"Of course."

She drank a mouthful of the bitter wine and went on. "You know, it happened the same way to many families that winter, it was that common. Losing two in one day, I mean. Yes, I knew several families who suffered that."

I frowned in puzzlement.

"We lost both our children in the same morning, Nora."

"Oh . . . no, no, no."

"I don't know whether it was God's cruelty or His compassion that made it happen that way, but it did."

Still fiercely, defiantly holding herself together somehow, she looked away from me and toward the darkened ceiling for the next part of her story.

"Merusha was first," she said, "near dawn, in my arms, at my empty breasts. She was dead for more than an hour before I would give her up to Andrei. He wrapped her in a woolen blanket from her crib. I asked Andrei if we could bury her, and he said we could, in Piskarevsky. You see, he had some dynamite from his work. He said the ground was frozen but he could blow a hole in it for her. We wouldn't stack her up with the other dead, Andrei said."

She looked at me directly now, faced me across half a century of living silently with her horrors. And I thought Eva Ramirez had a determined stare.

"And Misha?" I said.

"Beautiful Misha had been sick for weeks, the swollen ankles and potbelly of starvation. That morning, in our grief over Merusha, we had forgotten about Misha. When we came from our bedroom to the living room with Merusha's body, Misha was dead on the couch. He was as cold as Merusha, probably dead for longer."

Her voice remained hard, but now her tears came again, rolling from her soul in profusion. "I remember grasping Misha," she said, "grasping him by his face and kissing him, kissing him all over his face and neck, licking his cold cheeks, like a mother animal licks its dead." She wiped her cheeks. "Don't ask me why I didn't kill myself that day, Nora. I will never know why I didn't."

Anna gulped another mouthful of wine and I poured her more. Speechless, I waited.

"It was very cold that night," she continued, "probably fifteen or twenty degrees below zero, and the sky was clear. Moonlit and starry. We carried the bundled children to Piskarevsky, about two miles on empty streets—it was too cold for the German planes to bomb that night. I had Merusha, and Andrei had Misha and a sack with a shovel and the dynamite. We walked slowly. We were too weak to hurry, but we would not have wanted to, anyway. You see, what we had planned to do for our children over the next fifty years had to go into a single evening. All we had left to do for them now was to bury them. Do you understand, dearie?"

"I think so, Anna."

She smiled thinly. "We found a flat spot in Piskarevsky. Andrei laid Misha down, then shoveled away the deepest snow. He used the shovel to cut a narrow trench in the ground, then he set the dynamite and lit it. When it blew, the noise split our ears and the air filled with a spray of the hard chunks of earth.

"The hole wasn't big, but big enough—after all, the bodies were small. I handed the children to Andrei, and he arranged them in the hole, very carefully, adjusting the blankets that covered them. The children's faces remained covered by the blankets. We had kissed them at home and would not do it again.

"We filled the hole with snow and ice because there was no earth to return—it had been blown to bits. We knew this was not a proper grave, that it would become an open hole when spring came, or would be torn open by the bulldozers before that. But we felt that we had done something for the children, paid them some homage, not just tossed their bodies onto a pile. Our grief was so great after that we felt no cold or hunger for days."

Finally, Anna told me of their evacuation from Leningrad in March 1942, and of train rides through central Russia, through Cherepovets and Gorky, through Liski and Rostov, and finally to Pytagorsk, at the foothills of the Caucasus Mountains. The trains had been crowded and dirty and cold, she said, but at least there was food, the first food of substance they had eaten since November. At Pytagorsk, they lived in relative calm till the summer, when the city was occupied by the Germans. The Skrabinas, like thousands of others, were then captured and sent to camps in Poland, and from there to dozens of small towns throughout Germany.

Anna's story about her days spent working in a German munitions factory was familiar to me. It was the same chronicle Andrei had told me three years before. I had forgotten the details, but not the small fires that had burned in Andrei's eyes as he spoke.

"Anna," I said, "Andrei told me this part of your story. It was one afternoon just after my accident, when you and Meg were off somewhere. He told me how you worked in the factories, how you watched from a cave while the Allies bombed your camp."

Anna stirred, then reached for her wine, but she set the glass back down without drinking. "I think it's enough I've had."

She settled back against the couch and said, "Andrei told me he had spoken to you. But just about Germany, not of Leningrad or the children."

"I could tell from his face that there was more," I said, "but I wouldn't have asked. I felt privileged to hear what I did."

"Maybe that's why I'm telling you now. Because you had the decency not to ask."

"It was easier to keep it inside, Anna?"

"Easier?" she mused. "No, not easier. Until now, I suppose I just wasn't willing to bleed anymore."

We sat till after ten o'clock, till the orange streetlights had flickered on, and Meg had tucked herself into bed.

There was no blood of kinship between Anna and me, but

anyone watching would not have known that. We had not been embarrassed to touch, or even embrace, during the most poignant parts of Anna's account of her final winter in Leningrad. Anna's story had moved me deeply, had focused a hard, brilliant light on my love for my own Meg.

It was almost ten-thirty when Anna, her face tired and her eyes sad but dry, stood from the couch to leave. She said she would be fine alone that night: she planned to watch the news, then sleep.

As she walked across the living room, I noticed my purse still on the floor where I had put it earlier. "Oh, Anna, would you mind looking at something for me?"

"Of course not, dearie."

I picked up the purse and rooted past my gun. I extracted Lugotov's Leningrad map from the disarray of the purse and handed it to Anna.

Instantly, she said, "This is Leningrad."

"I know."

"Where did you get this, Nora?"

I ignored her question. "What do you think of the red X on the map?" I asked.

She fingered the X as if it might have a dimension of depth, a thickness that would tell her something. "It's in the Haymarket district. That's all I can tell."

"What's Haymarket?"

Eyes steady on the map, she said, "A place for the whores to collect. A place for gamblers and criminals. During the war, the black market traded there." Looking up at me, she said, "Nora, during the Siege, it was rumored that human flesh was for sale in Haymarket."

"What?"

"People were butchering humans to sell their meat," she said. "We were that hungry."

"They butchered the corpses?"

"Some were already dead, but it was said that others were murdered for their meat."

"Do you believe that happened?"

"Yes."

"How did you know, Anna?"

"People know. I had a friend who may have been murdered for that reason."

"Did you ever eat meat from Haymarket?" My question embarrassed me as soon as it came out.

"God, no!" she answered sharply. "Never! We went hungry. Anyway, we had no money to buy it even if we had wanted it."

She folded the map and slipped it back into my purse, then demanded, "Why do you have that map?"

"The map was found in the apartment of a man murdered on the North Side early this morning. He was Russian, Anna. But he was from Kiev, not Leningrad."

"How do you know Kiev?"

"His immigration records said so."

"I see." She kissed my cheek and turned to leave.

15

After locking the front door, I walked back to the living room and turned on the news. The lead story was Semyon Lugotov's murder; the Channel 6 videocameras had somehow made it to Eddy Street before Lugotov's body was out of his apartment. The images swam across the screen, and I spotted Karl Kramer, the Channel 6 news editor, standing in the stairwell outside Lugotov's open door. Kramer was a scourge to us at Area Six, always pushing for blood, more blood. As the camera panned over the sheet-white face and the bloody body of Lugotov on the floor, I shouted, "Kramer! You son-of-a-bitch!"

It wasn't five minutes before Anna telephoned. "Nora," she said, "I am watching the news, Channel 6. Are you?"

"Yes."

"This is the murder where you found the map of Leningrad?"

"Yes."

"Shocking."

I paused before asking, "Are you all right, Anna?"

"Yes, thank you. Good night, dearie."

I went to Meg's room, and knelt at her bedside. In the faint light from the street I watched her breathing, her small mouth gaping innocently, the smell of her breath not yet stale from sleep. After several minutes, I slid my arms around her and squeezed her to my chest, tight enough to feel her small ribs. Somehow Meg's warmth made me decide that yes, for now at least, I was a believer. It seemed like a revelation, and it gave me great comfort.

Soon I was in bed myself; the dinner dishes would wait till morning. My body felt the lightness of the wine as I removed my prosthesis. I lay back into my pillow and shut my eyes to dislodge the thought of Anna's dead children. Then, for a moment, I saw the fat man in the red car. He was a nameless, faceless man, but not for long. When his image left me, I realized that in listening to Anna's Leningrad story, I had forgotten to ask her about the man at the doughnut shop. Like the dishes, it would have to wait.

For the next half hour I tossed in bed, no nearer sleep than when I first lay down. Finally, I sat up and pushed my blanket aside. I pulled open the curtain and stared out at the black pitch of lake to the east. A row of faint, blinking shorelights marked the majestic, northward sweep of the dark water. I began to weep. I couldn't peg it precisely to Anna, or to Misha and Merusha, or even to wounded Eva or dead Lugotov. It was just there, a wide, timeless expanse of sorrow, filling me. With my hands to my face and thinking about nothing specific, I simply wept.

Thursday morning, Meg and I climbed the stairs to Anna's apartment as we always did on school days. The usual rap on her door produced no Anna, nor did several even louder raps. Finally, afraid, I used Anna's key that she had given me some years before, when we had traded keys to our apartments.

We found her in her bed, all but her face covered. Her form looked lumpy under the quilt, like a hunted animal tucked into a ball. A bitter frown covered her face, her eyes lusterless. Even Meg's hugs couldn't chase the monster away.

Anna barely spoke to me, would only say she had had a *bad night*. She wasn't sick, she said, just suffering a kind of aftershock from our talk the night before. I told her that her Leningrad story had granted me introductions to her children, and had allowed me to see Meg in a bend of light that gratified me. I said her story had moved me more than she could know. She thanked me with a small nod but no words.

In her kitchen, I made buttered toast and hot coffee laced with sugar. I left the tray at her bedside and encouraged her to get up when she could. She said that she would pick Meg up after school, if only I could just get her to school this morning, please. Of course, I answered, and I asked her to call me at the station if she needed anything. I would check on her after my workday was over.

By seven-thirty that morning, I sat at my desk thinking about Anna and fighting a headache I attributed to the bargain price of the previous night's wine. The corridor outside our office bustled with activity, the day shift nearly up to cruising speed.

Art arrived, and without greeting him, I said, "You were right about the key."

He sat at his desk. "Great," he said. "What key?"

"The one I found in Lugotov's hallway."

"Oh, yeah." He smiled and tapped his temple with his fingertip. "Don't test the memory of older men. It's embarrassing. Now, what was I right about?"

"The key opened the Ramirez box. How did you know?"

"I didn't," he said. "I guessed. But I've never been as trusting of Eva Ramirez as you have. I'm not sure why. Maybe that signature on the note with the money. That shit about 'a friend not an enemy.' "

"Okay, now try this one," I said. "The key also opened one of the other five mailboxes in the lobby. Apartment 2A. Explain that, Mr. Holmes."

"Maybe the money was put in the wrong box," Art said, "or maybe the Ramirezes are doing a joint venture with whoever lives in 2A. Have you checked out the 2A folks yet?"

"Not yet. But why the need for a common key?"

"You'd better get back to Hugh Thomas," Art said. He got up and started out of the office.

"Where're you going?" I said.

He frowned and waved a wad of rolled-up papers he had grabbed from the desktop. "It's Melchior time," he said.

"God, I forgot." Since Anna's Leningrad story, I hadn't once thought of Melchior touching me, let alone the Watson incident. "How'd you handle the accident report?" I said.

"I wrote there isn't a shred of evidence from the mechanics that would indicate a brake failure in Watson's car."

I smiled proudly. "Good for you, Art. You'll make mincemeat out of Ray."

"Yeah, and if I don't, look for me inside a sausage casing. Or worse, directing traffic on Michigan Avenue."

"You've got Melchior by the ass. You know it."

Art disappeared into the corridor as my phone rang. It was Dr. Dorner from the morgue at County Hospital, ordering me to come to the morgue, to come now because he had a problem with Mr. Semyon Lugotov. I questioned Dorner, but he would say no more—except that I was to bring the homicide team with me. It would be the first time in anyone's memory that a team had been summoned back to the morgue to recheck a body it had already delivered.

I left a note on Art's desk telling him where I was going, and asking him to start the license search on the red Ford Escort when he finished with Melchior. I phoned Alice Adams and told her to assemble a crew and meet me at County.

Five minutes later, I cranked the Fury and laid into her, roaring east on Belmont Avenue toward Lake Shore Drive. Since rush hour was in full bloom, I decided on the Wacker underground, the network of streets built under Michigan and Wacker Avenues, and parts of the Loop. It was a maze as dark and foreboding and stinking as an abandoned cellar. Dim lights shone from inside black metal cages bolted to the ceiling, and seams in the concrete above dripped water down onto passing cars. The streets were a study in potholes: blacktop as cratered as a moon under meteor attack. A longtime Chicagoan could get lost in the Wacker underground if she wasn't careful. Pity the tourist who might wander in driving a rental car: he or she had an even chance of ending up on a missing persons' list.

Ten minutes later, I ascended from the underground into a bright sun that pounded the Eisenhower Expressway white. The Damen Avenue exit put me just a block from County.

The County Hospital pathology staff would come to call it the most macabre incident in anyone's memory, even old Maynard Herman's, the autopsy assistant with forty years on the job.

They waited for me in a hallway whose walls were made of large, pale green cement blocks and whose air smelled of hospital antiseptic. I recognized no one but Vincent Dorner in his immaculate white lab coat. He was a square, dense man in his mid-sixties. In profile, his face was jagged, nose and lips in conflict. His gray, crew-cut hair looked tough enough to use as a wire brush. His life may have been somewhat sedentary, but there was no softness about any aspect of the man.

"Thank you for coming so promptly, Lieutenant," Dorner said to me as I approached. When he spoke, the others backed off a step, all except a small, young, hawk-faced woman who remained close to his side.

I loosened my coat. "You were very persuasive," I said to Dorner. "My team is on their way. What do we have here?"

Dorner touched the sleeve of the woman next to him. He said, "Miss Doel—Cecily Doel—opened the autopsy room this morning as she always does. She shrieked, and we came. Like Samaritans, I suppose. You can go in and see for yourself."

I looked to the closed double doors to my left. Then I said, "Cecily, may I call you that?"

"You may, ma'am," she said, in an obvious British accent. Her hands were knotted together on her Black Watch plaid skirt.

"Cecily, what time did you open the room?"

"Six-forty-five."

"Nothing unusual about that?"

"No, ma'am."

"And you were the first through the door today?"

"Yes."

"The door had been locked?"

"It was, ma'am."

My face felt the heat of the audience's stare. I had run out of questions. I thought, Haul ass into the room, Callum, before you seem any more stupid to these people than you already do.

"Excuse me, Cecily, Dr. Dorner."

Cecily smiled slightly; Dorner nodded.

I turned, pulled open one of the doors, and took two steps into the room. Nobody followed.

The sight ahead so staggered me that my hands jumped instinctively to shield my eyes. Sickened, I had all I could do not to drop to the hard tile floor. For an instant, blinded as I was by my hands, smell became my only useful sense, the sense that brought me the distinctive stench that circulated in the air of the room. I dropped my hands from my eyes.

What I saw was Semyon Lugotov hanging, stark and at full length, from the ceiling. A huge black iron hook roped to an overhead water pipe held his long and naked corpse, kept his toes floating in the air several inches above the floor. The hook, which gouged him under his left collarbone, tipped him grotesquely to his right, so far that his right ear touched his shoulder. His skin, white and bloodless except for the dark entry and exit tracks of the bullet holes through his belly, glistened with a thin coat of moisture from the dank air of the room. No blood leaked from his wounds because his heart, in its final, agonal contractions, had emptied all of it onto his apartment floor the morning before. His genitals were dark and shriveled.

I moved two steps forward, heard commotion in the hallway behind me and the door opened further, but I didn't look back. When I felt a hand squeeze my forearm, I turned to see Alice Adams. Her gaze fixed on the hanging body, she said, "Wasn't killing him enough?"

Alice and the team had finished their inspection, their routines of photographs and fingerprints. Now Dr. Dorner and I stood on opposite sides of the still-suspended Lugotov. The cool, thin light of the ceiling's fluorescent tubes ran over us. The sweet, almost rotten smell of the body, and the sight of the hook poking around Lugotov's collarbone, in and then out of his skin, still sickened me. I felt the same turmoil in my stomach as I'd had when I looked at the body in the Eddy Street apartment the morning before.

"I've seen a lot on the streets," I said, "but, except for the mob, I've never seen anything like this before. Have you?"

"Never," Dorner said.

"How could someone have found the body in here?" I asked.

"Not hard. Just search the body drawers—they're all left unlocked." He gestured to the wall of shiny metal drawers.

"He, or she, must have the strength of a bull to have managed this."

"I suppose," Dorner said, "or just be highly motivated. We're all capable of great physical feats when the circumstances are right."

"You'll be able to do the autopsy today?" I asked as I trailed him toward his office adjacent to the autopsy room.

"Yes."

At the office door, he stopped and turned to an assistant who stood near the opposite wall. "Unhook him," he said to the man.

"Unhook the poor bastard and lay him out on the table. He's first this morning."

Dorner's office walls were windowless and covered with narrow shelves. On the shelves, to my surprise and slight discomfort, sat a hundred or more yellow-white human skulls, precisely lined in rows, the empty eyes aimed at Dorner's desk. "Some office," I said.

Dorner lowered himself into his desk chair. "It's my collection. All these skulls came from people who committed violent crime. Very violent, I might add—murder or mass murder."

As Dorner spoke, I moved closer to the skulls, close enough to touch them. At first, I barely brushed them, as though they might be as fragile as the hollowed-out eggshells of Easter decorations. Then, more boldly, my hands began to touch the smooth tops of the yellowish brain boxes and my fingers explored the empty openings that had once held nerves, eyes, and lips. In a moment, I pulled my hands away, feeling they were an intrusion into the lives of the dead, as much a trespass as Lugotov's hanging. I thought of Misha and Merusha as I turned and walked to a chair in front of Dorner's desk.

"I inherited the collection from the pathologist who was in charge of the county morgue before me," Dorner said. "Those were the days when you could keep the skulls or anything else you wanted from bodies—in the name of medical science. All that's changed now, of course." He smiled ruefully. "These days I couldn't assemble a collection of white rats' skulls without an act of Congress."

"Why do you keep them?"

"Now? Oh, just as artifacts. They don't serve any scientific purpose. Originally they were saved to test a theory about the shape of the braincase in violent criminals. It's the science of phrenology, but it turns out there's nothing to it. The theories hold no water." He leaned forward and rested his folded hands on the desk in front of him. The knot of his tie made a perfect triangle under his starched collar. "Well, Lieutenant," he said, "do you have any leads that will bring this madman to justice?"

I dragged my eyes away from the skulls. "A few, yes. I think we're fairly close, actually."

"Are you looking for anything special from me? Drug levels, type of weapon—that sort of thing?"

"The ballistics might be unusual here. I'm interested to see if you find any bullets still in the body."

"I'll do full body x-rays so one doesn't hide."

"Fine. That should be about all."

"I'll have a preliminary report later today. You can call." Dorner got up from his chair as a gesture to move me from the office. "You know, Lieutenant, there probably won't be any surprises here. It looks pretty straightforward. I doubt that I'll be of much help."

"Okay, well—"

"Death by gunshot, the bullets tracking superiorly from entry to exit wounds, knocking off things in their way, things in that area like the liver, the spleen, the lung, death finally by exsanguination."

"Aren't the paths of the bullets unusual?"

"Yes, a bit, at first glance, they are. That's perceptive of you," he said. "I'll measure the angles out, but I'd say that if the victim was standing at the time of the murder, then the killer must have been shooting up from the floor. That's unusual."

"Lugotov was found with a gun in his hand," I said, "but it seemed unfired. He was lying just inside the door to his apartment."

"Not surprising, I guess—the unfired gun, I mean. Can you imagine opening the door and finding someone on the floor blazing away at you? How could you get a shot off?"

I changed the subject. "Dr. Dorner, how could anybody have

gotten in here to rope the body to the ceiling last night? Isn't there any security?"

Dorner slid back into his chair. "Security? That's a laugh," he said without a smile. "We're budgeted by the County. We're happy to have salaries paid and the lights go on. There's no money for security—and we haven't needed it. I can't remember anyone ever disturbing a body before."

"You don't lock the doors?"

"We lock the door Miss Doel opened, the door to the corridor. But this whole laboratory area communicates within itself, so once you're in the department, you can go anywhere without a key. The other door to the morgue leads to the blood bank and that's open all night—and it's usually busy all night."

"No one questions a strange face in the middle of the night?"

"There are strange faces there every night," he said. "Runners from the patient wards down here to pick up transfusions, donors for rare blood types that we need on an emergency basis. You might see anybody in the blood bank at three in the morning and never suspect a thing. One could slip in here, close the doors, search the drawers, slide a body out, and hang it, although it would take great courage to try. A deranged kind of courage, I grant you, but courage nonetheless."

I waited at the morgue for another hour, until the attendants had lifted and unhooked the stiffened Lugotov, then laid him on a stainless-steel autopsy table. Dorner used a small, hand-held electric saw to crack open the chest cage and a scalpel to slice the soft belly. In minutes the body gaped apart from the base of its neck to the root of its penis. For the next half hour, Dorner leaned over this yawning and smelly trench, his gloved hands speedily cutting out viscera, which he weighed and measured with complete dispassion. As he finished with each organ, he tossed it playfully in his hands, like a piece of calves liver in the butcher shop, before returning it to the dark hollow of the carcass.

My unusual interest in the dissection puzzled me at first. I knew I didn't watch out of any sense of arrogance toward the dead—since my own gunshot wound, I counted myself lucky just to be alive. I also knew my interest wasn't scientific: I had never had any curiosity in the forensic side of policework, and I didn't particularly admire Dorner's obvious deftness with his surgical tools. After some thought, I decided that I watched simply to prove to myself that I could watch, that I could stay that close to a dead body for that long a time and not snap. I had been aware for years that I feared the unburied dead greatly. The several dozen slain victims and criminals I had already seen—or even touched, for that matter—had not lessened my anxiety about how I would react to the next one. Watching this autopsy was a test for me, another experience to give me confidence that I would behave properly when I confronted death on my job again. Standing silent in a corner of the autopsy room, I was working out, just as an athlete works out on a running track.

16

L unch at McDonald's on Ohio Street: I sat alone in my parked car and watched the traffic whiz along toward the lake. As I ate, I thought of Meg, wondering if she liked the turkey sandwich I had packed her for lunch, not feeling more than a twinge of guilt about the two chocolate cupcakes I had hidden under a paper towel at the bottom of her lunchbox. The kid deserved them—what the hell. Anyway, what seven-year-old could face an afternoon of Sister Mary Aletius without a bit of chocolate? I looked forward to the weekend, when Meg and I could go out for lunch together.

On the way to the Area Six station, I saw Hugh Thomas walking on Western Avenue. I double-parked my car and tooted my horn. Thomas crossed the street and leaned against the Fury. The high noon sun shined on his balding pate. Without his half-rimmed glasses, he looked more like a tired beat cop than a reader of Plato.

"Craving some real policework, Nora?" Thomas asked, kidding. "Want to ride with us this afternoon?"

"No, thanks. Got a minute for a question or two about that key I told you about?"

"Shoot."

"That key does open a mailbox," I said. "In fact, it opens two of the six boxes in an apartment building. Make any sense?"

"Sure," Thomas said. "Either the locks were made the same by chance or by intention."

"Explain."

"By intention is obvious," he said. "It may be convenient for one key to open two boxes."

"And by chance? What's that? One in a million?"

"Hardly," he said. "Lever tumblers for the cheaper mailboxes are fairly generic. If you went to a lock-supply store today and ordered ten different mailbox locks and their keys, those few keys would probably open eighty or ninety percent of the city's boxes. Now, that's generic."

"Another question. Why would there be a one key slot above the whole bank of mailbox doors?"

"That slot's for the mailman. When the carrier turns a key in that lock, the whole bank of boxes opens out toward him, because the bank's hinged at the bottom. Then he can just dump the mail in without opening and closing each individual box. Great time-saver."

"Oh," I said.

Thomas said, "The key you have to the two mailboxes shouldn't fit the bank key."

"I know. It didn't."

I found Art in the station's small coffee room. The air was a fog of cigarette smoke.

"Goddamn, it stinks in here!" I barked.

Art sat at a table that held a coffee urn and an open, nearly empty box of sweet rolls. Wearing his necktie down and his shirt collar undone, he was reading the *Tribune* editorial page. Frankie Luchinski sat across the table, smoking a cigarette and drinking coffee as he stared at the gray cinderblock wall behind Art. Frankie wore his dark blue patrolman's uniform; the creases in his sleeves were as sharp as a knife's edge.

I sat down next to Art. "Let's keep the door open," I said. "Air this place out."

"Relax, Nora," Frankie said, then lit a new cigarette off the butt of the one he was finishing. Art looked up from the paper and smiled at me.

"Frankie, did you ever see what happens inside your lungs from those things?" I said, then gave him no time to answer: "Well, for your information, I just did. This morning, I was at an autopsy where the pathologist cut out a lung that was as black as mud. That was from cigarettes, Frankie."

It was an untruth—except for two penetrating bullet holes, Lugotov's lungs looked fine. I regarded my remarks to Frankie as only a minor deception in the name of public health.

"That's bullshit," Frankie said. "Once, I saw a piece of a lung from a smoker, and it wasn't black. It was pink."

"Where'd you ever see a piece of lung?" Art asked.

"When I was still on the street, on a beat, I saw the body of a gangbanger who was shotgunned in the chest. His lungs, his *pink* lungs, were oozing out through big holes in his chest. Nothing was black, just bloody and pink. And he was a heavy smoker, Nora. Three packs a day. Believe me, I knew the bastard before he was killed."

"Three packs a day? How old was he?"

"Nineteen."

"Nineteen? No wonder. They don't go black by nineteen, dummy. It takes a few more years."

"My ass, Nora," Frankie said, and sucked deeply on his cigarette.

I turned toward Art. "What's the matter with Sergeant Luchinski today?"

"I think it's because of my talk with Smilin' Ray this morning," Art said. He pushed the paper aside and slouched in his chair.

"What?" I said.

"Well, I put it to Ray, you know, about the ponies. It worked. I wedged him off that defective-brake shit on Watson's killer car. Then Ray had Frankie into his office after I left. Maybe they talked about the ponies, I don't know." Art turned from me to Luchinski. "Is that right, Frankie?"

"Fuck off about it, Art," he said. "What goes on between Melchior and me is my business."

Frankie flipped his cigarette into the coffee in his cup and started out of the room, reaching back for a sweet roll.

"Leave the door open, will you, Frankie?" I said.

Just before slamming the door, he said, "Get laid, Nora."

I jumped up quickly and opened the door. To Frankie's back, I called, "Thank God, never by you, Frankie. Get bit yourself."

I reslammed the door, then returned to my chair. Art said nothing.

"Christ, he's out of sorts today."

"He's okay, it's just Melchior," Art said. "I'll bet he chewed Frankie's ass royally for something or other, just because he was pissed at me."

"I suppose."

"You know, Nora, I remember one day a few years ago when Melchior cleaned me out good—you know, the kind that puts you in a blue funk all day."

"I know, I know."

"So what do I do?" Art said. "After work, I go home and yell at Helen for nothing. A few minutes later, she screams at one of the kids, and a few minutes after that, the kid kicks the dog. Then—get this—the dog runs over and bites the cat, who's cuddled up just sleeping in a chair."

I laughed. "The poor, innocent cat," I said, "bit in the ass because of Smilin' Ray."

"Yep," Art said, "shit just rolls downhill."

"So tell me about you and Melchior this morning," I said as I poured myself a cup of hot coffee.

A small but satisfied smile brightened Art's face. "Ray had me in to see the report about Watson's bad brakes. I said the car had been checked, and there was nothing to support that conclusion. Melchior said do it anyway, fake the report. I said no." Art shrugged and said, "That's it."

"C'mon, Arthur. Fart-face didn't give up that easily."

"Oh, he did mention something about me remembering what it might be like to be back on a beat all day—*every fuckin' day*, as he put it. I told him I didn't think that being on the street was all that bad, that there was a lot of corruption to fight on a beat, corruption like gambling. And I said I had heard the gambling was even involving police sometimes, police I happened to know. Those were the kind of guys it would feel good to bust, because they were such a discredit to the Force."

"Oooo!" I exclaimed. "That was a good one!"

"That shut him down. In another minute, he had me off the Watson case and said I should help on the Lugotov shooting."

I stood to relieve an ache in my stump. "Let's get out of this stinkhole. Let's go back to the office."

"Not before you tell me what went on at County. I saw your note on my desk."

"You're not going to believe it," I said.

"Huh?"

"They opened the autopsy room and found Lugotov hanging from the ceiling."

"What?" Art's mouth opened in disbelief.

"That's right," I said, "a dead man dangling from the god-damned ceiling. Someone had strung him up overnight. Used a rope and a big black hook."

"Shit," Art murmured. "Same guy who killed him?"

"Who knows?"

"Nora, I'm getting tired of this job and this city. Bunch of friggin' perverts and freaks."

"Now, Arthur," I chided, "where else can you see the White

Sox half the nights of the summer, or listen to Mozart while lying on the grass at Grant Park and eating fried chicken and smelling the lake?"

"Knock it off, okay? Let's go back to the office. I've got something to show you."

A steady breeze poured through the window of our office, washing the air clean. While Art ate his sack lunch, I sipped my coffee and recounted everybody's horror at seeing Lugotov slung from a water pipe. Art plowed through two sandwiches and a piece of cherry pie before I finished my story. More food still bulged from his bag, cookies that I knew had been baked by Helen.

Art knocked his knuckles on his metal desktop, his way of changing subjects. "Let me give you some good news. The car trace."

I brightened. "The computer went back on line?"

"It did, and I had time after seeing Ray to work on it."

Art pulled a folded piece of paper from his desk drawer and handed it across the desk to me.

Ill. #AFS 697 / Glazunov, Georgi / DOB 03-25-23 /
5564 S. Kenwood Ave. 60637 / Caucasian / 5 ft. 6
in. / 205 lbs. / hair gray / eyes brw /

"Glazunov, Glazunov," I muttered. "I wish it was Nikki instead of Georgi."

"He's sixty-three, and he's not Mr. Glazunov," Art said. "He's Dr. Georgi Glazunov. He has a Ph.D. in history, and he teaches at the University of Chicago."

"We have a record on him?"

"Not a thing—no more record than Eva Ramirez had. He's clean as a week-old dog bone, probably never even had a traffic ticket before his car got towed last Saturday."

"Then how'd you find all that out so quickly?"

"My high-tech search capabilities."

"What?"

"I opened the phone book," Art said. "It was right there, two phone numbers, one for his home, one for an office at the U. of C. I called the university's information office. They loved talking about themselves."

"We don't know if it was him driving the car Saturday," I said.

"We're *assuming* it was him in the car. Anyway, if we're wrong about the driver, at least Glazunov's a start."

I sucked at my teeth with an audible squeak. "He does fit Lugotov's fat man description, doesn't he? Five-six, two hundred pounds."

"It's him."

"What about the letter from Talitha?" I challenged. "What about the map? What about the ten grand in Ramirez's mailbox?"

"Look, we go with this till something better turns up."

"What does he teach at Chicago?"

"Russian Affairs," Art said. "In fact, he's the chairman of the department. Suddenly the map of Leningrad fits in, right?"

"Sure, right," I said, mocking. "Clear as crystal. Why couldn't I see it yesterday?" I reached across the desk and into Art's lunch bag for one of his cookies. "Can I have one?"

"Have all you want," he said.

I bit off an edge of cookie. "Do you happen to know where Glazunov is this afternoon, Art?"

"He has a two-o'clock class on Russian agricultural policy or some shit like that."

"And haven't you been a busy beaver?"

He grinned.

"God, these are good cookies," I took another bite. "How'd you find out about his classes?"

"I called his department secretary."

"She knows you're police?"

"Of course not. The secretary asked me if I was interested in the course, asked if I wanted to audit. Wouldn't need any special permission or anything. They must be short of students, the way she was pushing it."

"Do you want to go?" I asked.

"Are you kidding? Fifty-three-year-old blacks don't blend into the U. of C. student body."

"Some people will say anything to get out of a lecture on Russian agriculture."

The morning's thin clouds, dissipated by the brisk wind and strong afternoon sun, had all but disappeared as I drove south on Lake Shore Drive. I coasted along in the slower right-hand lane. I wanted to enjoy the lake as I drove, the bright triangular sails on boats whose owners already had them in the water this spring. These sailors would be the wealthy and the idle, rich enough to be sailing on a weekday afternoon, not at an office or driving a bus or selling shoes or working on the line in a factory. The boats always attracted me, not because I envied what their owners had, but simply because of their brilliant white and colored sails that broke the powerful monotony of the lake's blue-green surface.

Just south of the Loop, I passed rambling parks on the lake side of the drive and housing projects on the city side. The parks were gentle flats of cropped grass and weeds, with clusters of trees marking the bicycle and jogging paths. The projects were grim rows of skyscraping, window-boarded, pale yellow-brick buildings, staggering in their dreariness—the city's attempt to gather up the street-level spread of black poverty and stack it high into the sky, as though it might evaporate as it ascended into thinner air. It had been an instance of civic planning based more on the profits of favored construction contracts than compassion or logic, and the results were calamitous. Any faint hope the projects' residents might have had for improvement in their lives collapsed as they became high-rise hostages to crime and the loss of neighborhood.

I turned off the Drive at Forty-seventh Street, the Hyde Park exit. The University of Chicago was a few blocks south and west, an open campus that merged imperceptibly with the cityscape. I found the small Gothic building Art had directed me to and the second-floor lecture hall. The place was empty. After a minute of confusion, I spotted a handwritten notice posted on the closed door of the lecture hall, saying that Dr. Glazunov's class had been canceled for today but would meet tomorrow afternoon.

On a campus phone in the lobby, I called the Department of Russian Affairs. A woman answered on the first ring.

"Oh, hello," I said, surprised by the speed of the response. "My name is Nora Callum. I'm calling for information about the graduate program in Russian Affairs. I'm thinking of applying, and I'd like to speak with Professor Glazunov about that. Could he see me today?"

"No, the professor is ill this afternoon—home in bed, I'm afraid, or at his doctor's office."

"I see."

"But I expect him in tomorrow morning—by eight, I would say."

"Could I have an appointment then?" I asked.

"That's early, somewhat irregular, but I suppose he would see you. You say it's about the graduate program?"

"Yes."

"Master's or Ph.D.?"

"Master's or Ph.D.?" I repeated, stumbling on the question for a moment. "Well, both, actually," I finally lied.

"Oh, so you're interested in the dual-degree program?"

I darted into the opening. "Yes, that's right."

"Good. We haven't had a woman in that program for some time. That would be very refreshing. Well, then, I'll have you down for eight o'clock in the morning. The professor's office is Room 125 in Pick Hall. Are you familiar with that building?"

"I believe I know it," I said.

"And your name again, please?"

"Nora Callum."

"And your undergraduate degree is from which institution, Miss Callum?"

"From Illinois," I fudged. "Yes, the University of Illinois."

"Oh, yes, very good," she said. "We'll see you at eight then, Miss Callum."

17

itting in my car, I fished through my purse for the paper that held Georgi Glazunov's driver's license information. His home address was on South Kenwood, a half-mile north of the campus. I was there in five minutes, and parked in a spot that put the Glazunov residence in easy view, two houses ahead of me and across the street. The homes on this block were two- and three-story frames, all old post-Victorian beauties. Black wrought-iron fences or budding hedges enclosed the uniformly tidy lawns. Huge ancient oaks and maples thrived on the terraces and dappled the street and sidewalks with shade. The neighborhood looked solidly middle-class, an island surrounded by areas of the city that might euphemistically be described as marginal.

Although I saw no red Escort in the driveway, I waited several minutes to see if anyone entered or left the Glazunov house: it remained tranquil. I was tempted simply to go to the door, but I was afraid of spooking Glazunov. I had the identification of his car at the El station, but nothing else: no gun, no witness, no motive. If he was still in the city, still teaching this long after the first shooting, then, to a degree, I had the upper hand. I didn't want him feeling police pressure now, not when I still scoured for evidence.

Was I being too tentative, too indecisive? Was I playing cat-and-mouse?

My internal debate ended quickly. I decided that Glazunov had no reason to suspect I was this close to him, and, besides, I needed more time to think through my approach to the man. My appointment for the next morning would be soon enough.

I made the drive home in descending sunlight from the west and a chill lake breeze from the east. In Rogers Park, I stopped at a tiny grocery store near my apartment building and bought hamburger, onions, and bread for a meat loaf, some fresh green beans, and a freezer pie. As I placed my groceries in the car, I noticed the Sheridan State Bank across the street, and an idea came to me.

Sheridan State was a small neighborhood bank, a check-casher and a changemaker, an inconsequential part of the city's financial landscape. Devoid of any architectural note, the one-story brick building was salvaged only by its wide, floor-to-ceiling windows. When the sun shone, these lenses to the outside admitted great slabs of light to brighten the bank's dreary interior.

Inside, I passed an elderly, emaciated guard seated on a stool at the edge of the lobby. I hoped the life savings of Sheridan's depositors didn't one day rest on this man's brawn or quickness of reflex.

Three tellers were working. The remaining one, with no customers at his window, was a man, short and round-faced. I approached him.

"Good afternoon," he said blandly, making no attempt at eye contact.

"I'd like a money order," I said.

"Made out for how much and to whom, please?"

"For twenty-five dollars," I said, "and make it to Mr. Georgi Glazunov."

"I'll need you to write that out." He shoved a blank notepad toward me.

I carefully printed out Georgi Glazunov's name and pushed the pad back.

"That was for twenty-five dollars?"

"Yes."

"Then the total will be twenty-seven. Two dollars for the service charge."

I pulled the cash from my pocketbook and handed it to the teller. He counted the money before sliding it into his cash drawer, then turned to a typewriter on his back desk. He rolled a blank money-order form into the machine.

"Oh, sir," I called to him, "before you make it out, I have a small request."

The man looked up, indignation flickering on his face.

"On the upper right-hand corner of the check," I said, "opposite the bank's name, could you please type in the name of a payor."

"The bank's the payor, ma'am."

"Yes, I understand, but I wish this done for—for clarification. So Mr. Glazunov will know where the money's coming from."

"The money comes from the bank. The bank's the payor."

"Yes, but—"

"To imply anything else would be inaccurate." He stiffened his spine pompously. "And I don't wish to be inaccurate."

It was this inflated motion of his body rather than what he had said that pushed me to shift gears. I was tired, hungry, and anxious to see Meg. I decided to do something I rarely did in my own neighborhood. Opening my purse, I yanked out the small leather wallet that held my police badge. "Come here, please," I said, and motioned the man back to the counter.

As he walked the four steps back to the counter, I flipped open the wallet.

"My name is Lieutenant Nora Callum," I said with great resolution, yet quietly enough so that other bank customers took no notice. Staring hard at his eyes, I continued: "This money order is being prepared as part of an investigation. I have paid for the money order, and I want it made out as I said. I want it done now. If you delay me further, I will consider it an obstruction of police business. It's that simple."

The obstruction charge was a fabrication, of course, but it was the kind of thing that sounded harsh enough so that even the most stubborn citizen usually gave way to its threat.

"Yes," the teller said, "I think I understand now."

"Good."

"And whose name would you like typed in as payor?"

"Windy City Towing. And I want the address typed also. Do you have a telephone book?"

The man reached under a counter and lugged out the Chicago *Yellow Pages*. I rummaged through the volume for a minute. "That would be at 3614 North Elston Avenue," I said.

He pecked dutifully away at the typewriter till the order was completed, then he slipped it into an envelope and handed it to me.

"Thank you," I said sincerely. I smiled broadly, my generosity of spirit seeming to take him by complete surprise.

Home by six, I happily cried "Meg!" as soon as I opened my apartment door, but no one answered. I toured the bedrooms: deserted. I walked swiftly up to Anna's apartment and found it as empty as mine. For a moment, I became lightheaded, my stomach uneasy. I sat on Anna's couch to regain my bearings. Meg and Anna had to be fine: after all, they were a team, a wonderful twosome I trusted implicitly. They shouldn't be required to clear their every little adventure with me. If that was the control I demanded, then I might as well quit the Force now.

Back in my kitchen, I started the meat loaf. At seven o'clock I heard them at the front door, and I rushed from the kitchen. Meg gave a boisterous "Hi, Mom!" and I picked her up from the floor and squeezed her. Anna moved past us with a forced smile and no greeting.

"You two out gallivanting again?" I said to Meg, glad to feel her body against mine, no longer caring where they had been.

Meg giggled and said, "What's gallivanting? Hey, I smell meat loaf!"

I set her down and walked toward Anna. Her face was drawn, and she looked little better than when I had seen her in bed that morning. She agreed to stay for dinner, but only, it seemed, out of sheer lethargy.

The meat loaf was a great hit with Meg, her favorite, but Anna only picked at her food indifferently. When Meg left the table, I said, "Are you okay, Anna?"

She didn't answer, didn't even look at me.

Reluctant to push, I remained quiet. Finally, her face immobile, she surprised me with "I saw the noon news, dearie."

"I didn't. Anything special about it?"

"I see they hanged him."

Playing dumb, I said, "Hanged who, Anna?"

She looked up at me. "The man from Eddy Street. A man named Lugotov. The newsman told about him."

"Yes, I guess I did hear that was on the news," I said with a touch of curtness.

"They said the police were there. I thought it might be you, dearie."

"You're right," I said. "They called me this morning. Some maniac hung the body on an iron hook. We don't know who. I didn't say anything because it didn't seem like dinner conversation, especially with Meg here." I slid my hand across the table to her forearm. "Did it bother you because he was a Russian?"

Slow to answer, she said, "I think so, Nora. Yes . . . I think because he was a countryman. He would have been there when I was."

Silently, we did the dishes; then Anna left for upstairs. Meg was ready for bed by nine o'clock. As I sat on the edge of her bed and tucked her in, I said, "Okay, fess up, where were you and Anna today? Another doughnut shop visit?"

"How'd you know, Mom?"

It was a moment before I could say, "I didn't."

"Do you think we'll be going there every day after school?"

"I don't know." I swept her hair off her forehead, leaving my hand on her head. "Did you see the same man today, Meg? The one who buys you doughnuts?"

She smiled and nodded. "Can I ask him home for supper next time?"

I decided not to say more and risk disturbing her sleep. "We'll talk about it tomorrow. Okay?"

I switched off the light and sat with her in the dark, my arm draped lightly across her legs. The cadence of her breathing slowed, and sleep took her in minutes.

Back in my own bedroom, I changed into a white cotton nightgown and a raucous striped robe. Caitlin had bought me the robe just after my amputation, bringing it to the hospital one afternoon, roaring that its colors "will freak you out!" The gift touched me, but the robe was so garish that I couldn't bring myself to wear it unless I was alone. Ugly as it was, it reminded me of Cait and my parents, so I felt better when I wore it.

My clothes changed, I slipped my thigh from my prosthesis, then crutched my way to the living room. En route, I grabbed a pad of paper and a pen and shoved them into my pocket. In the worn stuffed chair near the living-room windows, I massaged my tired stump through my gown and robe.

The room was dim, brightened only by a single floor lamp that backlit the chair. Outside, I saw the circles of pale orange radiance made by the streetlamps standing at attention along

Fargo Avenue. At the end of the street, to the east, lay the smooth, even, impenetrable blackness of Lake Michigan. With Meg asleep now, the apartment became as quiet as the unseen lake: it was the kind of peace I needed for productive thought.

I drew a rough floor plan of Holy Name Cathedral, penciling in the confessional and Rita's water bucket. I made a small number 1 at a point in the center aisle, at the approximate site where Lugotov's Tokarev pistol must have been fired for its bullet to ricochet off the back wall and through Rita's bucket. Then, for the Nagant's point-blank firings into Eva, I drew the numeral 2 just outside the left-hand door of the confessional. I sorted through the sequence of shots according to Eva and Father Ritgen; I also thought of Semyon Lugotov's story of his chase as told to Steve Schwartz. I dialed Art at home.

"I hoped you'd be home," I said. "Sorry to bother you, but I need to talk."

"We went to the game, but we've been home for an hour, left after the seventh inning."

"Kind of early, huh?"

"Aww, Nora, the Sox can't do shit with the bats! What's up?"

"I've been thinking about the Cathedral last Saturday, now that we know that Lugotov's gun and probably Lugotov were there."

"I spent half the game going over the identical thing," Art said, "and I'll give you odds we're on the same wavelength. I'll know I'm right if you can tell me which train Lugotov boarded when he was chased up onto the El platform."

"Schwartz said the southbound train."

"That's it! It works!"

"All right, let's hear your version."

Art's voice was even deeper and warmer on the phone than it was in person: "Glazunov, the man who we have to assume had been stalking Lugotov, quietly follows him into the grocery store

Saturday afternoon. Lugotov has his gun with him because he's been chased for a week or two, and wouldn't you be carrying your gun if you had one?"

"I guess."

"Of course you would," he said. "Now, when Lugotov spots Glazunov, Lugotov panics and takes off, leaving the store. He runs east on Addison, finally turning in to the El station. He pays a buck and climbs the steps to the tracks. He thinks he's got it made, but no—oh shit!—here comes Fat Man huffin' and puffin' and trying to blow the house down. Before the train pulls away, Glazunov jumps on."

"So far, I like it," I said.

"I've got it right by you?"

"Damn right, partner."

"All right, so the train takes off south, headed for the Loop. After the Fullerton Avenue stop, it goes underground into the subway. Now, it's black in that tunnel—and noisy? Christ, those steel wheels screaming on the tracks—"

"And don't forget the train lights blinking on and off," I interrupted.

"It's enough to scare the hell out of anyone, especially if you don't know where you're headed. Okay, by the second underground stop, Chicago Avenue, our Semyon is ready to piss in his pants, just dying to do something—anything but stay parked in his seat like a dummy. So when the train stops at Chicago, he charges off, hoping Glazunov won't follow. But he does. Now they both climb the stairs out of the subway station and end up at the corner of State and Chicago."

"Picture them," I said, chortling, "these two old men coming out of the subway, one running after the other, probably both waving their pistols in the air."

"Yeah, comical," Art said, "unless, of course, someone is going to get shot, like Eva Ramirez."

"You're right," I said. "Sorry."

"Sure."

"Art, let me take it from here."

"You're on."

I continued the sequence: "Lugotov runs south on State. He goes past the Cathedral school, then nears the church itself. He's geting tired by now, and he knows Glazunov is close behind. Not having any better idea, he heads up the stairs into the Cathedral. Maybe he'll be safe in there, he thinks."

"But no luck again," Art said, "because Glazunov sees him and follows."

"Right. Now, inside the church, they both run by crazy Rita, first Lugotov, then Glazunov, probably neither one noticing her. Lugotov goes partway up the center aisle, then, suddenly, whips around. He's had it, so he fires a shot at Glazunov. This is the first noise that Ritgen and Eva hear from the confessional. Well, Lugotov's shot misses Glazunov by a mile, and the bullet ricochets off the grillwork on the back wall, then through Rita's water bucket. At this point, maybe Glazunov drops to the floor to avoid the shot; anyway, Glazunov somehow loses sight of Lugotov."

"This is where it gets hairy," Art cut in; "this is the real guesswork."

"I know, I know," I said, "but we must be right."

"You mean that while Glazunov is down, Lugotov either slips out of the church unnoticed or—"

"Or he runs into the confessional—into the *right* side of the confessional," I said.

"And Glazunov somehow thinks he's in the other box, in Eva's box."

"Yes," I said. "Now Glazunov pumps four slugs through the door."

"And into Eva. By mistake."

"By mistake."

We both fell quiet, the pause comfortable. Finally, Art asked, "Nora, how do you think they each got out of the church?"

"Glazunov must have left first, thinking Lugotov was dead in the box."

"And Lugotov followed in a few minutes, before Rita called for the cops?"

"Yes."

Art said, "Why did Glazunov assume Lugotov was in the left-hand box? That doesn't make any sense to me."

"Maybe he wasn't paying close enough attention after ducking Lugotov's shot," I offered. "Other than that, I don't know."

"Another thing. If Eva's shooting is such a big mistake, then why is ten grand sitting in the Ramirez mailbox a couple of days later?"

"I don't know," I said.

"That may be easy next to the big question."

"What's that?"

"The motive," Art said. "We don't even have a hint of a motive. And it's nothing common like drugs or sex. It's not that simple when a dead man is gored and strung up to a water pipe in the morgue."

"You're right . . ."

After a pause, Art said, "Let's sleep on it, girl."

"Okay."

"Let's start out tomorrow in the Cathedral, early. We'll look again at the church and the confessional."

"Is seven okay?" I said. "I've got an eight-o'clock appointment with Glazunov at the U. of C."

"Are you shittin' me?"

"No shit, Arthur. Didn't you know of my interest in a graduate program in Russian Affairs? A detective can't be a scholar? Why, my father would be bursting his buttons with me on the U. of C. campus."

Art chuckled. "Okay, seven it is."

I hung up the phone; the quiet of the apartment enfolded me again. I knew I still lacked crucial evidence for arrest and conviction: the Nagant revolver, a reasonable motive, and proof that it was indeed Georgi Glazunov who drove the red car, wounded Eva, and killed Lugotov. Still, I felt that I had the real prize, the identity of Glazunov. Jack Flaherty used to tell me not to decide who was guilty before developing evidence with the strength of prosecution. Convicting a hunch is as futile as playing the Lottery, he used to say. But Jack would have been wrong this time, I thought. Glazunov was the one, and he was close to my grasp. Grab him now; bring in the evidence later.

18

The ringing of the phone broke up my reverie. It was Anna. "Nora," she said haltingly, "Nora, I . . ."

"Anna, what is it?"

"I can't . . . but if I knew, I—"

"Anna, are you having pain?"

". . . a way, I need . . ."

It was only nonsense followed by more nonsense. "Unlock your door, Anna. I'm coming up." I strapped on my leg, grabbed my keys, and locked the door behind me. Meg would be all right for a few minutes.

Anna was sitting on her bed amid a tangle of covers and wearing a shiny, long-sleeved nightgown, a style that looked decades old. Her face was wet.

I took the phone from her and placed it in its cradle. "What is it, Anna?"

She shrugged her shoulders, her lips moving ineffectually.

"It's okay," I said, and took her cold hand. "It's okay. I'll sit with you a few minutes."

She nodded and managed a tight smile of thanks.

We sat together for fifteen or twenty minutes, the only noise a siren's whine from Sheridan Road. Then, pulling her hand from mine, she said suddenly, "It's the Siege, Nora."

"Still?"

"It's come back so hard lately."

"I'm sorry I brought that book home," I said.

"Don't be. I'm glad you did. I was a long time letting you all the way into my life, much too long. You've never been that selfish with me. This morning," she continued, "after you left, I was better, but then I saw the story of the hanging. That made me worse again."

"Why, Anna?"

"I suppose it reminded me of all the violence of the Siege, of Haymarket. Remember about Haymarket?"

"Yes."

After another few minutes of silence, I motioned her to lie back on her pillow. She did it without argument. I covered her and said, "You sleep. I'm going to sit awhile in the living room, just till you drop off. I'll lock your door when I go."

"Thank you, dearie."

I closed her bedroom door halfway and walked to the darkened living room. At her desk, I switched on a lamp and sat in a creaking wooden chair. I felt tired, but I knew I was nowhere near sleep.

The desktop was a clutter, as bad as John Dover's, and unusual for neat Anna. I read her *Tribune* for a minute, then lifted it off the desk to fold it. Underneath the newspaper lay a scatter of photographs, all of them black-and-whites edged with the yellow curl of age. I immediately recognized Andrei in the photograph on top of the pile. He stood alone in the picture, young and lean and square-shouldered. The next several pictures had all captured either young Anna or Andrei or both together, always smiling, as handsome a couple as I could ever recall seeing.

Three of the pictures showed a small boy: Misha, I supposed. In one of these photos he looked to be two, maybe three years of age. He posed on a pillow, his eyes pale, his smile dimpled and full. A small round hat sat comically askew on his head. The camera had caught his bare arms as they opened wide, his hands spread apart, as if to say, "Come to me, come to me, I love you."

In the smallest, grimmest of all the photos on the desk, I saw a half-covered newborn child, its sex indeterminable, its face nearly skeletonized in its thinness. As it lay on its back in a crib, the baby's fragile eyes looked half open, their gaze blank and unfocused. I assumed this was Merusha.

I laid Merusha's photo down, afraid to look any longer, fearful that I might start to break apart as Anna had. I grabbed the pile of photographs and spread them as haphazardly over the desk as I had found them. But when I reached for the *Tribune* to lay it back over the desktop, another photograph caught my eye; it had been half-hidden under the base of the lamp.

Black-and-white like the others, this looked to be the oldest photo of all, its images badly faded by time. Again, it was a picture of children, this time a boy and a girl, each six or eight years of age, standing side by side. They were holding hands. The boy wore a pale shirt and dark knickers, the girl a full white dress to her knees. They posed in front of a sunlit trellis of flowers. Their smiles were impish.

I had no idea who the children might be. Before I replaced the photograph where I had found it, I casually flipped it over. There was an inked inscription on the back.

The words struck me like a hammerblow. I closed my eyes. It was a full minute before I had calmed down enough to read the words again: *1920—Nikki and Talitha.*

Quickly, I turned the photo over to re-examine it. Much as I tried not to see it, the resemblance was there—yes, most clearly in the eyes, but recognizable even in the angle the jaw made to form the chin. It was Anna as a child, no question.

I rummaged in my memory for the letter from Talitha to Nikki that had been found in Lugotov's apartment. I couldn't remember the text clearly, only something about the birthmark on Lugotov's cheek. I slid the photograph halfway under the lamp, as I had found it, and opened the newspaper over everything.

I needed the letter, but it was downstairs, in my purse. As I stood up from the desk, I remembered the general appearance of the letter and recalled Art's remark that the type was even dirtier than what our Detective Division typewriters produced at Area Six. Quietly, I started around the apartment: merely hoping something wasn't true didn't justify inaction.

I found it as easily as if she had felt no reason to hide it. An antique Royal, it stood in full view on the floor of a closet off the living room. From my pocket, I pulled the sheet of note-paper with my Cathedral diagram. Breathing deeply, I rolled the paper into the typewriter. I struck only two keys: the "a" and the "e."

The letters snapped onto the paper: their open loops were as black with ink as those in Talitha's letter. There was no longer any question in my mind. Anna was Talitha.

Furious, I yanked the paper from the typewriter and crunched it in my fist. I stood and walked to Anna's bedroom. I found her in deep sleep, her mouth agape, air moving across her teeth in a faint whistle. There was no point in my staying any longer, not when she was in that kind of stupor. Anyway, I needed to settle myself. The photograph, the Talitha letter, the doughnut man—it would all wait till morning.

In my apartment, I checked Meg, who still slept with the conviction of the dead. I kissed her, and went straight to the kitchen for brandy and milk. I retrieved the letter from my purse, then returned to my living-room chair. I read the letter over and over again.

My dearest Nikki,

I am writing tonight because I am thinking of you and I miss you. Today I attended a lecture that brought many things back to me. You are strong in my thoughts now.

I am sad tonight, Nikki, and I needed to tell that to someone who would understand. I am thinking constantly of those who were with us through our worst months, those I cannot even bear to mention.

I would love to see you sometime, if there is a way we could do that. For now, with my love,

Talitha

PS—Today, at the lecture, I saw a man who seemed to know me, I mean, know me from our Vyborg district. When he looked at me and I saw his face, it put a fear in me and I don't know why. He looked your age, and he had a large spot on his cheek. My brain is rusty. Would you remember him, Nikki? Write if you can. Love, T.

Painfully, I admitted to myself that somehow Talitha—Anna—was tied to Lugotov's murder, and ultimately, to Eva's shooting. Although the letter did not incriminate her directly, her part seemed substantial. I assumed Nikki was a brother or cousin or friend, but I could take it no further. I had no under-standable link between the letter and the shootings that, until now, had seemed to be the work of Glazunov. But was this Nikki responsible instead? And if Anna was Talitha, might Glazunov be Nikki? And was either one the kindly man who favored Meg with chocolate doughnuts?

I switched off the lamp behind me and slipped out of my leg. I thought for a long time about the burden of Anna's grief, the terror she had been through, how often as a young mother she must have beseeched the Leningrad darkness to swallow her into itself, maybe forever. I shivered with the thought of Merusha's photograph. Then the impact of Anna's betrayal washed through my body, causing me to tremble fiercely. When my ragged muscles finally settled, all I could generate was a despondent, whispered "Fuck . . ."

Still sitting, I awoke at five in the morning, my joints aching. Outside, a steady drizzle streaked the windowpanes. Through patchy fog, Fargo's blacktop glistened under the streetlamps. The occasional honk of a car horn on Sheridan Road signaled the start of the city's day.

I made it to the bathroom where I had three aspirins and a shower. In my bedroom, I strapped on my prosthesis, then sat to dry and comb out my hair. I arranged it in its most formal manner, parted in the middle and pulled back snugly on my scalp. Next, I dressed in my navy, pinstriped silk suit and white linen blouse. A meeting with a Russian Ph.D., murderer or not, called for my very best.

The morning paper waited in the hallway outside my door. I picked it up, then woke Meg.

"It can't be time yet," she said, blinking at the light through flecks of sleep encrusting the corners of her eyes.

"But it is. It's six."

"But—"

"Let's go, Meg, now. Time for a shower. Get going or you won't have time to eat."

While Meg showered and dressed, I sat at the kitchen table drinking coffee. At breakfast, Meg said, "I like your suit, Mom. I mean, those little stripes."

"Thanks, honey."

"Do you have to see a judge today?"

"No. A professor."

"Professor? That means school, right?"

"Right."

Frowning, she said, "You're not going back to school, are you? Mom?"

I smiled and said, "Don't worry. No more school for this girl."

"Don't scare me like that." She spooned in a mouthful of cold cereal. A thin streak of milk broke from a corner of her mouth. "See, I figure I need you to help with my homework. I mean, if you're doing *your* homework, then you couldn't help me with mine. Yeah, like . . . the math. You know?"

"I know." I reached for and squeezed her warm bare forearm.

In another minute, she set her spoon down and said, "My stomach hurts."

"Since when?"

"Since this cereal. Maybe I better stay with Anna today. I don't want to be sick at school."

I leaned over and pressed on her belly. "Your stomach feels fine to me, Meg. You know, the last time you felt like this you weren't that sick, were you? It all worked out at school."

She turned her lip down with great melodrama. "But Sister doesn't know if I'm really sick or not."

"Sister will call me if she thinks you're having a problem. She's very good about that. C'mon, let's get your lunch together."

At six-thirty, Meg and I marched upstairs to Anna's apartment; Meg would wait there until it was time to walk to school. Anna, still in her robe, answered the door quickly. Her gray hair was wild from her sleep. She looked pale but fresh.

"Hello, Nora, good morning," Anna said, bending down and beaming at Meg's smooth, bright face. She was as maternal at seventy-five as she must have been at thirty, I thought.

We entered the apartment and stood in the small foyer. Meg

wandered off to find the television and "Bozo's Circus Show." I fidgeted with my collar and said, "You slept well?"

"Yes. You coming up did it, dearie."

"Good. Meg complained of a bellyache at breakfast, but it's nothing. She can go to school."

"Of course."

I stopped for the pause demanded by an unexpected shift of subject, then said, "Anna, while I waited for you to sleep, I sat at your desk for a time. I saw your pictures, of you and Andrei and the children."

"Oh," she said, with just a wisp of surprise, "I am glad you saw them. I have only the one picture of Merusha. It sat in the camera for over three years. We couldn't develop it until after the war. We guarded that camera with our lives. It was all we had of her."

I nodded and said, "Sometime I would like to talk more of Leningrad, if you wouldn't mind. I would like to hear about all of it, your family, your childhood."

"Come in, dearie, come in and have coffee with me."

"I can't now. I'm late to meet Art at Holy Name Cathedral. But I think we need to do it later today."

"Of course," she said. "You are learning many things about Anna Skrabina these past two days."

"Yes, I can see that. I'm glad for that."

"Me, too."

I stepped into the hallway. "Oh," I said as if the notion had just come to me, "do you and Meg plan to walk along Sheridan Road after school? As you have for the past two days?"

A quick, nervous flick of her head telegraphed her surprise at my question. Recovering immediately, she said, "I haven't really thought about it yet."

I started toward the stairway. For some reason I looked back, and when I did I saw Meg come to the doorway and stand close against Anna. Anna draped her arm over Meg's shoulder. Meg smiled at me.

Doubt pricking me like a shard of glass, I wanted to go back and stay with Meg, but Art would be waiting at the Cathedral, so I started away again. After two steps, Anna called to me. "Oh, Nora . . ."

I turned back. "Yes?"

"Be watchful. Pray constantly."

19

The rain descended across the city, softly and methodically. A slab of dense clouds and fog had amputated the city's two greatest skyscrapers—the John Hancock Building and Sears Tower—at mid-height, their top halves now lost in mist. On Lake Shore Drive, as the water fell from the sky, thousands of sizzling car tires spat it back up from the shimmering pavement. I drove southward through the spray and the traffic, my thoughts on Glazunov, my windshield wipers slapping time.

A few minutes before seven, I entered Holy Name Cathedral where Art, also early, waited for me at the rear of the church. Overhead lights dimly lit the cavernous sanctuary ahead. A scatter of parishioners, smudges of dark color—mostly loners, but some couples—huddled in their pews and patiently waited for the seven-o'clock Mass.

Art and I exchanged greetings; then Art said softly, "I forgot to tell you last night that I had a check run on the renter in 2A."

"You mean—"

"The Ramirez building. The mailbox thing."

"Anything?" I said.

"The landlord gave me a name. Schwartz ran it through for me on his shift. Gregory Kirkland. He's a middle-aged cokehead who's done time for rearranging his wife's face with a pipe. Sounds like the son of a bitch damn near killed her. Anyway, I stopped by there before coming here. No one's home. I couldn't bust in—no warrant or anything. I'll follow up later today."

I said, "It's probably a zero, but I guess we should talk to him."

"Any other ideas?" Art asked.

I thought of telling him about Anna and the photograph, but I stopped myself. I reasoned there was nothing worth saying until I had more, until I had talked with Anna. Maybe I stayed quiet because I felt Anna was still too dear to me to admit her part in the wrongdoing.

"Let's check the confessional," I said.

We started up the center aisle. Halfway up, to the great surprise of the few parishioners who noticed, I stopped and suddenly spun around to face the rear of the church. Saying nothing, I extended my right arm into the empty air and aimed my forefinger at the back wall, brashly simulating Lugotov's shot toward the pursuing Glazunov. Art's simple nod told me that he still believed in the chase sequence we had agreed on during our phone conversation.

We went farther into the church, to the temporary panels of plywood that now hid the wrecked confessional. We squeezed behind the blockade to see the still-doorless left-hand compartment and the dried splatter of Eva's blood on the plaster wall.

I moved to the intact right side of the confessional, pulled the penitent's door wide open, and let it go. It quickly snapped shut, its hinges controlled by spring-loaded automatic closers. "I thought this door might have been standing open when Glazunov shot," I whispered to Art. "If he had missed seeing Lugotov leave from a side exit, and if this door had been open, then he might have assumed Lugotov was in the left-hand box."

"Guess not," Art said, in a low church-voice, "not with those closers as strong as they are."

Now Art moved up and stepped carefully into Eva's open box. He tapped a knuckle on the screen that separated the priest's face from the penitent's; then he gave a gentle kick to the kneeler from which Eva had fallen. His right fist to his mouth, he stared intently at the kneeler. "Nora," he said, "back up a step, back away from me and the box. Go up against the plywood."

"What?"

"Do it."

I did, saying, "Arthur—"

He knelt down on the springy kneeler and said, "Now look up and tell me what you see."

I tipped my eyes up to the still-intact doorframe. "I see the green light bulb that just went on when you knelt. So what?"

"And the light does what?" he said.

"Tells when someone is kneeling. Tells when the box is occupied."

Without speaking, Art stood and walked to the right-hand box. He opened the door and walked in, and the door quickly closed behind him. From inside, his muffled voice said, "I'm kneeling now. What do you see?"

I looked up over the door of the box. "This light is still dark," I said. "Burned out, I guess."

I thought for a moment, my eyebrows contracting. Then I jerked open the door and blurted, "My God, Art, that's it!"

Art stood and started from the box.

Not waiting for him to speak, I ran with it. "See, Lugotov charges into this box while Glazunov is getting up—I mean, getting up from ducking Lugotov's center aisle shot. From the rear of the church, Glazunov probably sees Lugotov head into the confessional, but he's not sure which box. When Glazunov finally gets up here, he logically shoots through the only penitent's door with a lit bulb, Eva's door."

Beaming, Art opened his arms and hugged me. Apart again, he said, "You'd better get your ass out to the University of Chicago, girl. It's already seven-fifteen."

I screeched away from the Cathedral, heading south on State, then east on Congress Parkway till I hit southbound Lake Shore Drive. Speeding and tailgating and lane-changing recklessly, against all odds, I reached the University of Chicago safely, and by seven-fifty. I chose one of the several empty parking places on University Avenue, across the street from Pick Hall. With the collar of my raincoat snugged up against the weather, I rushed through the drizzle, and was relieved to find the building already open at that hour.

Room 125 was at the end of a dim corridor off the building's lobby. The door was closed, its glass opaque and dark. Glazunov's name and professorship appeared in black letters at the bottom right-hand corner of the glass. I tried the door. Locked. I walked a few feet to a wooden bench across the hall and sat to wait, but heard him coming before I got settled on the bench.

Professor Georgi Glazunov turned the corner from the lobby at one minute before eight o'clock. He walked quickly, his body undulant with the motion of his gait. He wore a billowing, ankle-length black raincoat, the kind a bishop might wear to his chancery office. His hat was tall and wide-brimmed, Roman and clerical-looking also, a style so old that it had recently returned to the fringes of fashion. Instead of looking to find his face, I looked quickly into my purse and grabbed for something, anything, that would make it seem as if I were otherwise occupied. Ironically, out came the Leningrad map, but no matter. Glazunov only glanced at me before unlocking his door and entering his office. He closed the door behind him.

With the click of the door, I drew in a shaking breath, my pulse speeding wildly. I was puzzled that my body was betraying me like this. Before, many times before, I had stalked thieving drug runners or vicious pimps, brutal rapists or child murderers, the city's worst vermin—those members of the species Art could only refer to as "human shit." I had hunted and touched scum and not felt my nerves kick up as this man made them do. Did I fear him because he was Russian, or scholarly, or because he appeared—on his surface, at least—to be more refined than criminals who made no pretense of sophistication or civility?

I slowed my breathing and soon felt calmer. I thought about arresting Glazunov now, but I quickly discarded the idea. I didn't have much—no gun, no witness besides Rita the crazy rug-scrubber, no motive—so I decided to let things play out a little longer.

My instincts told me to go with the fake money order from Windy City Towing. The graduate-student scam tweaked me uncomfortably; besides, I wanted to observe Glazunov's reaction to someone knowing his car had been towed last Saturday afternoon.

The phone inside Glazunov's office rang at five after eight: that would be Glazunov's secretary telling him of the graduate-student appointment. I unfastened my coat and gave full view to my silk suit, my badge of credibility. I fluffed my blouse slightly, then patted at my damp hair. I brought my hand back to my lap and laid it there in a feminine manner. It was showtime.

The door opened, and Glazunov stepped into the hallway. Keeping one hand on the doorknob, his eyes searched for me. He was dressed for the day's chill: a dark blue corduroy sport coat, a white turtleneck top thickly rolled at the neck, and wrinkled woolen pants.

I was initially struck by the cherubic softness of his face, the quality of benevolence. He looked more like an angel than a murderer—an old angel, to be sure, but an angel nonetheless.

His white eyebrows uplifted in inquiry, Glazunov said, "Would you be Miss Nora Callum?"

I swallowed and said, "What?" I paused; then, recovering, I said, "No, I'm afraid I'm not Nora whoever."

Looking perplexed, Glazunov said, "Oh . . . well—"

"Why do you ask?" I said, moving slightly to the edge of the bench. I felt my nerves in good control, my pulse rapid only because of the exhilaration that now charged me, that warm, familiar rush I always felt when I was this close to my quarry.

Glazunov said, "My secretary just called and said a woman named Nora Callum would be coming here at eight o'clock. Something about graduate work. I'm sorry for the mistake." He tipped his head courteously and turned toward the office.

I quickly stood and stepped forward. "Are you Dr. Glazunov?" I said.

Turning his face to me, he said, "I am."

"Well, I'm not Miss Callum, but I was waiting for you. May I come in for a moment?"

"I'm very busy this morning," Glazunov said, with a nervous smile.

"It would only be a minute. I have something to deliver to you."

"For a moment, then," he said, and motioned me into the office. "Leave the door open, please. For air."

The office was small and square, a cubicle walled with shelves and stuffed with an untidy assortment of books, binders, and stacks of papers—manuscripts, I supposed. A large, multi-paned window looked out to a courtyard sodden with rain. The room smelled of wood and dampness.

Glazunov sat at his desk near the window, then asked me to sit in a chair close by, between himself and the open door. He tugged at the soft clutch of his turtleneck. "And your name is?" he asked me.

"Frances Luchinski," I said promptly.

"And you said you had something for me?"

"Yes, I have," I said, staring at his fluffy mustache. I smiled and went on, "I have a small surprise for you—a refund check." I handed the folded money order across the desk.

Glazunov's thick fingers unfolded the check. He scanned its

contents deliberately. "I'm not sure I understand," he finally said, and looked up.

"You've overpaid your charge at Windy City Towing," I explained, "for the tow last Saturday. The bill should have been fifty dollars and the clerk charged you seventy-five. The last twenty-five dollars was a Sunday pick-up charge, which we suspended six months ago—you know, not wanting to be accused of price gouging or anything like that." I frowned my concern with Windy City's error, then finished with "The woman didn't remember that. She's a drunk. Sunday morning help is hard to find."

Glazunov nodded, his now tired-looking eyes never moving from my face. I felt heat in his gaze. For a painfully long half-minute he said nothing, and I wondered if he was thinking about denying the tow had ever occurred. Would he claim some mistake had been made?

He smiled, indicating that he understood about the clerk at the tow yard. "I did think the charge was a bit steep," he said.

"It was very steep. My apologies from the company."

"That's not necessary," he said, and settled into his chair. "If I might ask, Miss Luchinski, is this your entire job, just to deliver refunds?"

"Oh, no," I said. "I do many errands for the company, all over the city. We own tow lots on the West and South Sides also."

"You're so beautifully dressed to run errands," he remarked.

"Look good, feel good," I blurted.

"I see. Well, I'm still surprised by the personal delivery of this small amount of money. I would have expected a check by mail."

His observation now made the illogic of my visit as immediately obvious to me as it must have been to him. Struggling for a response, I delayed by standing and rearranging my coat. "We give this personal service because we're interested in your business, Professor. We don't just tow for the police. Much of our work is private, you know, towing your car if it won't start or if

A WIDE AND CAPABLE REVENGE

it breaks down on the road. We want you to think of us if that happens. That's all."

"Ahh, now I understand," Glazunov said, with gentle sarcasm.

"I'll be leaving now. Sorry for the bother."

He stood. "No bother at all, Miss Luchinski." He tipped his head graciously. "And thank you for the money. My wife and I may eat out tonight."

"Fine. Goodbye, then."

I spun quickly around, anxious for Glazunov not to see the flush of embarrassment that warmed my face. I was out of the building and to my car in minutes. With coat and collar pulled tight for comfort, I sat motionless in the car's dank seclusion. Riddled with self-doubt, I reflected on my visit to Glazunov. The principle of the visit, and my interaction with Glazunov, seemed a reasonably sound piece of work, but the flaw lay in the detail of the deception. Glazunov was right, of course: the small amount of the refund, twenty-five lousy dollars, made no sense for personal delivery when mail was available. And if Glazunov had called the Windy City office, no one there would have confirmed the story. In my exuberance, I had failed to substantiate the ruse. On balance, I had bungled the encounter. I'd have been better off going after Glazunov from a distance, hands off. Art would be properly disappointed with me. Discouraged, I laid my forehead to the cold steering wheel and listened to the soft ping of rain on the metal roof.

I sat in the car for probably half an hour, paralyzed by my inability to decide my next move. But Mother Time and Glazunov determined it for me.

Just before nine o'clock, Glazunov walked out of Pick Hall and turned north on University Avenue, heading away from me, a dark, spherical form moving urgently into the swallow of fog. He carried a leather briefcase. He made a quick turn to look back—so quick, I thought, that he could not have seen me in the murky weather.

I started the car. If Glazunov was now as suspicious as I felt he must be, then I could not be overly cautious. I may have botched our meeting, but at least the blunder may have forced his hand. I steered the car out into the street, determined not to let him slip away.

I drove slowly, my foot barely on the accelerator. At the first block, Glazunov turned onto East Fifty-eighth, the intersecting street. When he stopped at a car, a red Ford Escort, I slid into an empty parking space and waited, my engine running.

Glazunov set his briefcase on the ground, then fiddled with his keys before unlocking the door and getting into the car. He started the motor and drove onto University Avenue. I felt sure he was headed home, although the feeling was purely intuitive. Nevertheless, if I was right, then I could lay back a little farther than I otherwise might—I knew the Kenwood Avenue location of his house.

He was home in five minutes, and quickly out of his car and into his house. I parked some distance behind his car and waited, my engine shut off. It wasn't twenty minutes before Glazunov walked out onto his front porch and started down the steps. He lugged a large suitcase in his right hand. Immediately behind him came a woman, also carrying a suitcase. The woman was bundled against the weather, but I saw her graying hair and decided she would be about the same age as Glazunov. Neither spoke as they loaded their bags into the trunk. Before entering the car, they each looked briefly but intently back at the house.

20

almost lost them in the tangle of Hyde Park side streets before the Ford turned in to the parking lot of a bank on Fifty-fifth. Glazunov walked into the bank while the woman stayed behind. Twenty minutes later he emerged, a canvas bag tucked under his arm. Back in the car, he drove east toward Lake Shore Drive, then turned north.

The red Escort was easier to follow in the openness of the Drive, so I could afford to stay a few yards back, and in another lane. Wanting all my attention focused on this tail, I turned down the volume on my scanner. Art knew where I was: I had radioed him at Area Six while I waited outside the Glazunov house.

The morning rush hour had eased, and traffic barreled along, most drivers ignoring the slippery hazards caused by the rain. To the east, Lake Michigan heaved dark, rough waves toward a sky hung so low that it seemed one with the water. Ahead, the jagged downtown skyline was barely perceptible: the buildings' bold outlines had surrendered to the mantle of the storm.

Closing on the Loop, Glazunov stayed in the far right-hand lane, surprising me. The baggage he and the woman had carried from the house indicated they were traveling. I had expected they would take the Drive to the Loop, then go northwest on the Kennedy Expressway to O'Hare Airport. Or they might leave the city by train, from Union Station just west of the Loop.

That again would mean a left turn off Lake Shore Drive, an impossibility from the far right-hand side of the six-lane road.

But Glazunov stayed far to the right, ignoring any westbound exit. Soon we had passed the lakefront's complex of public museums and the Monroe Harbor Yacht Club, leaving the downtown behind. We continued north, on our left the coldly imposing steel-and-glass residential high-rises of the Gold Coast, on our right the yawning beaches at Oak Street and North Avenue. Farther north, the Drive cut through Lincoln Park, the deep green acreage that hugged the rocky lakeshore. An occasional inveterate jogger could be seen puffing in the rain along the twisting asphalt paths.

Glazunov's car never moved from its lane, motoring steadily along, courteously allowing other cars to enter from the ramps when necessary. He followed the Drive to Hollywood Avenue where the expressway bent west, away from the lake, then ended abruptly.

At Hollywood, Glazunov signaled to turn right on Sheridan Road, but was stopped by a red light. While I waited two cars behind, I heard my name being called on the scanner. I flipped up the volume: it was Mike Jewett, an Area Six dispatcher. "Lieutenant Callum," he said through the buzz, "contact base now. Our need is now."

I picked up my microphone. "Mike, this is Nora. What's up?"

"We have a call from a woman who says she's the principal of St. Ignatius school," he said.

"I know the place," I said, my heart already slamming my ribs. "So?"

"She says your daughter, uh—Meg? She goes there?"

"Yes, she goes there, goddammit!" I shot back.

"Hey, easy. Look, the lady says your daughter didn't make roll call this morning. She wonders if the girl is home sick, and you forgot to phone the school."

"She's not sick," I said. "That's all the woman told you?"

"That's it. Look, give the lady a call, will you?"

I hit the disconnect button. The light turned green, and Glazunov started up. I had two seconds to decide: either follow
Glazunov's right turn, or lose him by going west on Hollywood
toward St. Ignatius. The choice was self-evident.

Both Glazunov and the car between us turned right, clearing
my lane to proceed straight west. I floored the Fury, its rear tires
screeching; then I flipped on my siren.

To Broadway in moments, I squealed right, pushing toward Loyola Avenue, a residential street hemmed in by parked cars; here
I went west again. Not crashing the Fury took enough concentration that I could scarcely think about Meg.

I climbed the school's granite steps minutes later. Meg's classroom was on the first floor, its door standing open. Nearly breath-
less, I motioned to Sister Aletius, who was working at the
blackboard. She shook a gentle finger at the students to keep
them quiet while she came into the hallway. She was a trim,
white-haired woman in a gray flannel skirt and white blouse.

"Is Meg ill, Mrs. Callum?" she said, seeming puzzled.

"Meg had a little stomachache this morning," I said, "but I
told my sitter she was fine, to come to school."

"Nobody called," Sister said. "I asked the children if anyone
had seen Meg or her sitter—"

"Anna."

"Yes, Anna," she said. "We all know her. No one had seen
either one of them. I thought it was strange we had no notice,
because you always call."

I glanced into the classroom, finding the desk that I knew was
Meg's. Its emptiness froze me.

"Are you all right, Mrs. Callum?"

I heard Sister's words but couldn't respond. The image of Meg
standing under Anna's arm in her doorway early that morning

was all that registered for me. Anna's warning to me—"Be watchful. Pray constantly"—burned in my ears. In meeting Art and pursuing Glazunov, I had ignored my instinctive fear of leaving Meg with Anna. Now, filled with bitter self-recrimination, I stood staring at Meg's desk.

"Mrs. Callum?" Sister repeated, touching me on my shoulder.

"Oh . . . yes," I said, confused. "I'm leaving now, yes."

"Where to?"

"I don't know. To try and find Meg. If you see her, please hold her for me."

"You can count on it."

Back in my car, I looked blankly ahead at a row of simple apartment buildings, each with a terrace and a tree dripping rain. I was near panic. I thought about calling the Department—the Foster Avenue station was close by—and asking for a team to start a search with me, but I rejected the idea. That would have meant admitting Meg's life was truly threatened, and I was still too irrational to confront that possibility. I would start my own search back at home. I had given up on Glazunov: I didn't care if the man shot a hundred people and strung all of them up on black hooks.

I drove along Sheridan Road slowly, looking from one side of the street to the other, hoping to glimpse Meg. At Fargo, I turned toward the lake and drove toward my building.

Stunned, I jerked my head sharply in disbelief. For a moment, I stopped the Fury in the middle of the street, my reactions paralyzed. Just ahead, parked in front of my building, was the red Ford Escort. The driver's side was empty, but Glazunov's woman sat in the passenger seat.

I pulled into a spot about ten yards behind the Escort and shut off the Fury's engine. The wipers stopped in mid-cycle; the only noise now was the clatter of rain on the rooftop. I grabbed for my prosthesis, twisting it pointlessly on my stump. My mind could not claw away the tangle that besieged it. I only knew that somehow things were coming together.

I slid to the passenger's side of the car where I had a better view of the building. I wondered if Meg was in the building with Glazunov, and whose apartment he had entered. If it was mine, he probably would have forced his entry, although he might have a key: nothing would surprise me now.

I sat with my face close to the window, peering through the curtain of rain outside. I groped desperately for my next move. Finally, I decided to go for my apartment first, hoping to find Meg there. My route would be down the sidewalk alongside the building toward the alley, then up the outdoor rear staircase. Entry from the kitchen would be more likely to surprise Glazunov.

I glanced upward to my living-room windows, beyond the open white draperies, to see if a light might have been turned on. The room was dark. I fingered my .38 Special, in the purse slung over my shoulder, and considered the risk of gunplay if Meg was in the apartment.

I half opened the car door: the first drops of rain peppered my face. Looking up again before sliding off the seat, I noticed a lamp switch on, but not in my apartment. It was Anna's.

My pulse pounded in my neck as I squinted at her window. My face wet with rain, I watched and saw Anna's gray head come into view, then disappear.

I bolted from the car, slamming the door behind me, paying no attention to whether Glazunov's woman looked back at me or not. My coat flapped open in the wind and rain pelted me; my special linen blouse was quickly soaked. I charged down the sidewalk that led to the rear of the building, the limp from my prosthetic leg intensified by my running. The wooden steps were slick with standing water, and at the first-floor landing, I fell painfully. Quickly up again, I drove myself higher, my stump aching with the effort. In a short time, I had reached the second floor.

At my back door, I stopped for a moment to suck in a deep, calming breath. I pulled the gun from my purse and flexed my forefinger on its trigger. Quietly, using my left hand, I opened the door with my key and stepped into the kitchen. My ear cocked, I heard nothing but the rain whacking the wooden landing outside. Faintly, I called, "Meg," but I heard no answer.

With gun down, I toured the apartment, taking note that the breakfast dishes I had left in the sink had been washed and put away. In Meg's bedroom, none of her things had been disturbed. I walked back to the kitchen and used a towel to wipe my dripping face and my gun hand. I returned to the kitchen door, now hoping Meg was one floor above me.

I climbed the stairs slowly, unaware of the rain, thinking only of how dangerous to Meg the action might be in Anna's apartment when I entered. Anna's kitchen door was unlocked, so I went in easily. I moved toward the living room, still hearing nothing, my pointed gun directing my way.

The room was empty, except for Anna. She sat on her rose-colored couch, her chin tipped down, her cheeks shining with tears. She wore a dark skirt and a heavy white woolen sweater. She looked up in surprise when I broke into the room, my gun rudely in the lead.

"Where is she?" I demanded.

"Who?" Anna said, at first feigning ignorance while hurriedly wiping her cheeks with the back of her hand.

"Meg!" I shouted.

"She's—"

As Anna began to speak, Meg came around the corner from the bathroom. Smiling innocently, she said, "Hi, Mom."

I ran the short distance between us and wrapped my arms

tightly around her body. Tears squeezed from my closed eyes, and the gun dropped to the floor behind her. I let her go only when she squirmed from my arms and said, "What's wrong?"

"They called from the school," I said. "They didn't know where you were. I was scared."

"My stomach's better," she said.

From the couch, Anna said: "She complained after you left, Nora. I was sad, and I felt like company today. She didn't have to say much for me to keep her home. I just forgot to call school. It's my fault."

In my relief, I had forgotten Glazunov. Suddenly, I picked up my gun, then turned from Meg and Anna and ran to the front window. I looked outside and saw the Glazunov parking place was empty. The red Escort was nowhere up or down the street.

"Goddammit!" I said to myself, my jaws clenched. Discouraged and confused, I banged the butt of my .38 on the sill, then slid the gun into my purse, which still hung from my shoulder. I went to the couch and touched Anna's arm. "Are you all right?" I said.

"Yes, dearie."

I put my purse on the floor, then sat at the end of the couch away from her. I pulled my soaked, chilled blouse off the skin of my chest where it had stuck. "We have to talk, Anna."

"I know."

"Come here, Meg," I said. "Please, sit with me."

She did. I placed my hand on her thigh and squeezed.

"So . . . his name is Georgi Glazunov?" I said.

"Yes," Anna said.

"And the woman in the car with him?"

"Sophie—his wife."

"You know Glazunov."

"He's the doughnut man, Mom," Meg offered.

"Quiet, Meg—okay, honey? So you know Glazunov, Anna?"

"I do, yes. For more than fifty years I know him."

"From Russia?"

"From more than Russia, dearie," she said, with iron in her voice. Her eyes hardened with pride. "I know him from Leningrad, from the Siege. We were together then."

"As lovers?"

"Oh, my God, Nora, no! I was married to Andrei." She looked away from Meg and in a low voice she said, "Do Americans assume sex in all forms of togetherness?"

"No. I'm sorry. I—"

"Georgi was a teenager, and I was a mother of two small children. He was a neighbor, my young brother's closest friend."

"Mom—" Meg interrupted.

"Meg, you have to hush. Please. Okay, kiddo?"

She nodded, set her head against my side, then said, "Maybe I could watch TV. In Anna's bedroom."

I told her that was fine. When she left, I said, "Anna, you mentioned Georgi was your brother's closest friend. Who's your brother?"

"Nikki."

"Where's Nikki?"

"He lives in the Vyborg district, where we were raised. It's a section of Leningrad."

Relieved as I was about Meg, I still felt myself trembling at the notion of Anna's involvement in Glazunov's violence. But my thoughts were too disorganized to bring up the letter to Nikki just yet. "You came to this country with Glazunov?"

"No, as I said the other night, Andrei and I came from Germany. Georgi and Sophie came from Leningrad. They were ahead of us by a year or more. He was already a university student when we came."

"University of Chicago?"

"Yes," Anna said, "and he was a brilliant student. When he finished his Ph.D., the university knew they could not afford to let him go. They asked him to start up a department of Russian Affairs. It was the first department—"

I interrupted with "And you have kept in contact with the Glazunovs since you came to Chicago?"

"Fairly close. Neither of us had any children. Andrei's and mine were dead, of course, and the Glazunovs were never able to conceive. We had that and the Siege in common. Those are the strong bonds, dearie. Bonds of shared death do not fade with time."

"Then you see them regularly?"

"When Andrei was still alive, before I became close to you and Meg, we would see them several times a year. Sometimes, during summers, we would vacation with them in northern Wisconsin. They own a cottage there. Andrei and Georgi would have a wonderful time fishing together."

In my lap, my intertwined fingers clinched each other. My anger with Anna, my sense of having been betrayed by her, kept disrupting my thoughts. I asked, "Why was Glazunov here today?"

Anna blew her nose into a handkerchief, then said, "He told me he met with someone this morning, and now he knew he had to leave the city. He was here to say goodbye to me."

"Then you know where he's going?"

She ignored this question, preferring instead to look obliquely toward the rain-smeared windows.

I slid across the couch, near enough to the woman to take both her thin hands in my own. The yellow light of a lamp cut across our laps, highlighted them, but our upper bodies were obscured in the room's dimness. I already felt guilty about being angry with Anna. With a faint hint of apology, I said, "Anna, I have to tell you that Georgi Glazunov has committed two crimes, two serious crimes."

She said, "I know that he shot the lady in Holy Name Cathedral." Then, in a quieter, more measured voice, she added, "And he killed Lugotov."

I slid my hands from hers. "How do you know Glazunov shot those people?" I said.

"Because he told me."

"This morning?"

"No," she said, "when I saw him briefly the last couple of days."

"With Meg? At the doughnut shop?"

"Yes."

"Goddammit, Anna!" I cried. "What's going on here?"

She winced.

"I'm sorry," I said, immediately regretting my curse, language I tried never to use in front of Anna. "It's just that I don't understand what this is between you and Glazunov. I can't put it together. Please, Anna, make sense—please."

"Georgi met me to tell me what he had done," she said methodically. "I mean, killing Lugotov and wounding the woman a few days before."

"You knew he had planned those things?"

"Of course not, but I was not surprised to hear about Lugotov. The shooting of the woman was an accident, a pure accident."

I stood and walked to the window. This person who had nursed me through the losses of a leg and a husband, who had become a second mother to Meg, seemed so surely involved, at least complicitly, in Glazunov's acts of murder and attempted murder. But still I was reluctant to accuse her—not until the pieces were fitted together.

"Anna," I asked, returning to the couch, "tell me about Eva Ramirez. Do you know her?"

"No."

"And Lugotov?"

"I knew him from Leningrad, also from the Siege."

"He was not from Kiev?"

"No," she said.

"But the Immigration Service records say so."

"Then he lied."

"Okay, did you know Lugotov was living in Chicago?"

"Not until a month ago . . . when I found him."

"Explain," I pressed.

"It happened by chance," she said. "At the time, I didn't know who he was, but that ugly thing on his face—"

"The birthmark?"

"It scared me. I knew I recognized it. It meant something to me, something fearful, but I couldn't place it."

"Where did you see Lugotov?" I asked.

"At the downtown public library. It was the noon lecture series on the Second World War that I told you I had been attending. Remember?"

Unsure, I said, "Yes, I think so."

"The lecture that day was on the German Siege of Leningrad. For some reason, Lugotov was there—drawn by the subject, I suppose."

I said, "Anna, you're telling me you found a man you knew nearly fifty years ago in a city ten thousand miles from here? How do you expect me to believe that?"

She tilted her shoulders toward me for emphasis. "It can happen, dearie. It's happened to Nazi war criminals many times. I mean, years later they're spotted on another continent by someone from the camps. Some man in Cleveland was arrested just lately. Did you see that?"

I shrugged ignorance.

"People never forget those kinds of things," she said sternly, "never. Don't you believe in Providence?"

"I haven't thought about it lately," I said, exasperated. "You're confusing me."

"Stay with me, dearie. It'll become more clear."

It had goddamn better, I thought.

I said, "Okay, you saw a man with a birthmark. Then what?"

Anna settled back against the couch. She said, "That night, I wrote a letter to Nikki. Hearing the lecture and seeing pictures of the Siege had made me sad. And then, there was this man who disturbed me. I told Nikki all of this."

I reached into my purse and pulled out the photocopy of the letter. I said, "Are you called Talitha?"

One of Anna's eyes twitched and her head jerked forward. "Why?"

I handed her the letter. She scanned it.

"Where did you get this?" she said sharply.

"It was found in Lugotov's apartment. Someone had mailed it to him before he was killed."

She stared at me without speaking, her eyes pleading for something I didn't understand. Finally, sadly, as though I had broken some sacred trust, she said, "How do you know I am Talitha?"

"A photograph I saw on your desk last night. It had the words 'Nikki and Talitha' on its back. You were easy to recognize. You still have the same beautiful features you had as a child."

I hoped the compliment might draw her back to me, but she only nodded without expression.

"Why are you called Talitha?" I said.

She shook her head and waved a hand at me, as if to tell me to be still. The name had somehow put me even more deeply into her life. As her eyes glistened, she placed her fingertips to her cheekbones. Her fingers pressed there briefly, then came away to fold in her lap. Quietly, she said, "It was a very personal name. Only my family called me that, just Nikki and my parents—especially my father. Not even Andrei. I was given the name as a small child."

"Any special reason?"

"As a name of affection," she said. "It's Hebrew. It means 'beautiful young girl.' My father began using the name instead of Anna. He learned the name from Russian Jews who were our friends." She paused before saying, "Only Nikki would call me that now."

"It's a lovely name, Anna."

"It brings back everything for me."

"I understand."

She took in a large volume of air, then let it out with a halting, rippling sound in her throat. Calmer, she said, "You think I had something to do with Lugotov's murder, don't you, Nora?"

21

said nothing; the muscles in my face were so tense that I felt their hardness under my skin. We were exactly where I needed but didn't want to be: Anna as an accomplice to murder. My police training told me to build the case for her guilt, but all I could think of now was how to extricate her.

Twisting her rump on the couch, Anna said, "I suppose I did have something to do with Lugotov's murder. I did find him, after all. And I wrote the letter to Nikki."

"But the letter says you didn't know who the man was with the spot on his face," I said.

"I didn't, not until I talked to Georgi."

"You met at the doughnut shop?"

"Twice," she said. "Georgi has been phoning me these past few days. Two days ago, he said he wanted to come to Rogers Park to see me. I decided we could meet shortly after I picked up Meg at school."

"And?"

"At the first meeting, he said he had killed Lugotov the night before." Her gaze dropped to her lap. "Yesterday he told me about the hanging. That's why I've been upset, dearie."

"Anna, how does one letter result in all of this?"

She looked up. "Because when Nikki received my letter, it

struck him that the man I described might be Lugotov. Nikki telephoned Georgi to tell him."

"Nikki knew Georgi was in Chicago?" I asked skeptically.

"They have kept their friendship over these years," she countered. "Do you find that so strange, Nora?"

I did not answer.

"We were all from the same neighborhood in Leningrad's Vyborg district. We all starved together, lost family together. Everybody knew of Semyon Lugotov and his birthmark. Before he had a beard to hide it, we saw it every day."

I nodded grudgingly. "And how did Georgi find Lugotov?"

"It couldn't have been easier. Georgi said he found Lugotov's name and address in the phone book. Lugotov was either too stupid or too brash to change his name when he came to this country. When Georgi began watching him, he knew it was Lugotov." With a shake of her head, she added, "Georgi must have been shocked. Imagine, Lugotov in Chicago, right under his nose."

"Glazunov had been looking for him before?" I said, surprised.

With a thin, ironic smile, she said, "Since January, 1942."

"What?"

"Oh, not actively. Georgi, like many survivors, had given up finding him. Georgi's feelings of revenge had probably been long forgotten, completely dormant."

Only more bewildered, I said, "Anna, you're assuming that I know what happened in Leningrad in 1942."

"It's coming," Anna said, "a little slowly, I know, but it's coming. You see, I am trying to unwind the feelings of half a century, and that's not easy. Like talking about my dead Misha and Merusha, it can hurt too much to . . ."

"I don't mean to push, but—"

"What I am trying to do, dearie, is to explain Georgi's reasons for the shootings."

"Explain?" I said. "He's killed a man and nearly killed a young mother. Can you explain that away?"

Anna stood from the couch and walked to the window. She peered out for a moment, her back to me; then slowly she turned and retraced her steps. She stopped short of the couch, yet close enough for me to notice her faint, soapy smell. Standing as tall over me as she knew how, she clasped her hands in front of her. I saw her face flush with resolution, and her eyes rage like blue fires, small and distant. Finally, she said, "Semyon Lugotov was a murderer, Nora."

"What?"

"A murderer, I said. During the Siege, he murdered Leningraders, dozens of them. Georgi is one of the survivors who knew that."

I felt the room's air tear through my open mouth. I said, limply, "That's ghastly."

Anna sat near me on the couch. She laid her hand gently on my forearm. "We're not done yet, dearie," she cautioned. "There's more."

"Fine, okay, I'm—"

"Lugotov murdered them for their meat," she interrupted. "To make them into meat patties to sell to the starving who still had a few rubles left to spend. He was a butcher. You would call him a *goddamned* butcher."

"My God—"

"He murdered and cut up his victims in Haymarket. You remember the map of Leningrad you showed me with Haymarket marked with an X?"

"Yes."

"Georgi must have sent that to Lugotov. As a taunt, I suppose, along with the copy of my letter."

"Tell me more about Haymarket," I said.

"He usually strangled them," she said, "but maybe he shot

some. It was not important. If he did strangle them to death, it wouldn't have taken much effort, not at that point. They were usually already half-dead from starvation."

"You have proof, Anna, proof that Lugotov committed these murders?"

"Nora," she said, "everybody in Leningrad knew about the murderers like Lugotov. Would people lie about something like that?"

I didn't reply, just shook my head.

"There is more, dearie."

"What?"

She inhaled deeply again. "Lugotov also killed small children for their flesh," she said. "They were said to be better catches because they were more tender."

I cringed, trying to hold my face and body still.

Then Anna said, "There are horrors from Leningrad you don't know yet, Nora, other outrages that need to be considered before making judgments about us Leningraders. But I'm done talking about this for a while." She choked on her words.

For a moment, I was afraid to speak to her, afraid of what communion with her might lie ahead. We fell silent, each of us absorbed with the turmoil of our thoughts.

I spoke next. "I'm sorry, Anna, believe me, I'm deeply sorry about what happened to Leningraders at the hands of Lugotov. It was unpardonable."

"Unpardonable. Yes, that's the right word."

I moved a few inches closer to her, but was reluctant to take her hands into mine again. "Anna, do you see anything wrong with what Georgi has done?" I asked.

She looked away from me into the incandescence of the lamp at her other side, as though her answer might be found in the glow. Her eyes fixed, she slowly said, "In my view, it was wrong, yes. But when I talked with him this morning, he said that he sees he had become crazed by the need to kill Lugotov. The vengeance seemed justified, he said. He was doing what a Leningrad court should have done years ago."

She paused before adding, "But even at that, he's already remorseful. Georgi is a kind man, dearie, not a killer."

"Why didn't you ever tell me about the Glazunovs, Anna?"

"Because they were Leningraders. Talking about them would have led to Misha and Merusha and the Siege." She sighed faintly. "It was stupid of me, because you and Meg have become my family . . . if I might say that?"

"You know you can."

"It was too painful to tell. I wanted to—God knows I wanted to—but I could not find the strength, especially with Andrei gone. The longer I waited, the harder it became. Can you see that?"

I nodded my head, and my attention suddenly shifted to thoughts about chasing Glazunov. I felt better. "Where did Georgi go, Anna?"

"What?"

"I think you heard me," I said delicately. "They had suitcases in the car."

She leaned forward and propped her chin in her hands, aimlessly scanning the carpet in front of her. In sunlight, the color of the carpet was lime green, but that day it had lost all its freshness and had somehow taken up a dark, biological shade.

Unrelenting, I repeated, "Where did he go?"

"I am not sure."

"Can you guess?"

"Big Sand Lake," she said suddenly, not looking at me.

"Where?"

"To the summer cottage in Wisconsin."

"They're driving?"

"They must be." She brought her eyes to mine. The guilt she felt over her admission was evident.

"How far is it?" I asked.

"Six hours."

"You know where it is?"

"Of course. Didn't I say it was the place where we went for summer vacations?"

"Is there anyone else who might know for sure if he's going there? His secretary, maybe?"

"I doubt it." Anna hesitated, then said, "Evan might know."

"Who?"

"Evan, the caretaker for the cottages at Big Sand. Georgi may have phoned him to open the cottage. It would still be closed this early in the season."

"Can you call this Evan? I'd like to know for sure that's where Georgi's going."

"I have his number," Anna said.

She left the couch for the bedroom and her telephone. While she was gone, I paced the room, flipping through my options, shuffling responsibilities, possibilities, deciding. Anna returned in several minutes. "Evan said Georgi called this morning and is on his way. Evan's already got a fire going in the cottage."

"I'm going there," I said. "I have to follow him. Tell me how to get there."

Anna mechanically smoothed her skirt with her hand, then announced, "I'm going with you, dearie."

"I'm sorry, you can't. This is police business. You're a civilian."

"You're going to need me to talk to him for you," she said. "You're planning to arrest him, aren't you? You're not planning to shoot him?"

"We don't shoot people unless they're shooting at us. We want him alive, not dead."

"Then you need me to talk to him for you. He's despondent."

I turned Anna's idea over in my mind. The use of civilian help in making an arrest for violent crime ran counter to all Department policy, but Anna did have a point. If Glazunov could be tracked and caught, Anna was probably more likely to convince him to surrender than I was. "Okay, you can come," I said, feeling like a renegade.

Anna's bedroom, which faced the alley and had only one small window, was even darker than the living room. Meg slouched in a chair, mesmerized by the television. From the bedside telephone, I dialed Art at Area Six.

"I've found him, Arthur," I said, a spark of excitement in my voice. "Glazunov's the one, no question. I have a witness of sorts, even—someone he told of the murder after it happened."

"Okay, girl, where are you? Let's pick him up."

"I'm in Rogers Park, in my building," I said. "But he's not here—in the city, I mean. He's headed for Big Sand Lake."

"Where?"

"It's in Wisconsin."

"Aw, shit, that lets us out," Art said dejectedly. "We have to turn it over."

A pause while I pulled absentmindedly at my lower lip. A garbage truck rumbled down the alley outside.

"Are you there?"

"Yes, but only for a minute," I said, not a fleck of uncertainty in my voice. "I'm going after him, Art."

"What? C'mon, Nora, get off your high horse. Wisconsin's not your jurisdiction, and you can't do a thing about it. Now, get back down here and we'll get some help."

"I said I'm going after him. You'll understand later when you hear it all."

"You can't make an arrest in Wisconsin," he said. "Do you understand that you can't bring him in from there?"

"I understand that. I'll get a local cop to do it."

"What local cop?" Art ranted. "You think they have local cops? They're all cheeseheads up there, Nora, maybe throw in a few deer-hunters and fishermen. Oh, that's it—get a cheeser game warden to go with you and make the arrest. Arrest Glazunov for not having a valid fishing license."

"Keep talking," I said. "I'm feeling even better."

"I'm not."

"Don't worry. We'll be fine."

"*We'll*? What's the *we'll*?"

"My baby-sitter's going with me."

"After Glazunov?"

"Yes."

Silence intervened for a moment before I said, "Art, are you still there?"

"Goddammit, Nora!" he exploded. "Your baby-sitter can't go with you! She's civilian!"

"It'll be all right. I need her."

"Are you sick? Have you gone fuckin' crazy on me? Do you understand me? Are we both speaking English?"

I smiled. "I'm fine, really. This will work out. Take my word for it."

After a moment, he said, "Okay, do it."

"I intend to. Thanks, Art."

"Yeah, thanks. Oh, what about Meg? Need me to pick her up from school?"

"No, she's with me now. I think I'll drop her off at my sister's."

"Okay."

"I'll make this up to you," I said.

"Sure, sure. Can you give me a new set of coronaries?"
I laughed.

"Say, be careful, girl. I haven't noticed Glazunov to be full of good humor lately. You might be next."

"Bye, Arthur. I'll keep in touch."

22

With Anna in the passenger's seat and Meg in the rear, I barreled up the Kennedy Expressway at seventy miles per hour, my Fury's grand, gas-hogging engine humming quietly, showing no strain. On days like this, when even the lakefront was grim, I found the Kennedy intolerable. Huge billboards, all garishly colored and lit, stood chaotically near ancient, rusting factories, buildings embraced at their edges by piled refuse and ash heaps. Then, there was the scatter of loose hubcaps and hurt, abandoned cars on the road's shoulder, and the blanket of general litter and grime that dusted the weedy upsweep of ground leading to the side streets. For years people had referred to the crumbling neighborhoods and parkways that bordered this expressway as "the uglification of Chicago." It was the city at its visual worst, and I felt personally embarrassed by it.

At eleven o'clock, we finally passed from the jangling sprawl of the western suburbs into the flat, broad hush of the Illinois prairie. Half an hour later, as the rain tapered to mist, I turned off at Marengo and drove to Cait's home. Cait was happy to watch Meg for the day, and I should just call if I wanted Meg to stay the night. Before I left, Tim, Cait's oldest, had Meg by the hand as they headed for the barn.

When the highway turned north to penetrate Wisconsin's

southern border, we left the interstate. Bladders full and stomachs empty, we came to a truckstop named The Oasis. No camels rested, only dozens of trucks and a mammoth plastic milk cow in the middle of the parking lot. The pink paint had been worn off the cow's teats by the inquisitive hands of vacationing city children who would probably never come closer to a dairy farm than this patch of asphalt.

Inside the restaurant, Anna and I perched on counter stools and ordered lunch. While we waited for our food, I asked, "Anna, did Georgi know how he made the mistake of shooting Eva?"

Anna, with her elbows on the counter, sipped ice water from a scratched glass. "He had no idea how that happened. He said he left the church thinking Lugotov was dead in the box."

"When did Georgi find out?" I asked.

"That Eva was shot, not Lugotov?"

"Yes."

"I don't know. On the news, maybe?"

Anna's replies were coming quickly, the tone of her voice showing no reluctance. She was concealing nothing. I didn't mention the burned-out confessional light; there was no point in plumbing the subject.

A waitress clattered silverware onto the countertop in front of us. When she moved away, I drummed my fingernails on the Formica and said, "You know, Anna, there's a sticky point about Eva here. A couple of days after she was shot, her husband walked into the Eighteenth and handed over ten thousand dollars in cash—said he had found it in his mailbox and it wasn't his."

"Ten thousand? It was that much?"

"You knew about it?"

"Just that Georgi told me yesterday how guilty he felt about shooting Eva Ramirez. He had even been calling the hospital to see how she was feeling. He told me he left her family some money as atonement, but I had no idea it was that much." She smiled and said, "Didn't I tell you Georgi was a good man?"

"It was thoughtful of him," I said. "He's a man of great contradictions."

"No, he's not at all," Anna said sternly. "There has not been an ounce of violence in Georgi's life until the past week, dearie. Since then, he's shot Eva purely by accident, and he's killed Lugotov. Like I said earlier, the murder was justice that should have been delivered years ago. I believe that firmly. I know what you have to do, Nora, I understand it, but I still believe Georgi is innocent in God's eyes."

"And hanging the body on a hook?"

Now she put her hands to her face, over her nose and mouth, and looked straight ahead, away from me. I let the question go unanswered.

When the food came, I wolfed down a cheeseburger and french fries. Anna had a grilled cheese, for which she showed no appetite. It lay moribund on her plate while she drank hot tea and stared vacantly at the chrome coffee urns and the malt mixers. With her thin, bent shoulders jutting up in her raincoat, she looked as brittle as I had ever seen her.

The weather worsened as we made the northern half of the state: the temperature dropped into the upper thirties, and the day was now more like winter than spring. When the rain returned, it came steadier and harder, blown by an unyielding, chilling wind from the north. The rain pounded the barnyards and haystacks and dairy herds all across Wisconsin. Water collected in puddles in the fields and along the gravel roadsides.

For the first hour after we left the truckstop, Anna remained solemnly quiet. Finally, I said, "What are you thinking about, Anna?"

"The war, I think, mainly the war."

Anxious to get her talking, I said, "Tell me how it started. How did you first know? Were you bombed or what?"

Surprisingly quick to answer, she said, "Oh, no, dearie. No bombs at first. We were on vacation in the forest south of Leningrad. I heard it announced on the radio, on a broadcast by Molotov, one of Stalin's men. I was cooking in our rented cabin when I heard it. It was about noon—a hot day, really blistering. Andrei was outside with Misha, near the lake. We had had a wonderful, long walk around the lake that morning, before the heat came."

"How old would Misha have been then?"

"Four years."

"And your daughter? Merusha?"

"I was pregnant with her that summer." After a pause, Anna said, "She lived for one month, dearie. Did you know they both died on the same day?"

"You told me that the other night."

"Oh, yes. I suppose I did, yes."

Now Anna lapsed into another silence for thirty miles or more. Then, suddenly, she said, "You know, dearie, there were some weeks we had to go to the lobby of our building every night."

"Why, Anna?" I said.

"The firebombs. It was phosphorus they dropped on us. Those bombs screamed as they fell, and if they hit nearby, the floor shook. I always held Misha tight, but that didn't stop him from shaking. And it wasn't just the children who shook. Even Communists made the sign of the cross and prayed."

Out of the corner of my eye, I saw her cross herself; then she adjusted herself in the seat and went on in free flow.

"One night, after we returned to our apartment from a raid, Misha began sobbing in my arms. He couldn't stop and he couldn't speak. He could only cry. Odd, because he had been so quiet in the lobby, his eyes pushed wide open with fright, but quiet. When Andrei came into the living room and saw Misha sobbing, he took him from me. Andrei sat and wrapped his long arms around Misha, nearly swallowing the boy into his chest.

He rocked Misha for an hour—maybe more—while he sang him a Russian lullaby. The sobbing stopped but Misha stayed mute. Then Andrei tucked Misha's face under his own chin and rocked some more till they both finally slept. I watched the two of them by the light of a fire that burned in the building across the street."

She touched a hand to her lips. "Funny, I remember that so. I wish I had a photograph of Andrei holding Misha that night . . . but I guess I don't need one. It's all still so clear. Strange what sticks with me through the years."

Then, as if her spring had wound down once again, Anna fell silent. My thoughts moved randomly from Anna's Leningrad stories to Glazunov's dilemma. The things Anna had told me about Lugotov back at her apartment had finally begun to sink in. The thought of a butcher like Lugotov not paying with his life for what he had done seemed abhorrent. And then there were the murders of the children: I was beginning to understand the powerful motive for Glazunov's vengeance. Not an excuse, I decided, but surely a mitigating factor.

At a town called Indian Bend—stop sign, white frame church, small grocery, two-pump gas station, and brick-walled tavern with a picture window—we left the interstate for the secondary roads. Now closer to the fields, we could see the first shoots of infant corn plants poking from the inky, wet soil. Only inches high, the leafy spikes were all symmetrical in their rows, rows that rushed by the car like long, moving green stilts. By midafternoon we were deep into North Woods, every road tightly enclosed by tall pine and birch, walls of trees that pressed in on the narrow blacktop and held out what little light the afternoon offered.

In the dimness, Anna spoke again. "What will happen to Georgi when you arrest him, dearie?"

"He'll be charged. Probably with a count of first-degree and another of attempted murder."

"But he was crazed, Nora. Won't that help him?"

"It could, yes, of course. It might mostly matter who defends him."

"You mean which lawyer?" Anna asked.

"Yes. It seems the truth, whatever that is, is not always definable. Then the lawyer means a lot. His or her manner in court."

"But you think he will go to jail?"

"A good chance. But you can't tell. I've seen them turn murderers loose who had far less going for them than Georgi."

"But you will help to keep him out of jail, Nora?"

I thought for a moment before answering. "I need to talk to him, Anna," I said. "Let me talk to him before saying."

"Would you let him escape, Nora? Today, I mean. Just let him go?"

I gripped harder at the Fury's steering wheel. Startled by the question, I couldn't answer her.

After another fifty or hundred miles—who could know?—I glanced over and noticed Anna dozing, her mouth hanging slightly open, her head back against the headrest. Listening to the steady drum of the rain, I thought again about Anna's dead children. It seemed an incredible burden of sorrow for one person to bear, and still go on. And, as awful as Anna's Leningrad horrors sounded now, nearly fifty years later, I knew the retelling couldn't approach what it actually must have been like to live through that time. I realized how much I had come to admire this woman sleeping next to me. And to think that I had known her for these several years and had never asked about her past, never shown a proper interest in her life and feelings.

As the terrain swept into deeper valleys and taller hills, the rain began to pelt the car more violently, and Anna awoke. "You had a good nap," I said.

She was quiet for a moment, wiping moisture from her eyes. "I was dreaming."

"About what?"

She smiled. "It wasn't one of those crazy dreams. It was a dream of memory. It must have come from all the talk we've had today about the war."

"You don't have to tell me, Anna. It's okay. Really."

"No. I want to."

I switched off the radio which had been quietly playing in the background.

"My dream was from that first day of the war," she said. "I remembered that morning I told you about, the lovely time we had had at the lake—Andrei, Misha, and me. The heat, the sun, those things we had wished for through the long winter. That may not sound like much, but it was as wonderful a morning as I have ever had in my life."

"Don't say it doesn't sound like much," I said.

She nodded. "Next, we were back in Leningrad—we had taken the train home after the announcement of war. Our apartment had been closed up all week, and it was hard to sleep in the heat. Then, just as we dozed off, the ground cannon began firing at German planes overhead. The noise was terrible. It felt like it would split our ears."

As Anna talked, she kept her eyes rigidly ahead. "We all went to the small vestibule in the building till the bombing ended—in about an hour, I would say—then we walked back up to our apartments. I put Misha back to bed, then—"

She stopped and turned to me, a small, crimped smile on her lips. "After Andrei and I came back to our bedroom, we lay in bed on our backs. It was nearly dawn by then, and the air in the room had finally started to cool. I can remember we held each other for quite a long while, and then, instead of sleeping, as I had expected we finally would, we made love."

She spoke the word "love" so quietly it barely floated over to me. "I can even still smell him—can you imagine?"

Not pausing for an answer, she continued. "It was enchanting, moving with him like that. It took us out of our day and night of horror. It was like a sanctuary where the war could not intrude. Hitler and Stalin gave no orders there."

She paused thoughtfully, then, with a slight, embarrassed laugh, said, "It was Andrei's idea, dearie—making love that night, I mean. He said he wanted to feel the baby kick him in the belly as it had been kicking me."

By now, I had slowed the car considerably, my attention riveted to Anna and scarcely on the road. When I next looked from the road to her face, I saw a broad smile.

"This memory of mine may not sound like much—a couple makes love thousands of times in a long marriage. But that time was so special to me because somehow I used the memory of it to help me survive Leningrad. I mean, when I was starving, when my family was dying around me . . ."

"It's the most beautiful dream I have ever heard, Anna. I've never had a dream like that in my life."

"But you still have Meg."

"Of course," I said, "and so do you."

Anna nodded her head. "I do, yes. And I have you, Nora. Thank God for that."

We spoke no more till Big Sand. I felt profoundly honored that Anna had told me these things. Then it struck me that I had come to love this fine Russian woman.

23

We left Phelps—a small, unremarkable town carved into the North Woods—behind us in fog. By four in the afternoon, we were on Highway 17, eight miles from Big Sand Lake. Ahead, to the north, we heard soft, distant rumbles of thunder. The fog had thickened, visibility down to a hundred feet, so I drove the road slowly.

Anna showed me the way, and except for the fog, the last miles were easy: a straight shot, no turns, only a series of high, roller-coaster hills whose tops were lost in the afternoon's dimness. The newly budding trees along the roadside were dark green and dripping, while the dead ones, the broken and black ones, grew only mold and yellow fungus.

At the last mile before the turnoff, an arrow of lightning brightened the insides of the thick clouds above. I felt the tension swelling in me, almost beginning to overtake me. Most murders I had worked on required weeks or months of effort, and by the time of making an arrest, I often felt choked by the familiarity of the case, my initial outrage at the killing usually in decline. The last hours before bringing in the killer tended to be tedious and anticlimactic, rarely frenzied.

But not so this day. It had been less than a week since I had knelt next to an unconscious and bleeding Eva Ramirez; only two days since I had seen Lugotov's body stretched out dead at his door; and just over a day and a half since I had seen that same body dangling grotesquely from a ceiling pipe. This case had taken little time to develop, and it felt as explosively compressed as any I had ever been involved in.

"This is the turn," Anna said, pointing at an unmarked break in the trees on our right.

I slowed the car and turned down into the dip of a drainage ditch, then back up to the level. The road ahead was narrow and made of half-broken asphalt and rutted gravel. Rainwater had collected here and there in the low spots; a dense overhang of trees so darkened the way that it seemed more night than day. On our right, behind a solid wall of forest, lay the eastern edge of the lake. On our left was the grassy airfield that brought vacationers in summer, but now had dwindled into a treacherous mud flat lit only by an occasional shine of lightning.

"Go around the curve up ahead," Anna said, moving to the window for a better view. "The cottages will be on our right. Georgi's is the fourth."

I took the curve; the Fury was barely creeping, but my mind raced with the dilemma that had been building in me for miles. I knew it was why I felt so agitated as I approached Big Sand. Was I prepared to arrest Georgi Glazunov? And if I was, and he resisted, was I willing to shoot him?

Through Anna, I had come to sympathize with Glazunov, to realize that he was not a cold-blooded killer like the ones I faced on Chicago's North Side—the kind who would just as soon shoot you as look at you, the kind who killed out of avarice, or malice, or simple boredom. I had come to see Glazunov, unlike them, as a still-grieving son of Leningrad who did what any system of justice should have done: punished Lugotov by taking his life. Was Glazunov's execution of Lugotov really any different, morally or ethically, from the State's doing it? In the same circumstances, I could see myself giving in to that kind of vengeance, demanding the proverbial eye for an eye.

And I also knew that the mechanics of allowing Glazunov to escape from Big Sand couldn't be more obliging. I had no jurisdiction in Wisconsin, so I could not arrest him myself. And where could I find local help? In Phelps, a two-intersection town now encased in fog and rain? Of course not. Even if the town did have a policeman, he was probably sitting in a windowless tavern fortifying himself against the weather with warm brandy. Before I could be expected to find decent professional help, Glazunov could be allowed to run to Michigan's Upper Peninsula, or even Canada.

"Now, there it is," Anna said, sounding uncannily calm, "there's Georgi's place. The second cottage ahead. Stop here for a minute."

I did as ordered. Craning my neck, I looked through the rain-spotted windows at a neat yellow frame cottage attended by huge pine and birch trees. The birches, heavy with water, leaned their supple branches over the cottage. The roof was busy with water rushing for the gutters. There wasn't a light in any window. The building was some thirty yards ahead of us and twenty yards off the road.

"Looks pretty quiet," I said.

"Drive up a little further," Anna said.

We idled slowly forward until Anna stopped me well short of the red Escort parked at the side of the road.

I slipped the Fury into Park, then rustled through my purse. I brought out my .38, holding it backward, by its black barrel. Anna looked away. I found the gun's chambers fully loaded with cartridges. I was ready.

"You said you weren't planning to shoot him," Anna said, turning back.

"I'm not, Anna."

"But—"

"If he shoots at me—and he might, he seems so crazy with

what's happened—if he shoots at me, I'm going to have to return the fire. Do you see that?"

She broke a small smile of understanding. "I suppose so, dearie."

I slipped the gun into my right-hand coat pocket. Seeing the cottage, I felt better somehow, less anxious about what I was going to do. And my body wasn't responding with the same shaking betrayal it had for a time that morning, when I had seen Glazunov in the hallway outside his office. Feeling the strength of my fingers on the gun's handle somehow made me think of Jack Flaherty, my dead mentor.

And then, in just another instant, I resolved what I would do with Glazunov.

I would arrest him, arrest him under any pretense, then suffer the procedural consequences later. My job was to bring in killers—any killers—and Glazunov was a killer, even if of a different ilk and from a different time. Even if his mistake in shooting Eva had nearly been tragic, and even if his murder of Lugotov had been Biblical in proportion, these crimes were still murder and attempted murder. I hadn't been trained to abet a killer's escape, and Glazunov was here to escape.

A round of thunder sounded close overhead. I decided to leave the car here, but to keep it running. I turned to Anna and said, "What might happen here may be hard for you."

She nodded.

"You might want to stay in the car. It's dry in here."

"No, I'm going," she said resolutely.

"Then you'll have to stay back at least, in case there is gunplay."

"I will."

I paused for several moments. "Anna, for a while, when we were driving, I thought maybe I should let Georgi go, let him run to Canada or wherever he's headed. I thought that because you've helped me understand why he did what he did. I can sympathize more with him now. He didn't kill like Lugotov killed."

"No, he didn't."

I glanced down at the floor of the car, then back up into Anna's pleading eyes. Softly and deliberately, I said, "But now I've decided I can't do that, Anna. I can't let him go. He's shot two people, one of them completely innocent." I looked away again, then continued: "I would like to let him go . . . for you, Anna, because I love you . . . but I can't do it."

When I turned back, Anna's face showed her assent. "I know you can't, dearie. I'm not sure I really believe what I said earlier—about the eyes of God, I mean. I suppose there's no justification for what Georgi has done. In front of God, I think even Georgi probably knows that."

I buttoned my coat and pulled the collar up around my neck. I refingered the gun in my pocket.

"But I want to be with him when you do it," Anna said, "and with Sophie. You can understand that?"

"Yes."

I noticed a light come on in the back porch of the cottage. A door opened and Glazunov emerged, bundled in his long raincoat and wearing his dark, floppy hat. I inhaled deeply. "There he is," I said as he walked down a stone path to his car.

With the Fury's engine still purring, I quietly opened my door and slid out, careful not to close the door behind me. I told Anna not to turn off the engine and not to move until I had made my first contact with Glazunov, until I had seen his reaction.

The rain was falling in a steady, loud drone. My collar wasn't tight enough to keep it out, so my neck and blouse were quickly wet. My hair was soaked before I had walked a dozen steps. The footing, with deep puddles and loose gravel all the way, was difficult for me with my prosthesis. I moved carefully toward Glazunov; now he was at his car, opening the trunk, his back to me. He couldn't have heard me approach, because the pounding of the rain drowned out everything in the background.

When I was about thirty feet away, I reached into my coat pocket and grabbed my gun. I would not bring it out now, not just yet, but it must be ready. I narrowed my eyebrows into a frown of concentration and called out, "Georgi Glazunov!"

Glazunov turned, surprised, straining to see who now walked slowly toward him through the rain. "Who's there?" he said.

"My name is Lieutenant Nora Callum," I said. "I'm from the Chicago Police Department." I eased the gun from my pocket, but kept it at my side, against my right thigh. "You're under arrest, Mr. Glazunov, for the murder of Semyon Lugotov and the shooting of Eva Ramirez."

Glazunov straightened, but said nothing, looking as though he were trying to see me better as I moved closer. Finally, even with my hair drenched and falling onto my face, I decided he must have recognized me as the woman outside his office, the woman with the absurd story about the towing refund. For a second, and only that, he seemed ready to say something, but nothing came. Suddenly, he turned and ran.

"Stop!" I shouted. "Don't make me shoot!"

But shoot I couldn't, even though my finger made good early pressure on the trigger, even though the shot I had at him was an easy one, the kind I had drilled hundreds of times before on the firing range. My finger simply froze on the trigger.

Glazunov ran ahead of his car, down the road, his gait matching his short stride and his weight. To his right lay more cottages and the lake, to his left a row of scrub pine and young maples and birches. Several yards past the car he turned in to the thickness of the trees.

I was shaken. Minutes before, in the car, I had felt the strength to go ahead with this, and now I couldn't squeeze off a shot, just a simple wounding shot to bring him down. At first, I decided to return to the car and follow him in the Fury, but when he turned in to the trees, I knew the car would be worthless. I started running too, my pace no smoother or quicker than his. For an instant, I looked back for Anna, and saw her leave the car and follow. And from the cottage ran another woman, this one coatless—Sophie Glazunov.

Ahead, Glazunov cut quickly through the narrow row of trees to his left. Beyond them, he broke into a broad meadow of tall wild grasses. The meadow was mound-shaped, with a slight central rise.

I went into the trees, just behind him. Thunder banged more frequently now, the crashes coming closer and closer. At the base of a tree, my unfeeling plastic left foot caught in a tangle of vines and weeds. Going down face first, I struck my forehead on a tree trunk and opened a large gash across my right eyebrow. I lay on the muddy earth dazed, hearing the echo of the shot my gun had fired randomly when my hand hit the ground.

It was several seconds before I was able to raise my face out of the mud. Blood now ran down my cheek, mixing with dirt and rain. The musty smell of mud was thick in my nose. I didn't yet know I was cut, my face so wet with rain that I didn't sense the blood on my cheek.

Intent on following Glazunov, I pushed myself to my feet, then fought through the remaining tangle of trees and under-growth. Panting with effort, I entered the meadow where Glazunov now stood on the central rise.

"Glazunov!" I shouted again, and Glazunov ran again. He crossed the rise, and for a moment, I saw only the top of his white head, his hat long gone. The rain was driving down in near-blinding torrents, the wind throwing it so hard that the gash on my eyebrow was washed clean by its force. Thunder pounded the sky remorselessly.

I started up the rise. I felt no pain in my face, but my stump ached from running. At the top of the rise, I found Glazunov again, now standing below me, near a broken wooden building some twenty yards ahead, at the edge of the meadow. It was a roofless, ancient barn with two walls missing and two still clinging together. Glazunov stood in the crotch of the walls, facing me.

I was puzzled that he didn't run around the walls and into another stand of trees just beyond. I looked for a gun in his hand and saw none. I started toward him again, my gun at my side, against my thigh.

"Georgi Glazunov!" I yelled through the hammering rain. "You're under arrest! Come away from there!"

Glazunov still said nothing. I moved closer, now elevating my gun from my side, as if asking it to lead my way. But I didn't need the gun: Glazunov was done. Spent, he stood motionless, dripping and strangely transfixed. Fear stretched across his face, like that of a terrified, trapped animal. I lowered my gun to my side. Anna and Sophie ran past me to him.

24

Still suffering almost half a century after their torment should have ended, the three Leningraders tramped ahead of me in single file, up the soaked stone path to the cottage. Stout Sophie dutifully led the way, Anna next, then Glazunov. Out of habit, I clutched my gun in my right hand, but it wasn't necessary. Docile Glazunov had given no trace of resistance. The rain, mercifully, had eased to a drizzle; I may have heard a songbird calling from high in a birch. My left hand pressed the handkerchief Anna had given me against the cut on my forehead. My stump hurt with each step, as though I might have torn loose some scar during my fall.

Once inside the cottage, the others formed into a circle and seemed to await my direction. I glanced quickly about the large, square room where we stood. Ahead of me was a bay window, and outside that, a lawn pitched gently downward toward the gray, choppy water of Big Sand Lake. At my left, a wood fire licked us with orange light and perfumed us with a fragrance like none I had ever smelled. On my right, a long hallway, lit by a ceiling lamp, led from the room and ended at the doorway to a kitchen. The fire warmed the air around us.

I took Anna's handkerchief from my forehead; the bleeding had stopped. My hands and clothes were streaked with dirt and blood from my fall. "Please, we should sit," I said.

Anna and Sophie chose a couch near the fireplace. Glazunov the gentleman remained respectfully quiet until they were seated, then spoke: "I would like to get out of my coat, Lieutenant."

A benign request.

"Sure," I said. "Of course."

He turned and started down the hallway. My good leg exhausted, I dropped into a nearby chair and watched him closely. Halfway down the hall, he slipped from his long black coat and hung it on a rack on the wall. The dripping coat glistened under the light like a huge, dark fish hooked through its mouth.

When Glazunov returned to the room, I stood and patted him down—arms, torso, and legs—with my left hand, my right one still holding the gun. He carried no weapon. I asked him to sit in the chair across from mine. I returned my gun and its threat to my purse, then put the purse on the floor near my chair.

At first, everybody seemed too tired to speak; the fire provided the only sounds we heard. Finally, into the vacuum, I launched, "Professor Glazunov, do you know who I am?"

He nodded.

"May I call you Georgi?"

An identical nod. He was in the same blue sport coat and white turtleneck that he had been wearing at his office that morning.

"You may call me Nora," I said, "if you like, that is."

Anna gave me a small smile of thanks at my offer, an option that Georgi would never choose to exercise.

"We will drive back to Chicago tonight," I announced. I waited for a response, but the three Leningraders remained silent, so I went on. "But before we leave, I would like to ask you some questions, Georgi. For my sake."

With this, Anna rose and said, "I'm getting Band-Aids for your forehead, dearie. In the kitchen, Sophie?"

Sophie answered yes. They left in tandem: schoolgirls too fearful to travel alone.

Now Georgi settled his girth back into his chair. The features of his round face looked as soft as a cotton doll's, his snowy hair and mustache soaked by the rain. His eyes were as dark as coal.

"Would you be willing to answer questions without an attorney present?" I asked him.

"I'll answer," he said.

I had no plan of inquiry, so I started at the beginning, at Holy Name Cathedral. "We have you at the Cathedral on Saturday afternoon, chasing Lugotov, but how is it that you shot Eva Ramirez?"

"An accident," he said. "I thought Lugotov ran into the box after he shot at me in the back of the church. I thought I was shooting him through the door, but it was the woman. I still don't know where he could have been."

"We think somebody was in the other box," I said, "probably Lugotov. The light above the door was burnt out."

"Oh," Georgi said flatly, not seeming to care. But then he added with sincerity, "How is the woman?"

"Very well," I said. "She's expected to go home from the hospital in a day or so."

"Without residuals?"

"What?"

"Her wounds will heal without future problems?" he explained.

"I think so," I said, then added, "Nothing beyond her psychological scars, that is."

"I feel very badly about her wounding, Lieutenant." He seemed to be opening just a crack to me now, though his tone was still despondent and without animation. "She wasn't meant to be there."

I offered a smile just wide enough to tell him that I believed what he said. "The money you left was very generous, Georgi."

"You know that? The amount?"

"Juan Ramirez, Eva's husband, brought it into the station. We have it."

Surprised, Georgi said, "The man must be a saint."

I needed to backtrack for some confirmations. I said, "Tell me, how did you know Lugotov was in Chicago?"

"From Anna's letter to Nikki. He sent it to me from Leningrad. We both knew who it was that Anna saw at the library but couldn't identify."

"Nikki knew Lugotov?" I said.

"As well as I did. Like me, Nikki was beaten by him when we were boys. Lugotov was a bully long before he was a teenaged murderer. If you're beaten like Nikki was, you don't forget."

"How did you know where Lugotov lived?" I asked.

"The phone book."

I moved on. "Next, we have you in Lugotov's apartment building, sometime between midnight and 4 a.m. That would be Wednesday morning."

Georgi folded his hands. Speaking deliberately, he said, "It was three in the morning. I couldn't sleep. You won't understand this, but I felt wild with knowing he was still alive and Eva Ramirez had been shot. I went to kill him that night, no matter what happened to me. I didn't give a damn."

"And he opened the door to you? With his gun in his hand?"

"I waited on the floor. I shot up into him before he could look down. He never got a shot off."

"We found a key on the floor where you'd waited. The key opened the Ramirez mailbox."

His eyebrows lifted in mild surprise. "I didn't know I dropped it," he said. "I haven't thought about it since I left the money in the box."

"Where did you get the key?"

"There's a shop for keys and locks in Hyde Park. I went in and told the man I had lost the key to my mailbox. He believed me. He sold me a few keys and said he expected one of them would probably work."

The women came back to the room carrying cups and a porcelain pot steaming with tea. While Anna tended to my forehead, Sophie filled the cups and passed them around with a sugar bowl. She apologized for having no cream. For a few minutes, nobody spoke except to thank Sophie for the tea; we were satisfied to warm our bones with the sweet brew. As I drank, thoughts of Meg distracted me.

Days later, I would reflect sorrowfully on what little value my police training had been to me that afternoon. Oh, my instructors had taught me matters of protocol, and the rubrics of how to manage this situation or that, and when to sense projected danger becoming real, and how to act like the model citizen. But what about the day when your personal construction of the world turns upside down, flip-flops onto its head? What then? And worse, whom might you call for help if you suddenly feel yourself aligned with a murderer?

The questions would go unanswered.

The heat of the tea now burrowing inside me, I said, "Before we go, there's one more thing I wish to ask, Georgi."

He set his cup on a table next to him; his motions were unexaggerated but somehow grave. He placed his hands on his knees and looked directly at me, his eyes giving me permission to inquire.

"Why now?" I said. "Why kill him all these years later?"

"Because I had the chance," he said without hesitation.

"Did it mean that much? Still?"

"She doesn't understand it yet, Georgi," Anna interjected, "the justice, I mean."

"Then I will give you some details, Lieutenant," he said. "Do you know of the Siege of Leningrad?"

"I have read some about it," I said, "and Anna has told me more."

"Then you know we were all starving to death . . . well, most of us."

"Yes."

"It's in books, isn't it?" he said sardonically.

"Yes, it is," I said.

He paused to inhale deeply—for effect, I thought. "Let me tell you a story, Lieutenant, a story from the Siege. It is one that circulated through Vyborg, our district. It is probably one of many similar stories told in Leningrad during those years. Some people knew the stories to be truth, others said they were only myth. You're an intelligent woman, Lieutenant. I'll let you decide about this one."

I felt a galaxy apart from these people and what they had experienced and whom they had known, as though I had been dropped onto a remote planet that orbited a distant star. An alien in this room, I shifted in my chair.

Georgi sat unmoving except for his lips and the occasional blink of his eyelids. He started with "Imagine yourself in Leningrad, in January, 1942. The Haymarket section. Picture a young man, a sixteen-year-old—a boy, really—who crouches at the end of a long room, his bony buttocks resting uncomfortably on his heels. The gray, exhausted look of starvation is evident on the boy's face. His hair is stark: patches of thin brown stubble struggle to survive among fields of baldness. His haunted eyes languish so deeply in their sockets that they seem irretrievable."

Georgi spoke beautifully, his faint accent only complementing his English, the rhythms of his speech mesmerizing. He seemed to be looking straight through me, to the other side.

"Since entering the room thirty minutes before, the boy hasn't moved, Lieutenant, except for his shivering. But it isn't the cold that makes him tremble, because his thick canvas coat manages to hold what heat his body generates. No, he quivers because of what he sees suspended in front of him."

I felt my forehead wrinkle in a frown.

Georgi went on: "What the boy sees are frozen, naked bodies—two skinny women and one skinnier man—hanging in a neat row, on great black hooks screwed into the ceiling beams. The women have been hooked through their pelvic bones because women's pelvises are wide, for childbearing, and easy to snag. This folds them at their waists, you see, and, somehow, their doubling over makes them seem only half as grotesque as their male companion. He has been slung up by his collarbone, his hook entering under the bottom of the bone, then emerging in the pale softness at the base of his neck. He hangs out at full length, like beef, but right side up."

I gasped audibly at the image: closing my eyes, I saw Lugotov in the County morgue, just in front of me, dangling and sweaty and sweetly-rotten-smelling. Two quick deep breaths to settle my stomach and I opened my eyes.

Georgi pushed on. "A thin spread of ice covers the white, lifeless skin of the three. The temperature this night will bottom at twenty degrees below zero, Lieutenant, and that kind of cold always brings the ice. Now, near midnight, winter moonlight shoots through the room's windows and dances across the bodies. The cold light charges the bodies' tiny ice crystals, millions of them, transforming them into blankets of diamonds. The dead are motionless, but the sparkle of their skin changes minute by minute as the moon ascends."

Georgi took a sip of tea and continued, his delivery still lyrical. If he hadn't told this story before, he had, at least, rehearsed it in his head a thousand times.

"The boy stands slowly and stiffly. In a minute, he feels himself loosen, his joints ready to carry him forward into the moon's brightness. He steps ahead, closing on the first of the two women's corpses, now noticing its heavy scent. Standing at arm's length, he brushes his hand across her icy buttock, then bends and fingers the tangle of hair that hangs from her scalp and touches the floor. Her age is unclear. Thirty? Fifty? Who can tell? Death and cold have washed the markers of age from her face, her face with its open mouth and broken teeth.

"Then the boy moves to the second body, this one as bare and frozen and ravaged by starvation as the first. This woman's lank arms hang down slackly, as in comfortable sleep. Her fingers point beneath her where a pancake of dark blood is frozen into the floor's sawdust. The boy doesn't touch this body, but before he turns his face away, he stares at the empty bags that were her breasts.

"Now, shuddering, the boy starts toward the last body, the man, the one whom he has come to this warehouse to find. He shuffles ahead with his eyes half-closed, unsure if he will be able to open them when the time comes. When his foot bumps into something on the floor, he looks and sees the dead man's thigh and leg that have been hacked away from his torso and now lie beneath him. The sight of the bloodless leg bends the boy at his waist and sickens him. He swallows quickly to keep from vomiting."

In my lightning rush of anxiety, Georgi disappeared from in front of me, melted into a white hot light that was all my eyes could make out. My stump suddenly screamed with the same pain I had on the night I had been shotgunned. I couldn't see Anna in the blinding light, but I heard her. "You're okay, dearie?" she asked.

"Fine," I lied.

"She's had an amputation herself, Georgi," Anna said.

"I'm sorry, Lieutenant," Georgi said.

"It's nothing," I said. My vision was beginning to clear. Georgi's ovoid form was sharpening again. "Go on with your story. Please."

"Now, as the boy regains some balance, he slides his feet closer to the corpse, all the while moving his vision upwards from the floor. His brain sorts out the images: the man's remaining leg, his icy genitals, his skeletal chest. At the man's neck, next to the long shaft of the hook, the boy sees a deep rope burn of strangulation."

A brief pause, then Georgi said, "Now the boy moves his eyes over the final hurdle, onto the body's colorless, emaciated face and its stubbly beard. Without a sound, he steps forward and squeezes the body tightly around its waist. He begins to weep. It is his father."

I gasped.

"May I finish?" Georgi asked me.

"Of course."

"The boy stands entranced," Georgi said, "embracing his father's body for a full hour, his tears chilling on his cheeks before they fall from his chin. In his grief, he cannot feel the pull of time, or even the cold, or his hunger. Nor does he hear the footsteps that thump softly across the floor behind him."

Georgi shifted slightly in his chair, his first move in several minutes.

"This is a tall, powerful eighteen-year-old who moves in on him, Lieutenant. This boy's cheeks are full and rosy. His hair's soft yellow color and bushy texture show that he has been eating, and eating regularly. When close enough, the eighteen-year-old chops his thick forearm hard across the back of the grieving boy's skull.

"For a moment, the shock of the blow causes the younger boy to clamp harder onto his father's trunk, but then he releases and drops to the floor, falling on top of his father's butchered thigh and leg. Before he can slide off, he feels a kick in his gut, a kick that throws him over onto his back. He looks up and sees the face of the eighteen-year-old, a face that he recognizes and half-expected to see. You're with me, Lieutenant?"

"Yes."

"Now the younger boy starts to rise," Georgi said, "making it to a crouch before he is knocked back by more hard kicks, these into his testicles. He rolls again, scraping his face across the floor. As he spits blood and sawdust, he feels himself being lifted up from the floor and hauled to the door. Thrown onto the building's outside staircase, he spills down its long course to the street below. In his pain, he still notices somehow that the moon has disappeared, and dense white snow now falls through the night, snow made of huge flakes that stick crazily to his bloody face."

Apparently finished, Georgi sat quietly, as did Anna and Sophie.

After a minute, Georgi finally said. "I lived this story. The snowflakes on my face, the kicks in my testicles, my strangled and butchered father."

"You are the boy?" I said. "And Lugotov—"

"Yes," he said.

"Jesus," I whispered, my fingers at my lips.

Georgi probed, "Did you see Lugotov in the morgue? Hanging, I mean?"

"Yes." I shuddered. My eyes were filling with tears that I tried to hold back.

Anna looked at me. "Nora, it was payment in kind. Hanging Lugotov, I mean."

I could think of nothing to say.

Then Georgi said emphatically, "On the way home that night, Lieutenant, I resolved that if I was ever given the chance, I would kill Lugotov. I would need no forethought, no wringing of my hands. I would simply kill him, God on my side. By dumb luck, I was given that chance this week, and I didn't waste it. What I did to Mrs. Ramirez was accidental but wrong. What I did to Lugotov was not pleasurable to me, but it was just. I try to think that my killing him was justice without vengeance . . . but I doubt if I'm that pure."

He paused for a moment, then asked me, "Do you know Shakespeare?"

"Some. A little."

"Shakespeare is a hobby of mine," he said. "If an instructor is sick, I will sometimes teach it to the undergraduates."

"I see."

"Have you read *Othello?*"

"A long time ago," I answered.

"Then you might remember a scene when Othello speaks about his bloody thoughts and how they goad him on, and will goad him until swallowed by what he calls a capable and wide revenge. Othello's need for revenge was nursed by naïveté, Lieutenant, but not mine. My father's murder and butchery were not works of my imagination—I saw his hanging body; I kicked his butchered leg. My revenge against Lugotov may have been delayed, but it was wide and capable."

Georgi stopped there. Spent, we all sat where we were, nobody moving. It was quiet in the room: we heard only the fire snapping and the drizzle kissing the rooftop.

25

The phone was near the doorway where we had entered the cottage. My call to Cait was brief—so brief, in fact, that she probably thought me rude. I told her we would be leaving for Chicago soon, and yes, yes, I was all right. She said Meg was fine, and that Tim and Meg had spent the afternoon slopping hogs. I smiled weakly at Cait's jest, but couldn't find the energy for a retort. She said Meg wanted to spend the night.

Next, I called Area Six and spoke to Art. We agreed that as soon as I was within the city limits, I would radio the station to call him at home. He said he wanted to help with Glazunov's formal arrest.

The notion hatched in me instantaneously, probably during the short walk back to my chair. It must have erupted from inner turmoil, from Georgi's story, like a new bird poking defiantly out of its eggshell, needing light.

Now, seated in my chair, I formed it into words. Counter to all rationality, I said: "Georgi, there is a piece of me that says I should drive back to Phelps with Anna, to look for a local police officer to arrest you. It would take half an hour or more. You would have some time here with Sophie, alone. Even if there are any police in Phelps, they wouldn't know I've already been here."

The women squirmed on the couch, stunned by the implicit offer of escape. Georgi, a sphinx, never moved.

My sedition startled me, yet I felt strangely liberated by it. Feeling more the renegade as the minutes passed, I looked for a rationalization, and found one. I decided that no code of law could measure the injury sustained by Georgi Glazunov almost fifty years ago. Anna had put it right: Lugotov had received payment in kind, nothing more. I understood that my proposition to Georgi was no way to run a society or a police force; still, I managed to justify Georgi's escape to myself, neglecting to consider potentially enormous and enduring consequences to me and, therefore, to Meg. The grief of the Leningraders had overtaken me.

"And if I leave while you're in Phelps?" Georgi asked.

"I will list you as a fugitive," I said firmly. "You will be chased."

Georgi turned in his chair and faced Sophie. They spoke to each other as if Anna and I were not in the room, a bedroom dialogue: after fifty years of marriage, they needed no touching; their eyes were like fingertips.

"It's a chance," Sophie said.

"We're nearly seventy," Georgi said. "Aren't you tired, love?"

"What?" she said.

"The running, I mean. We barely made it here today."

"But—"

"How would it be for us?" he said to her. "How much time do we have left together? To end it being chased like criminals?"

Sophie sighed. "She did say that you have a defense. Do you believe her?"

Georgi shrugged. From the side, I saw his chin quivering. Sagging in his chair, he looked devoid of all strength. The tears that ran down his cheeks gave me a sense of the awful hole in his soul.

Finished reading him, Sophie turned to me and said, "Don't

go to Phelps, Lieutenant. We will go back to Chicago with you. We will defend Georgi in court, try for an acquittal."

I had nothing left to offer or to say. I could only ache for them.

Later, dreams about the coat would haunt me: nightmares that would soak my gowns in cold sweat and leave me shivering under my blankets. Not the noise, or the blood-colored message, or even the blood itself. It would be the coat, my unpardonable mistake that would creep through the nights on tiger's paws to claw me.

"We will all go in my car," I said. "We'll have to decide what to do with your car later, Georgi."

He nodded.

"Does anybody want something to eat before we leave?" I asked. "It's a long drive, but I'd rather not stop along the way. We should eat here."

Everybody said no.

"Then let's move out," I said. "Oh, anybody besides me need the bathroom?"

Georgi raised a hand shyly. "Yes, please," he said.

"Okay," I said. "We probably all need to go. Where is it?"

"At the other end of the hallway," Sophie said.

"You first, Georgi," I said.

He stood and started down the hallway. I turned from him and quietly said to Sophie, "I'm not sure about his chances—with a jury, I mean."

"No?" she said.

"It's hard to say if a jury could really understand what happened to him in Leningrad. But at least Eva Ramirez has lived and will be well. Her death would have made things much different, much worse."

"You know a lawyer, dearie?" Anna asked.

"I think so. I'll call tonight when we're back. She should meet us at the station."

"Thank you, Lieutenant," Sophie said. "I'm grateful Anna has you for a friend."

My first look down the hall was just by chance. I turned back to Sophie and Anna, and it was still another moment before I felt something barely out of sync, an irritation as small as a stray eyelash on a cornea. I shifted my eyes back into the hall for a second look. In a blink, all my underpinnings collapsed beneath me.

His bishop's coat was gone from the rack on the wall.

"Goddammit, Georgi!" I screamed from the bottom of my chest. My hand was already on the gun in my purse, my body already lifting from the chair.

The women across from me jumped, looking for an explanation, but I was tearing across the room. I banged my shoulder on the hallway wall, then drove ahead the half-dozen steps to the empty coatrack. I saw the closed door to the bathroom to my right.

My gun hand up, my left hand went for the doorknob, but the explosion of noise from behind the door stopped me in mid-reach. I froze for a moment, my body fixed like an insect on a pin by the intense crack of sound, by the thunder that now pounded into the hall and split my ears painfully. The bathroom door flew open, and Georgi crashed out against me, knocking me into the jutting coatrack, the force reopening the gash on my forehead. I felt new blood rush along my eyebrow and down onto my cheek.

He dropped nearly soundlessly to the hard wooden floor, a wet, black heap. His aim had been flawless: his shot entered smoothly and innocently under his lower jaw, then broke through his mouth and into the bottom of his brain. When the bullet had left his skull, it took with it the whole top of his braincase, as though a small bomb had detonated inside. Now the smell of gunpowder was all around him. Blood eased from his wounds. His Nagant revolver, no longer hidden in his coat pocket, was half-covered by his pudgy face.

In horror, I touched my face and felt my own warm blood. For an instant, I feared his bullet had somehow blown through his skull and entered mine. Then, realizing I had only split open my forehead on the rack, I jerked my head up and away from the horror of his corpse, and my eyes inadvertently found the bathroom. The mirror over the sink carried the message he had printed in scarlet lipstick. In huge, uneven letters, it said "I love you, dear Sophie—"

26

Georgi was buried in a cemetery near the University of Chicago, and I took a morning off work to attend the funeral. Anna and Sophie—they were living together now, one floor above me—were there of course, and a few faculty and students from the university. The day was warm and dry, but the ground was still soggy from the storm two days before.

A machine had cut a hole in the soft earth, and Georgi's casket was lowered inside. An aged, worn priest of the Eastern rite muttered something in Russian, but said nothing else, offering not a shred of consolation to Sophie. A simple stone cross made the grave's headstone. On the cross was carved:

GEORGI GLAZUNOV
1923–1988
BELOVED HUSBAND OF SOPHIE
LENINGRADER

As our small group walked away from the grave, Sophie thanked me for coming. I felt deeply for her, but could think of nothing to say that might soothe her. There was no reception after the services, so I took Sophie and Anna to lunch at a small, dark restaurant near the university.

We all ordered, but no one had the stomach to eat much. But

we did talk at least, three bowed mourners circled at a table, each hung in black cotton or silk, each more interested in elegy than food.

Sophie said she knew Georgi had packed his Nagant in his coat that morning, but it never occurred to her that he would use it, not on me and certainly not on himself. My voice cracking, I admitted my mistake in not searching Georgi's coat when he went to hang it in the hallway. Sophie fussed at her hair, and told me not to brood. Georgi had pulled the trigger, she said, not me. She also said that she had always believed that most lives, especially lives like Georgi's, turned on bigger gears than simple chance or oversight. Gentle Sophie, forgiving Sophie. How could Georgi not have loved her?

Back at Area Six, I argued with Melchior about the ten thousand dollars that Juan Ramirez had brought into the station. Sophie wanted the money returned to the Ramirez family, and I argued for her, but Melchior would have none of it. He bellowed for a while about the rules of evidence, and I gave up quickly. I felt lucky not to be in front of a disciplinary board for following Georgi over the state line.

I wouldn't talk, not even to Art, about the afternoon at Big Sand. I filed the required reports and said nothing more. Once, I tried to tell Meg what had happened, but the words hung in my throat like paste. Meg laughed it off, telling me I was a *weird* mom.

Months later, as autumn deepened and the air sharpened, I returned to Georgi's cemetery. I found his grave easily, his white cross the simplest marker in the area, but now with an inscription that had been added since the funeral. Sophie, I assumed, had had it done. The tiny, slanted script read:

> Though your sins be like scarlet,
> they may become white as snow.

> Though they be crimson red,
> they may become white as wool.

I knelt next to the cross for a long time, and I felt the memory of Big Sand sting me. I thought about the misery that Georgi and Anna and even Lugotov had been through almost a half-century before, and I felt profoundly sad. After a while, when the cold of the ground seeped into me, I left.

On the way back to the station, I stopped on State Street, across from Holy Name Cathedral. I sat in the Fury and saw a hard white sun burning the church's stone facade. I listened to the bells tolling the noon Mass, watched people go in through the mammoth doors, even saw crazy Rita leaving to refresh the water in her stinking bucket.

I entered the church and walked to a side pew. The confessional where Eva Ramirez had been shot was new, the blood-stained carpet replaced. Two months before, on a lovely summer evening, I had run into Eva and her family at a lakefront festival. While Juan took Meg and his boys for ice-cream cones, Eva and I sat on a bench and talked about kids and school and the price of groceries. Meg came back and I stood to leave, but Eva caught my arm to bring me back down. She hugged me briefly and tightly; Juan turned away in embarrassment, and the kids giggled. I hadn't seen Eva since.

The Mass started; the priest was a slight young man with eyebrows too blond to be seen from my pew. I was looking for a lift in my mood, although I was too stubborn to do the prescribed standing and kneeling with the rest of the congregation. I remained sitting, thinking about Georgi Glazunov, thinking that he had been a man who was, indeed, white as snow, white as wool. I took no pride in my part in his final days.

I wondered how Sophie was doing in the months since Georgi's death—she had left Anna's place for her own home just a week after Georgi's funeral. I knew Anna visited her regularly: Anna said they were sharing their widowhood over lunches in franchise restaurants and afternoon movies in deserted theaters. I had been remiss in not calling or visiting Sophie when her life was so wounded. Anna never would have treated me that way.

The Mass rambled on, and I found myself comforted by those cadences of speech and chant so familiar to me since childhood. The temper of the church—the smell of hardwoods, the flush of light in the stained glass, the squeaking pews and kneelers—allowed for reflecting, something I did too seldom.

My thoughts drifted to Melchior. Since that midnight in his office, he hadn't conceded the slightest apology, but nor did he harass me further. He could have justifiably disciplined me about the final hours of the Glazunov case, but he allowed that to slip by, and I was grateful. Nonetheless, the thought of his ham hands on my breasts still humiliated me: I had told no one. I thought about my recklessness with my .38 that night: I knew I would draw it again in a similar circumstance, maybe even use it if I was desperate enough. Introspection had not unwound my confusion about my feelings.

The Communion of the Mass began, and I was surprised to find myself in line with the parishioners. When the priest placed a host in my hand, I looked straight into his clear eyes, as though I were daring him to notice me. For a moment, I thought he studied me specially, but I'm sure he didn't.

Back in my pew, I said no certain prayers, but I began to sense a kind of absolution for Big Sand, maybe just the amnesty granted by one's presence in a church, but absolution nonetheless.

After Mass, I drove to the station, and I went to Arthur. With the door to our office closed, I told him things that I should have told him months before, but was too ashamed to admit to. I told him how badly and expensively I had fucked up in not searching Georgi's coat. And I told him I had made a wrongheaded offer to Georgi, but that I still didn't know if I would always be able to separate sentiment from responsibility.

I needed to tell Art those things because he is my partner, because we are dependent on each other, sometimes for our very survival. White or black, woman or man, one-legged or two, we wash across each other, like tides over a beach. We require the greatest trust in one another: we need to know to whom we are really tied.

When I finished my little discourse, Art said nothing, but, instead, wadded up a sheet of paper into a ball that he lofted toward my head. As I ducked, Art grinned, and as he did, a young officer knocked brusquely on our door and piled into the room. He said a Rush Street pimp had just been machine-gunned to death by a maniac in the Oak Tree Grill, and that the word was now out on the street that the pimp's whores would all be dead by morning. Art jumped first, was standing in an instant. "C'mon, girl," he crowed to me, "c'mon! Let's get our asses over there! Now!"

I smiled broadly at him, and reached for my purse and gun. We were off.